Losing My Home/
Losing My Mind

Losing My Home/ Losing My Mind

A Work of Philosophical Fiction

DAVID B. MYERS

RESOURCE *Publications* · Eugene, Oregon

LOSING MY HOME/LOSING MY MIND
A Work of Philosophical Fiction

Resource Publications
An Imprint of Wipf and Stock Publishers
199 W. 8th Ave., Suite 3
Eugene, OR 97401

www.wipfandstock.com

PAPERBACK ISBN: 979-8-3852-0848-7
HARDCOVER ISBN: 979-8-3852-0849-4
EBOOK ISBN: 979-8-3852-0850-0

01/05/24

For my quotation from Deuteronomy in the Tanakh:
A line from Deuteronomy is from the Tanakh, the new Jewish Publication Society translation. Copyright, 2003.

For my quotations from the gospels of Matthew and John in the New Testament:
Lines from Matthew and John are from the Holy Bible, New International Version, Zondervan, Copyright, 2022.

For quotations from *The Myth of Sisyphus* by Albert Camus:
Lines are from *The Myth of Sisyphus* by Albert Camus, translated by Justin O'Brien. Vintage International. Copyright, 1955, renewed 1983.

For my quotations from *Nausea* by Jean-Paul Sartre:
Lines are from *Nausea* by Jean Paul Sartre, translated by Lloyd Alexander. New Directions. Copyright, 1959.

For my quotation from *Beyond Good and Evil* by Friedrich Nietzsche:
Lines are from *Beyond Good and Evil* by Friedrich Nietzsche, translated by R. J. Hollingdale. Penguin Books. Copyright, 1990.

For Aaron and Christian Myers, my son and grandson,
both lovers of literary imagination

Contents

1. The Stranger

YOUR LIFE CAN BE turned upside down in the blink of an eye. I had just returned from my daily walk. That's when it happened. Saturday. It was a calm and beautiful summer morning in Winterville, a small college town in northwestern Minnesota. Yes, the calm was noticeable, with no trace of the strong winds we frequently get in this part of the Great Plains. Winterville, lying east of and next to the Red River of the North, about a hundred miles from the Canadian border, is one of the windiest cities in the country, putting Chicago to shame. On that rare windless morning, the sky was clear and bright blue. At that moment, as I was walking up the steps to my condo, I had no worries or fears. I felt at peace. When I experienced such moments, I called them nirvanic. Nirvana as a permanent state I had ruled out long ago. But, at that moment, my life was, on balance, good. I had experienced more than my share of these peaceful moments. That would soon end.

I entered the unlocked door to the foyer where there were mailboxes and a locked door that led to the condo units. A digital clock above the mailboxes read 9:12 a.m. This foyer area is where guests buzz in. It's a very secure building. The entrance door to the foyer is locked from ten in the evening to seven in the morning to prevent homeless people from spending the night there. This was a response to finding a person sleeping in the foyer overnight, more than once. We often found cigarette butts on the floor. Our condo association decided that we needed to lock out this squatter—really all trespassers. In the winter here, when the temperature can sometimes be cold enough to kill an unhoused person, that may seem like a cruel thing to do. But we—I also so voted—decided this was only prudent, a way to protect our valuable property. Feeling guilty about this, I posted on the outside door a list of shelters with addresses and phone numbers. Ironically, I would soon become a member of the unhoused community that our condo association decided to lock out.

I lived on the third floor: 301. The Red River Park Condominiums had been my home for about four years. Or at least I thought I lived there. The door leading to the condo units is always locked. When I reached into my pocket, I couldn't find my keys. Had I somehow lost them on my walk? Unlikely. Maybe I had absentmindedly forgotten to take them with me. I had done that before, locking myself out, and then, when I returned from my walk, requested someone in the complex to buzz me in. There is no camera in the foyer. I always identified myself. Since residents of this small condo complex knew each other's voices, and even the voices of relatives and friends, there was no security threat in letting someone in you couldn't see, as long as you recognized the voice.

When I happened to glance at the mailboxes, there was, to my surprise and puzzlement, a different name in the slot for 301. A name other than mine. The name on the box for 301 now read Louis Johnson. Louis Johnson? What? An odd joke? I saw that all the other names on the mailboxes were correct—that is, they were the familiar names of people who lived in our small complex. This upscale building has only twelve units. Residents were congenial neighbors, always ready to help one other in small and even large ways. I pressed the button for my neighbor across the hall in 302, Juliette Prowess, with whom I had enjoyed wine and good conversation once a week.

"Juliette, I forgot my keys. Would you please buzz me in?"

"I don't recognize your voice."

"It's Nathan. Nathan Feldman."

"I'm sorry: our policy is not to let anyone in we don't know."

"Juliette, someone has removed my name from the 301 mailbox and inserted the name Louis Johnson. You must be in on this odd prank."

"No one replaced your name. It's Louis's mailbox; he has lived here for ten years—in unit 301. He's on vacation. Maybe you have mistakenly entered the wrong building."

"Juliette, please stop this foolishness and let me in."

"Sir, you're beginning to scare me. I'll have to call the police if you don't leave."

That curt rebuff marked the end of my life as I had known it. The end of my life as a person who owned a lovely spacious two-bedroom condo—with a balcony that I had spent hours on during the summer: reading, writing, listening to music on my cell phone through my buds, or simply sitting there to take in the many nearby large beautiful oak trees, with their very green leaves. Our winters seem never-ending—the name of our city could not be more apt—and so our trees are depressingly barren most of the year. In this part of the world, green leaves are never to be taken for granted. When I wasn't traveling during the summer, this balcony was my private outdoor retreat. Now it no longer appeared to be my balcony. It supposedly belonged to Louis Johnson, someone I saw as an occupier.

When I reached for my billfold, it too was missing—not in the left back pocket I usually put it in when I went for my daily walk. Perhaps I had also forgotten to take it with me. I had deliberately not taken my cell phone. Often, I left it behind because I didn't want anyone to interrupt my peaceful—often meditative—walk. At that moment, although I couldn't know it, I had also in fact left behind everything I thought I knew about myself and my world. My once comfortable life as a well-off university professor became a thing of the past. Would I ever recover it? I didn't know. All I can say is that I now fondly and nostalgically remember it as a peaceful, academic life of luxury, one in which I had my summers free to write, bike, hike, and travel abroad. One in which I, as a well-paid single man, had plenty of money to spend on things like eating out several evenings a week at good restaurants, vacations on breathtaking coasts in various countries, two-week jazz cruises, and much more: things whose costs I never thought about. And, being both environmentally attuned and relatively affluent, I had a new beautiful teal green all-electric Nissan Ariya. Or at least my memory told me that I owned such a vehicle. Now, suddenly and shockingly, I seemed to have only my legs as a mode of transportation—and I possessed only the clothes I was wearing.

After being locked out of what I thought was my home, I walked around in a daze, not knowing where to go or what to do. This didn't make sense. I was at a loss in trying to understand what was happening. I saw a police car and flagged it down. Maybe this patrol vehicle was in the area because Juliette had called the police to report a suspicious intruder. After the policewoman lowered her driver's side window and asked what was going on, I tried to explain my confusing situation to this at first cordial cop. It was of course an incredible story: I was locked out of my condo, someone had changed the name on my mailbox, and I couldn't get my neighbor across the hall to buzz me in. A neighbor and good friend who said she didn't know me! The policewoman wasn't buying it. I could tell she was trying to smell my breath. Was I slurring my words?

Then, when this cop failed to get a whiff of alcohol, it became clear to me, after I continued to describe my puzzling condition, that she probably judged me to be a mentally ill homeless person. And I noticed that she was staring at something I hadn't seen before. It appeared to be a fresh wound on my left wrist, a newly forming scar from what appeared to be a long and very deep cut, like someone had sliced the top of my wrist with a very sharp knife. The healing wound was not close to any veins—so, the policewoman probably didn't see it as an attempted suicide. And there appeared to be cut marks on my upper left arm, faint scars not as serious as the one on my wrist. I had no memory of what caused these wounds. Later I would discover that these were ominous signs of something I would be shocked to learn. Given the cop's reaction to me, I was thinking that I could easily be mistaken for a mentally ill person living on the street who had recently been attacked—or perhaps who had been in a fight with someone wielding a knife.

After all, our homeless population was growing larger by the day and within it were of course individuals disconnected from reality, perhaps because they could no longer afford the meds that kept them sane—or refused to take them. My clothes could have belonged to such a person: grungy jeans, a dirty old torn T-shirt, and well-worn sneakers, crumbling Nikes that seemed to mark me as an impoverished person who had to travel mainly by foot. One of these old shoes had even been repaired with masking tape. Although I usually wore expensive attire—a friend accused me being a dandy—when I went for my morning walk during the summer, I didn't care how I looked. I took a strange pleasure on my walks in not dressing up, in looking sloppy, even as appearing to be a member of the unemployed proletariat. I could see why, to the policewoman, I—speaking nonsense, unkempt, and poorly dressed—must have looked like a wandering and confused unhoused man. Before we could continue our conversation, this cop received an emergency call and told me she needed to leave. Apparently, she judged this call to signal a greater threat than I seemed to pose.

Not knowing where else to go, I walked toward the state university a few blocks away that was my place of employment, the place where (I believed that) I worked nine months of the year, with the luxury of summers off, a schedule I had enjoyed since kindergarten. That is, nine months of school and three months of freedom—an ideal life I had taken for granted. My salary was very good because the leaders of our teachers' union had been aggressive and successful in working for yearly increases in pay. Our salaries were so high that the local paper, *The Winterville Forum*, published the highest ones, including mine, on the front page with our names—as if to say "look where your tax dollars are going," implying that we were overpaid. COVID had, however, dealt a blow to our enrollment, and so the days of salary increases were probably over. I have to admit I felt a little guilty about how well I was compensated for nine months of work—really not even nine months because we had close to a month off for winter break and a week off for spring break, not to mention a scattering of many other holidays. That at least was what my memory told me. But it appeared that memory was the very thing I could not rely on anymore.

I was desperately hoping that my memory was not entirely untrustworthy. As I walked toward campus, I remembered being at this university for ten years, having tenure, and also, at the age of forty-one, being awarded the title of Full Professor of Philosophy—which meant, if the department could still get it, another boost in salary. I was an up-and-coming well-published scholar and a Neo-Marxist critic of advanced capitalism. In my mind, Marxism, with some revisions, was very much alive and relevant in an age when this heartless economic system was still wrecking great havoc on both humans and nature—a mortal danger that needed to be disassembled. Neo-Marxism provides a critique of late-stage capitalism that goes beyond mere economic analysis to incorporate insights from other traditions, such as feminism, existentialism, psychoanalysis, critical criminology, and queer theory.

I also recalled being a member of Democratic Socialists of America. There were those—including my Republican friends, few in number—who mockingly described me as a "bourgeois socialist" and dismissed me as hopelessly utopian in my thinking and clearly hypocritical in my style of living. As I approached the university, I remembered being a radically left professor who enjoyed an affluent life while condemning the exploitative society that made such a life possible. I was well aware that some might see as hypocritical my preaching socialism while living a life of great privilege and disproportionate wealth. My memory told me that two years ago I received a large inheritance. I don't recall money ever being an issue for me—at least not until my life changed on that beautiful Saturday morning when I suddenly found myself homeless.

Entering the university grounds, I suddenly realized that I had never appeared on campus so poorly dressed and so mentally messed up—now even questioning who I was and whether I belonged on this campus.

Questioning everything my memory told me. Even feeling embarrassment. Embarrassment? That made no sense. My earlier encounter with my neighbor and the female cop had shaken me, causing me suddenly to doubt everything I thought I knew about myself, about my world. My name was no longer on my mailbox and Juliette had treated me like a complete stranger—indeed as a menacing intruder. I walked nervously into Larson Hall, the building that housed the Winterville State University Philosophy Department, climbed the stairs, and went straight to my office on the third floor. Or what I thought was my office. Again, a different name was on what memory told me was my office door.

Although summer school was in session at the university—which I never taught because I never needed the extra money—very few people were there on a Saturday morning. But the WSU Philosophy Department secretary, Marge Cook, was in her office. Marge was a talker who often carried on long conversations during weekdays when she should have been working. I remembered that she often worked on Saturday mornings because almost no one was around and she could catch up on her work: filing this, filing that, following instructions for creating philosophy exams, word processing student evaluations of professors, etc. Fearing the response that I in fact was about to get, I nevertheless greeted her by name. She looked puzzled. Always friendly, she smiled and was polite.

"I'm sorry. I don't remember your name."

Rather than answer her, I apologized—sheepishly saying, "No, I'm sorry"—and quickly walked away. Apologized! Why did I apologize? I was embarrassed because Marge didn't recognize me. This brought the stunning realization that I had suddenly become a complete stranger in what I thought was my academic community. Would I now be a stranger to everyone I believed knew me? My heart sank, my stomach was queasy. I felt sick. A dizzying nausea I had never before experienced hit me, much like that described by the existentialist philosopher Jean-Paul Sartre in his first novel, titled *Nausea*. Existential nausea. A confusing feeling of being absolutely lost and completed alienated. All at once, I was inexplicably homeless in what had become an absurd world. I experienced a sudden disorientation, a sensation of losing my mental balance, a kind of ontological vertigo and frightening light-headedness. It was a sense of being existentially unmoored, with no solid ground beneath my feet. Although most contemporary philosophers consider existentialism a long dead movement, I found that it spoke to me—and most of my students—with its themes of alienation, absurdity, abandonment, freedom, and being thrown into the world. Now more than ever.

My head was spinning. A bad dream. That's all this could be. But then I dismissed that explanation, one I would revisit later. I had entered a Kafkaesque world, the kind I taught my students about when we discussed the writings of this dark spirit, Franz Kafka, the novelist of strange fiction who was born in Prague but wrote in German, dying of tuberculosis at forty. Maybe the term "Kafkaesque" is overused and may not be the right description of my situation because Kafka never wrote a work of fiction about a character who suddenly is no longer recognized by anyone in his community. Still, it's a term that has come to mean nightmarish and strange—and that was how my world now felt. Perhaps I could more precisely describe my situation as daymarish: a distressing experience similar to a bad dream but occurring while one is awake. I was feeling like a character in an old Twilight Zone episode, waiting for Rod Serling to enter the scene to tell his viewers about Nathan Feldman's sudden fall into complete anonymity.

Who was I? Without my wallet, I had nothing that would confirm my identity—driver's license, university photo ID, credit cards, library cards, etc. It struck me that I couldn't prove I was Nathan Hillel Feldman, forty-one-year-old academic who lived at 413 10th Street South, Unit 301, Red River Park Condominiums, in Winterville, Minnesota. Was I no longer the Nathan Feldman who worked at the state university—the professor who taught Introduction to Philosophy, Existentialism and Literature, Nineteenth-Century Philosophy, Contemporary Marxism, The History of Political Philosophy, Personal Identity Theory, Philosophy of Religion, World Religions, and Philosophy of Friendship, to list my varied teaching duties, half of these courses (except the Intro course) taught alternate years? I had taken pride in the diversity of my course offerings. Was this clear and strong memory of myself as a professor of philosophy at Winterville State University really false? Was that possible? It seemed so.

Having struck out at what I thought was my residence and my place of employment, I was thinking of turning to the synagogue community I remembered being a member of for a decade. Since it was Saturday morning, there would be a service at 10 a.m. and an *oneg* afterwards. I was in walking distance of Shir Shalom (Song of Peace), the Reform synagogue where, as I recall, I sometimes attended Sabbath morning services, but more often only attended 9 a.m. Torah study because I loved arguing with fellow Jews about our very flawed sacred texts. Although a religious skeptic, I did have faith moments, but they were far and few between. Most of the time I felt the absence of God. I called myself a soft atheist because I was open to belief in God and sometimes, although rare, could believe.

A significant percentage of the dwindling number of liberal American Jews who regularly attend Torah study and synagogue services are probably atheists or agnostics. This is probably true even of Reform rabbis—individuals professionally trained in seminaries to lead Torah study and prayer services. I suspect that liberal rabbis, in large numbers, doubt the existence of God, with many seeing prayer as nothing more than theological poetry that speaks to the heart in a mythical way, and seeing the Torah as the creation of anonymous imaginative writers, a collection of crudely edited-together ancient Jewish legends. So, among Reform Jews, I was not unusual in my tendency toward doubt and disbelief. For me and countless other liberal and progressive Jews, Judaism was not about belief but, at its best, about compassionate action, the true locus of holiness. I was, like many of my fellow Reform congregants, a social justice Jew who happily embraced what right-wingers consider a pejorative term: "woke."

And there is nothing more disgusting to many on the extreme right, especially white nationalists, than progressive Jews who work to welcome immigrants of color, triggering the slogan they repeat at their rallies, "Jews will not replace us," a mantra that means that they will not let Jews replace white men with dark aliens. I was one of those Jews who, supporting a long-established Jewish pro-immigrant organization called HIAS (Hebrew Immigrant Aid Society), welcomed immigrants and refugees from all over the world, something that apparently triggers a fear of white genocide among white nationalists. One of the most important commandments in Judaism, mentioned thirty-six times in the Torah, is welcoming the *ger* or stranger, meaning resident alien.

Although at times this country may seem to be overrun with immigrants, especially illegal ones from south of the border, we progressive Jews believe this country should do what it can to accommodate those escaping from dangerous places or simply looking for a better life. Now—how cruel—I was an alien in my own community and my own country. After all, as it would turn out, I could no longer prove my citizenship, my status as a legal resident of the United States. I was now a pale-skinned illegal alien, a white sojourner in my own land, apparently not recognized by anyone. I had become the ultimate stranger.

I thought about reaching out to my rabbi and fellow congregants for help, but what good would that do? I assumed that the synagogue would have no record of my membership and of course my rabbi would respond: "Nathan who?" Members of what I thought was my synagogue probably would not even allow me, now a complete stranger to them, to sleep in the basement of our temple. Strangers were not permitted to enter our synagogue! Antisemitism was on the rise again and many Jews felt under threat. Because of repeated attacks on synagogues in the United States, Shir Shalom had actually adopted a new rule in order to keep members safe: Never let in someone you don't know, the same rule they had at the condo complex. They might as well have put a sign on the synagogue door saying: *Strangers not welcome!* An anti-Jewish rule—a violation of a moral law in the Torah. Such was the unfortunate time I lived in when I most needed fellow Jews to welcome me.

At that moment, it looked like I was condemned to be a wandering— and wondering—Jew. A man without a home—and without a country. It didn't help that I was an only child whose parents had died when I was an infant. I was orphaned at this early age and then adopted by a Jewish couple when I was two. Since I was a Jew by birth, the adoption agency thought this was in my best interest—I am grateful to them for that. And, to add to my loss, my adoptive parents had both died two years ago in a car crash. Thus, the sudden large inheritance. But, alas, this appeared to be only my mythical past. It seemed that my recollections were unreliable: these memories of my adoptive parents and the inheritance were probably not trustworthy. Now I felt like a twice orphaned son. In reality, I seemed to have no family. I felt completely alone—like a motherless child. I thought about reaching out to those who I thought were my good friends. But why should I expect them to recognize me if my secretary and my neighbor across the hall failed to do so? Here I was, one of the few professors in the country who taught a course on the philosophy of friendship, now friendless. I should probably say that I only thought I taught such a course.

Judaism had not really prepared me for losing everything. I, fortunately, also had a Buddhist practice—or a memory, however unreliable, of such a practice—and the Buddhist tradition did offer techniques for helping me to cope with my crisis. I remember being what some call a Jew-Bu. I alternated Jewish and Buddhist practices and was a dual-belonger, a member of both a synagogue and a sangha. I was attracted to what is called socially engaged, justice oriented, Buddhism, similar to socially engaged Judaism. I recall fancying myself as a Jewish-Buddhist-Marxist committed to repairing a damaged world and ending all forms of capitalist exploitation, not only the exploitation of humans, but also the exploitation of nature and animals—exploitation done for the sole purpose of multiplying profits. I saw capitalism as a coldly calculating and ethically indifferent economic system oriented toward one end: maximizing returns on investments. Yes, I remember myself as a Jewish-Buddhist-Marxist teacher who never hid his philosophically plural self. Students seemed fascinated by my multiple identities and causes, and perhaps I played this up to fill my classes. Or so I recall.

I remember aspiring to true Buddhist liberation, understood as the readiness to let everything go, to give everything away, calling this *virtual renunciation*. It was really only the theoretical—*as if*—act of letting go of all that I possessed, of cultivating a state of mind oriented toward recognizing that nothing I owned was permanently mine. The resources of the earth should not be any individual's private possessions. This dimension of Buddhism comported with my Marxism. Again, it was of course only an intellectual transcendence of private ownership. It never occurred to me that one day being propertyless would become my actual condition.

Now, instead of virtual renunciation, I faced actual poverty. I had no choice. I was no longer in a position to give everything away, to give up all that I owned. It was simply my state of being. Although I was in shock at suddenly being homeless and propertyless, I remembered all those mornings of Buddhist meditation when I attempted to cultivate equanimity—a mental state that, if realized, enables one to remain calm in the face of catastrophe, in the face of everything falling apart. My world had literally collapsed. I no longer had any material possessions to hold on to, to claim as belonging to me, my personal possessions. But I was not really prepared to live out this renunciatory Buddhist vision, to live out the ideal of nonattachment to things. As should now be clear, I remember myself as a Marxist who, despite my theoretical critique of the private ownership of wealth, highly valued my private possessions. Now I owned only the clothes I wore.

Buddhism had encouraged me to transcend my hypocritical acquisitiveness and to prepare myself to lose everything, even to be disposed to give up everything I owned. This is what Gautama, the Buddha-to-be, had chosen to do in leaving his life as a prince in search of personal peace. He chose actual renunciation. Prince Siddhartha left behind the luxury of palace life and all his possessions—and indeed all those he loved—to wander in a forest in search of a solution to the problem of suffering. The Buddha-to-be had literally given up everything he owned, believing that voluntary poverty was a necessary condition for true liberation.

I was now involuntarily destitute—against my will, absolutely impoverished. I was of necessity as poor as Gautama had freely chosen to be. But, to repeat, I had not chosen this life. It came to me. Now I would need to draw on Buddhist wisdom to deal with having the ground pulled out from under me. I was glad I had this second spiritual practice because—to reiterate something important—Judaism did not really psychologically equip me to deal with this in the way Buddhism did. Judaism had motivated me to be generous toward the poor and to support local homeless shelters—and to work for a radically different society, one in which there would be zero poverty. But Judaism had not prepared me for losing everything, including the basic income I needed to pay for food, clothing, and shelter. My Buddhist practice, with its themes of impermanence and change, had at least encouraged me to mentally prepare myself to lose everything—had alerted me not to be surprised if I did. Still, it became clear to me, when I suddenly had nothing, that I had understood this Buddhist message in only a theoretical way.

Judaism had encouraged me to be generous with my wealth, with my surplus income and to try to avoid giving in such a way as to humiliate the recipient, and so to give anonymously if possible. Buddhism did the same. As I have admitted, I was never radically generous, as generous as I could have been, should have been. Now I had nothing. Unlike Buddhism, Judaism never made a virtue of poverty—or saw a life of complete renunciation as an attractive spiritual option. Again, both traditions highly value generosity: Jews call this *tzedakah* and Buddhists call it *dana*. Even the poorest of the poor in both traditions were called to find a way to be generous, something that might take a nonmaterial form. But it was not clear to me, now that I had nothing, what, if anything, I could give to others. What nonmaterial gifts did I have to share? It seemed to me that I had nothing to offer anyone. Would my fellow unhoused brothers and sisters be interested in being tutored in philosophy, in learning about Plato or Nietzsche, in solving the problem of how we know other minds exist, or in understanding different concepts of the nature of beauty? Probably not. I had become a person absolutely dependent on others for survival—for both material and moral support. I needed help in every way. I suddenly felt completely impoverished: economically, relationally, and psychologically.

Because of my practice of giving away at least some of my income, I knew where to find shelter, food, and clothing. My memory told me that I had made modest financial contributions to a local food pantry and had even volunteered at a local homeless shelter where, it now occurred to me, I might now become a resident, if those running the shelter would allow in someone who had no form of identification, who was a cipher. Who would remember even my modest giving and my occasional volunteer work? Did this actually happen? In truth, it was as if none of these things ever occurred, as if I, Nathan Feldman had never existed. The well-off Nathan Feldman who shared some of his wealth seemed to be a figment of my imagination.

That I now possessed nothing—had no source of income—was disturbing enough. But, even more disturbing, I had also lost all of those I loved, everyone I cared about and who I thought cared about me. It was as if I were dead to them. *As if* is not really accurate: I *was* dead to them. When they looked at me, they saw a total stranger. Not to be recognized by those you believed knew you well is devastating. I had never felt such loneliness. It was like being abandoned by everyone who mattered in your life. You recognize them, but they stare through you or past you. They no longer know who you are, no longer share a history with you. Whether you live or die only matters to you, no one else. Losing all of one's possessions and losing one's home are awful enough. But the feeling of being completely cut off, separated, from those you love and who you thought loved you—who fail to recognize you, even when you are in the same room with them—is unbearable. I had become an invisible man.

At my most paranoid, I thought I was being made invisible—made an outcast—simply because I was a Jew. When feeling persecuted because of that, I obsessed about the long history of Christian antisemitism. For centuries, the Jew was treated as the despised Other that the Christian majority wanted to make disappear—and was literally made invisible by being confined to a ghetto. Until relatively recently—in historical terms—a Jew's very existence was objectionable to Christians. I remembered—as an adolescent in Bryan, Texas—being called a Christ killer by a Catholic friend. Didn't he know about Vatican II? Maybe his parents were the culpable ones who, ignoring Nostra Aetate, told him that the Jews killed their Lord and that all Jews had inherited this guilt for the worse crime conceivable. I was told by other Christian friends that I was going to hell if I didn't accept Jesus as my personal Lord and Savior; we Jews, who reject Jesus as deserving eternal torture. The cross became for Jews over the centuries—and became for me as an adolescent in conservative Bryan, Texas—a source of great anxiety and fear.

In the nineteenth century a new secular form of antisemitism emerged, based on treating Jews as a diseased and unclean race. Racial antisemitism. How could I forget that day in high school walking home after school when two young budding Neo-Nazis beat me up, breaking my nose, calling me, repeatedly, "a fucking oven-dodging Jew"? How I could I forget that? It made me feel like human garbage. The message seemed to be this: vanish from our sight or we will cause you to disappear. We will beat you to a pulp and then incinerate you. I thought about the countless pogroms in Russia and Eastern Europe and then the murderous hate in Germany that gave rise to the Shoah. Is it any surprise that Jews in diaspora, wherever they lived, began to believe everyone was out to get them, experiencing what could be described as rational paranoia?

In my mind, at my most paranoid after becoming homeless, I saw myself as singled out for abuse, and this had everything to do with being a Jew. Jews have, almost from our beginning as a people, experienced hatred simply because we were Jews. Given our history, if Jews really were the chosen people, we seem to have been chosen to be victims of mass contempt and mass murder—and we have been accused of every crime imaginable. So, if there is a God, maybe this God actually hates, rather than loves, Jews. That is what the first generation of Jews leaving Egypt felt, according to Deuteronomy (1:27): "It is because the Lord hates us that He brought us out of the land of Egypt to hand us over to the Amorites to wipe us out." In place of the term "Amorites" Jews could, over the centuries, substitute any number of other Jew-hating communities all over the world who wanted to do the same. We can imagine Jews who survived the Holocaust saying that "it was because the Lord hated us that He handed us over to the Nazis to wipe us out." No doubt, many Jews have reasonably thought this—that God hated them—given a long history of repeatedly being made a denigrated people wherever they lived. Thus, even many Jews who believed the chosen people myth have also thought this: it would have been better for us if God had chosen another people.

My paranoia was reinforced by the antisemitism I saw resurging all over the world. Neo-Nazis and white nationalists seemed to be thriving and spreading hatred of Jews globally, blaming Jews for the decline of white culture, the decline of what they believed should be normative: white supremacy. I was told by my adoptive parents (in apparently another false memory) that I was a descendant of Holocaust survivors and should never forget the Third Reich's project designed to make every Jew vanish from the face of the earth, to see the Jewish people literally go up in smoke. The Shoah has sometimes been described as the culmination of "the longest hatred." In fact, it obviously was not the culmination, but only another chapter in a never-ending antisemitic saga of never-ending hatred.

Like a mutating virus, adapting and taking ever new forms, antisemitism was now a threat coming not only from the right, but also from the left, from progressives who identified Jews with Israel and Israel with occupation and oppression. Some non-Jewish progressives, like radical Islamists, even question Israel's right to exist. I was not uncritical of Israel, but there seemed to be a double standard, one standard that applied to the obviously very flawed, and maybe even deteriorating, democracy of Israel and the other standard to her clearly undemocratic Muslim neighbors. Still, Israel's gross mistreatment of Palestinians was exacerbating antisemitism. And at the time I am narrating this, Israel is again, in retaliation to a vicious attack on its civilians by Hamas, waging yet another war on Hamas that is causing countless Palestinian civilian casualties. This of course has increased hatred of Jews globally. A divine plan?

Thus, when paranoia possessed me, antisemitism became one answer I gave to the following question: Why am I suddenly homeless and forgotten? Why was this happening to me? I had never been someone who thought much about cosmic justice. I had peacefully accepted what Albert Camus calls in his novel *The Stranger* "the benign indifference of the universe." But now, no matter how irrational and self-serving these questions, I wondered: How can this be? Why me? What did I do to deserve this? The universe suddenly felt personally hostile and alien: malign. I was a homeless Jew, an estranged Jew that the universe seemed out to get. After the life I so well knew was suddenly taken from me, I sometimes irrationally felt—and this was part of my recurring paranoia—that the cosmos itself was antisemitic and that I was a target of hostile natural forces simply because I was a Jew. Judeo-centric cosmic paranoia?

Seeming to confirm my view that even the natural world was a threatening antisemitic place, I had a very disturbing experience that seemed to reveal nature's antisemitism. As I was walking down the street on the first afternoon of my new homeless life, the wind suddenly gusted and did something astonishing. Disturbing what had been until that moment a calm and beautifully clear blue Saturday—this powerful wind marked an ominous change in the weather, bringing dark clouds out of nowhere, creating an oppressive overcast feel to the day. I then noticed twigs from a tree, whipped by the wind, falling on the sidewalk in front of me, creating a pattern. When I looked down at the twigs, I saw that they had fallen in such a way as to form what looked like a swastika! I was shocked. Was I seeing things? I looked again, and, yes, the twigs were arranged in this disturbing shape, and, before I could look a third time, because this seemed so incredible, the twigs blew away. At that moment of extreme paranoia, I felt that even the wind and the trees had become antisemitic: hostile toward Jews, toward me. If Jews are paranoid, it is not without reason—but that afternoon my perception of the universe as out to get Jews, and thus out to get me, was of course extraordinarily irrational and pathologically egoistic. I knew this intellectually, but my gut was telling me something else.

God-forsaken, universe-forsaken, and people-forsaken—I felt existentially forlorn and absolutely abandoned. Even alienated from my very self, the self I thought I knew so well. I began to doubt my sanity. Was I losing my mind? Had I already lost my mind? Given what I had experienced since my fateful return from that walk on what had been an ideal summer morning, could I accept what appeared to be the case: namely, that memories of my life were unreliable? I seemed unable to remember my actual life—and was somehow remembering a fictional life. Was I suffering from a strange form of amnesia? Had I somehow suddenly and inexplicably forgotten who I really was? Or had everyone else forgotten who I was? That made no sense. It seemed more likely that my memories were betraying me, conspiring against me. The source of my problem appeared to be psychological, inside of rather than outside of me. My mind was obviously playing tricks on me—making it impossible for me to remember my actual past, my actual identity.

I could not prove even to myself who I thought I was. In desperation, I stopped at the public library to use a computer there. It occurred to me that one way I could confirm my identity was to access my Social Security account, with its identifying number that had been mine since youth. I was now wondering if even this form of national identification was discoverable. When I put in my username and password, it was just as I feared: the Social Security Administration did not recognize my password or user ID—and would not let me change either to access my account because there was no account. That meant that there was no Social Security number for a

Nathan Hillel Feldman who lived in Winterville, Minnesota. Without this fundamental identifier, even though I was impoverished, could I qualify for any kind of county benefits—for example, SNAP? If I could not provide my SS number, would I be able to get basic government food assistance? I feared that I would become completely dependent on handouts. I might need to beg for food money, and have to experience the predictable disdain of those who would view me as a bum, a social parasite.

And who would employ or train me for a job if I couldn't provide my federal ID number? Without that, did I even exist as an American? Of course, I could search for employers who hired illegal aliens—because that is what I now was. I was living in this country without the credentials I needed to remain here. Did I need to start fresh and create a new identity in order to survive—to create, by hook or crook, the credentials that would allow me to find gainful employment? That might mean stealing someone else's Social Security number. Did I, in order to survive, need to engage in identity theft? Had it really come to that? Incredibly, the answer seemed to be yes.

2. Time Out of Mind

I LEFT THE LIBRARY feeling profoundly discouraged and confused. Where would I sleep? I decided to spend the first night of my new life in Red River Park, close to what I had, it appears, mistakenly thought was my place of residence: Red River Park Condominiums. I would sleep—or try to—in this beautiful large park next to the Red River of the North. This river originates at the confluence of the Bois de Sioux and Otter Tail rivers, and, because of the incline of the terrain, flows north, emptying into Lake Winnipeg. I felt fortunate that it was not winter when the temperature can drop well below zero, making survival outside a long shot.

Although it was very cloudy, there was no rain in the forecast. My on-line weather search while in the public library revealed that. I was desperate for something to be thankful for, and that was the best I could do—gratitude for weather nice enough to camp out. Spending the night in a park was my preference because I couldn't bring myself to go to a shelter, to have to associate with other unhoused people. Maybe I felt superior to them, telling myself I was not really one of these fallen creatures. I still thought of myself as a respected professor of philosophy, an accomplished academic. I could not yet accept the fact that I was now simply one among Winterville's growing faceless, homeless population. I still had my pride.

I had never been a camper—even disliked the very idea of it, prefer-ring, when in the woods, to rent an upscale nicely appointed cabin with ev-ery convenience, including a built-in bar and indoor jacuzzi—so all of this was new to me. That's what I recalled. I would need some kind of bedroll if I was going to sleep in the park and make it my new home, at least temporar-ily. I walked to the Winterville Salvation Army Thrift Store and explained that I was completely broke. All I wanted was a sleeping bag. Fortunately, the short and stout elderly woman in charge, gray hair in a bun, wearing a drab Salvation Army uniform and a large cross around her neck, found a well-worn army-green sleeping bag and simply gave it to me. It was rolled up inside an old ratty-looking gray slipcover that tied at one end. She also gave me a Salvation Army baseball cap to protect my bald head from the sun, her assumption being that there would be sunny days ahead, something at that moment I found hard to believe, literally or metaphorically. In line with her missionary obligation, she gave me a tract about Jesus, about how his blood was shed to save all people and how the fire of the Holy Spirit purifies believers. I didn't tell her I was a Jew who refused to accept Jesus as my Lord and Savior. I greatly appreciated her kindness and generosity, even if she believed that everyone who rejected Jesus would eternally suffer the pain of hellfire.

After leaving the store, I walked toward Red River Park, Salvation Army baseball cap on my head—turned forward, not backwards, the way I remember many of my male students wearing them, something that I found irritating—with a sleeping bag over one shoulder. I began to see myself as others were now seeing me: a poorly clothed unhoused forty-something man carrying a bedroll. Was I a pathetic sight? The Salvation Army cap would be a dead giveaway, like an ad saying *I'm a homeless person*. I thought perhaps I should make two cardboard signs, both saying: *Broke and homeless. Please help*. I could hang the signs on my chest and back while standing in the median area of a busy boulevard, holding my cap upside down to receive donations. I had seen an increasing number of people with such signs—but it never occurred to me that I would ever become one of these desperate individuals.

I decided, for the time being, to forgo an appeal to the charity of drivers. How often had I stopped to give such a person money? Consistent with my impression of myself as grudgingly charitable, I can't remember ever giving anything to these individuals, rationalizing my lack of generosity by presuming that my contribution would be wasted on booze. As I recall, I always tried to make sure my charitable contributions were well-used and that they went to reputable 501c3 charities. One Jewish tradition actually calls for Jews to respond positively to all of those who ask for help, even if we suspect that these beggars are not truly needy and will use our donation unwisely. I had ignored this call to be gracious. Although willing to give, I was also very cautious in making contributions. Of course, these memories of my life—whether positive or negative—were probably, given the evidence, memories corresponding to nothing in reality.

I finally made my way to the park. Hours seemed to have disappeared. Time I couldn't account for. It was already early evening. Although I hadn't eaten anything since breakfast—my memory was that my last meal, a bagel and yogurt, was on the balcony of my condo—I had no appetite. I just wanted to rest, to sleep, perchance to dream. I was experiencing extreme fatigue. The day had taken its toll. Maybe a night's sleep would refresh me. When it became dark, I found a place to sleep on the backside of the park restrooms. By 10 p.m. the park was empty. No sign of even one other homeless person. I was happy I had it to myself. Many of the homeless lived in tents close to the shores of both sides of the Red River. Having sweated a lot during this long and disturbing day—both from anxiety and all the walking—I felt dirty.

Before bedding down, I walked into the vacant park restroom and washed my face and upper-body, using several wet paper towels that I covered in soap from an almost empty dispenser. Since I kept my head shaved—a frequent solution for vain men who are losing their hair who may even think this makes them look more virile—I didn't have to worry about dirty hair. And I didn't need to shave my face because I had been one of those bearded professors. That was my memory. Maybe in reality I was a bald bearded crazy homeless man imagining that he was a professor. I noticed in the mirror that, in addition to the long fresh scar on my left wrist and minor ones on my upper left arm, there was a small scar on each side of the top of my skull. Had I symmetrically cut my head while shaving it? Or perhaps, as speculated earlier, I'd been in a fight in which my head was cut along with my wrist and my upper arm. And perhaps I had suffered brain damage in this fight. Thus, my amnesia.

My facial hair didn't yet look too scruffy. I would eventually have to trim my beard to keep it from getting out of control. I needed to try to appear presentable and not look unkempt or smell unbathed. I washed my well-worn, torn, and now smelly T-shirt in the sink and put it on wet because its dampness felt cool to my skin on what was a very humid night. Brushed my teeth with a wet finger. I would need to pick up a toothbrush, toothpaste, soap, a razor (to keep my head shaved), travel shaving cream, scissors for my beard, used clothes, and other necessities from the Salvation Army, an organization I would come to appreciate in spite of its Christian missionizing. Would the old SA woman also give these away?

Sleep was difficult during my first homeless night. After catching a few winks, I woke up completely disoriented, thinking, when I opened my eyes, *So, this was not a nightmare.* Upon awakening that first morning in the park, I felt more frightened and confused than ever. Church bells were ringing: the sound of Sunday morning. Unspeakably depressed, I immediately thought of a Kris Kristofferson song—*Sunday Mornin' Comin' Down*—where he sings about the loneliness of empty sidewalks on an early Sunday morning. I felt completely alone.

I hid my sleeping bag in thick brush near the park—so I wouldn't have to carry it wherever I went. Was this my new life? A life that made no sense. I had clear and strong memories of my past that were now useless and probably unconnected to my actual past. My life seemed a complete mystery. I obviously had another name and another past—one different from that of the apparently nonexistent Nathan Feldman—a real past I couldn't remember but desperately wanted to discover, recover. But when, on that first Sunday of my new homeless life, I spent time again at a computer in the public library, I wondered what I should google. I looked around at all of the mostly ragtag people sitting at the twenty computers and realized that I was now part of a new community of unhoused individuals who spent their days in the library doing whatever entertained them on a screen: games, searches for long lost relatives, employment opportunities, images of a different life.

I again reminded myself that if I wanted to make it economically, I needed to find a way to craft a new identity—including getting a valid Social Security number—that would allow me to make a living. I could, with some help, create a false photo ID. Maybe a fellow unhoused person, perhaps someone convicted of fraud or identity theft, could be of assistance. The homeless population included—in addition to the mentally healthy who lost everything through some great misfortune, the mentally ill who lost their way because of a lack of treatment, and addicts who were simply looking for the next hit of their preferred intoxicant—those who could not find work because of their criminal record. Thus, if I could only discover in this subcategory of the homeless a person skilled in the creation of false identities, I would be good to go. Getting phony credentials would, however, require money because no one with the skill to create these materials was going to do this for free. I was penniless. To get money, I might need to rob someone or rob a convenience store. I couldn't believe I was contemplating this, but I was. Somehow, I needed to find the funds necessary to create a new identity—and that might require theft. My survival might depend on this.

Assuming I could manage to get the money needed to create my new self, who should I pretend to be? Whoever I really was, I somehow had a knowledge of philosophy. Could I create a new identity as a professor of philosophy, with phony transcripts from the undergraduate and graduate schools I thought I attended: the University of Houston and Texas A&M respectively? Why not! I assumed that my knowledge of philosophy was made possible by undergraduate and maybe graduate studies somewhere. My memory, even if unreliable, was that I received a BA with a philosophy major from the University of Houston, the downtown branch, and, to be near my parents, I earned a PhD at Texas A&M University very close to Bryan where my parents lived. My recollection was that as an adopted child and only son, I was emotionally close to my adoptive parents—that I highly valued our relationship and their love.

Of course, in Google searches I found no record of a person with my name who received a BA from the University of Houston or earned a doctorate in philosophy from a university in College Station. Texas A&M—founded obviously as a place for agricultural and mechanical learning—may seem a surprising place to have an outstanding PhD program in philosophy. But it did and still does. The now deceased charismatic teacher, pragmatism scholar, and philosopher of American culture and American literature, John McDermott—a transplanted New Yorker who in later years looked like a Hebrew prophet, with his huge head of white hair and bushy beard—had built the Texas A&M Philosophy Department into one of the finest in the Southwest. It now has twenty-two full time professors of philosophy, all accomplished scholars. Of course, that may change with impending budget cuts due to the pandemic.

Did my brain manufacture memories of graduate studies at A&M, working on a dissertation under the supervision of Professor Dieter Hoffman, completing a dissertation titled "Marx, Nietzsche, and the Future of Political Philosophy"? I confirmed that Hoffman—a specialist in nineteenth-century European political theory—is a member of the Texas A&M Philosophy Department and was there during what would have been my doctoral study years. I have a memory of renting the upstairs of an old house across the street from the A&M campus and even recall the address. A Google search confirmed there is a house at that address, with a photo of the house as I remembered it. How could I not have been there and know this?

Before that, I have a memory of growing up in nearby Bryan, Texas in the home of my parents, Theodore and Sarah Feldman, Jews who moved there from Boston. That is what I remember my adoptive parents telling me because I was only four when we moved. I have no memory of Boston. I recall that we attended Bryan's Congregation Beth Shalom, a Reform synagogue, a place that welcomed everyone—even in this conservative city—including those who identified as queer and trans. Are my memories of my loving parents, our life as Jews, and my childhood in Bryan, Texas a creation of my imagination? Apparently so, because, tragically, I could find no evidence that this couple ever existed. That, to repeat, was like losing my adoptive parents a second time and like being orphaned three times.

There must be some explanation of how I, if I am not who I think I am, can have memories of living in various places, including Winterville, with a detailed knowledge of these locations, recollections of facts I confirmed by doing a little research. This means that not all of my memories are unreliable. If something happened to my brain, it was extraordinary. Beyond abnormal. And before that happened, I must have lived a life that enabled me to attain the knowledge that is contained in what I call *memory*, a word that was, in my case, seemingly a misnomer when it came to memories of my past. Whether memory is the correct term, I did have within my mind a genuine knowledge of actual places and actual persons. My mental condition—disorder?—seemed to be *sui generis*. After many hours in the public library searching online the topic of memory abnormalities, I could find no medical research that described anything resembling my case.

When I failed to get into the condo complex that I thought was my place of residence and then had a conversation with a policewoman who obviously did not believe what I was telling her, maybe what I saw in the cop's eyes—seeing myself as she probably saw me—was correct: namely, that I was a mentally ill person who had become homeless. In fact, I was homeless. Was I also mentally ill? Or was I suffering from some kind of memory aberration that was not really a mental illness? Could this be an extraordinary malfunction of my brain, one in which I suddenly lost knowledge of who I really was—with my brain somehow inventing a fictional person and phony memories? Just as in dreams when the brain invents a strange new world or even a new identity for you, corresponding to nothing in reality, so this could be happening in waking life. And I kept coming back to the idea that if amnesiacs can forget who they are, maybe my condition was simply a more complicated case of amnesia. A behavioral health care professional would in fact later suggest this diagnosis.

The more I reflected on what I had lost, the more disturbed I became. I had no one to turn to, no one I could confide in—no one who might help me. Dead ends everywhere. No friends, no home, no obvious way back to the life I thought I knew. Feelings of hopelessness began to overwhelm me. I was feeling so desperate that I contemplated suicide. After all, I had lost everything. Did I really want to try to create a false identity that might be easily discovered? I seemed to be kidding myself about starting over. The very idea of beginning again suddenly seemed impossible. I fell into deep despair. What did I have to live for? My urgent and recurring question became "Why not commit suicide?"

I remembered the opening sentence of a book that, when I was seventeen, introduced me to existentialism. This sentence is found in Albert Camus's *The Myth of Sisyphus*: "There is but one truly serious philosophical problem and that is suicide." Camus says this in the next sentence: "Judging whether life is or is not worth living amounts to answering the fundamental question of philosophy." He tells his reader that, compared to this vital question, all other philosophical questions are mere games. My (admittedly unreliable) memory told me that during my senior year, while browsing the meager philosophy section of the library of Bryan High School, I discovered this collection of essays—*The Myth of Sisyphus*—that Camus had written when he was a young man.

I recalled how consoling it was to know that a respected French philosopher and novelist reflected on the fundamental absurdity of life and the question of whether suicide was a rational response to that. Camus, in what was an unconvincing argument (absurd reasoning?) makes the surprising case that awareness of life's absurdity demands that we *not* commit suicide. Whatever the merits of Camus's argument, the point is that during that time—when I was a very lonely, unappreciated, misunderstood, and sometimes suicidal Jewish teenager searching for meaning—I was amazed to come across a respected thinker who was willing to write about both the absurdity of life and suicide. I had to have this book—immediately. I urgently needed to make it mine. So, I stole it from the school library. That would be one of many books I illegally appropriated as an adolescent, with some books much more valuable than others. Or so I recalled.

At that moment in my high school library, I decided that when I entered college I would become a philosophy major and spend my life trying to answer Camus's foundational existential question, answer it for myself. I wasn't satisfied with Camus's answer. That's what I remember—or, should

I say, misremember. In any event, my current condition brought home in a very deep way Camus's theme of the absurd, of an absurd world. That idea—absurdity—kept popping into my head. What could be more absurd than living in a world where, suddenly, no one knows you and all your personal memories are no more real than dreams, recollections of things that, apparently, never happened? What, indeed, is the point of living in a condition of such extreme alienation from everyone and everything you love?

I could commit suicide, or . . . Or what? Well, I could work to discover what happened to my mind, who I really was, and how, if my memories were false, I could have the detailed knowledge I possessed of people and places. Didn't I need to give this more time, time to try to figure out what was causing my confused state of mind? Time to find an explanation of who I really was? As I was reflecting on my bizarre condition, an odd, really fantastical, question occurred to me: Could I be a character in someone's novel? Maybe the author of this work gave me the memories I have. Many novelists write about themselves, masking actual events and experiences by inventing a fictional character to tell their story. Maybe that's what I was, who I was. Perhaps I was a fictional character created by a retired professor of philosophy turned novelist, drawing on the memories from his childhood, schooling, and life as an academic. Of course, this was itself an absurd hypothesis, one I did not arrive at rationally. It was obviously a preposterous explanation of who I was—but I could not entirely let this idea go. I'll return to this literary explanation later.

More plausible was the hypothesis that I suffered from catastrophic memory loss that strangely manifested itself as false memories and the false belief that I was Nathan Feldman, a professor of philosophy at Winterville State University. Again, I could find no evidence that something like this could happen to a person's brain, but I seemed to be proof that this in fact was possible. What I found most puzzling was the fact that my seemingly false memories were populated by actual human beings I seemed to know a lot about—even if they failed to recognize me. That is what made my situation different from the standard case of amnesia. My seemingly unique condition was worth serious investigation. I decided, for the time being, that I needed to try to discover the nature of my mental aberration. Thus, I put off suicide temporarily in the hope of finding the truth about what had happened to my brain and who I really was.

3. The Missing Person

I DECIDED THAT I hadn't been thorough enough in my previous online research. In a renewed quest for self-discovery, I returned to the Winterville Public Library to do research on memory loss, mental illness, and even missing persons. But, again, I came up short, finding nothing helpful. I couldn't discover anything that would enable me to understand what had happened to my mind, to explain my inability to remember my actual past while remembering a fictional one—a fictional past that was, paradoxically, filled with real people whose lives I could accurately describe, although they claimed not to know me. These individuals seemed surprised when I provided information about them that they confirmed was correct. They seemed puzzled that I, a stranger to them, knew so much about their lives— and this seemed to make them want to avoid me.

Typical was my experience with a faculty member on campus I talked to after my disillusioning visit to the Winterville University Philosophy Department, after not being recognized by the secretary of the department, a woman I remembered knowing for ten years—a person I thought knew me well. Following this man on campus, I called him by name, Wilfred James, as he was walking toward the WSU Student Union. When he turned around, and gave me a puzzled look, I, maybe showing off, named the courses he taught, the university committees he was on, the place he received his PhD, the names of his wife, children and their ages, his Golden Retriever's name and age, the place his family usually spent winter break, and much more. He seemed uneasy about what I knew and clearly wanted to get away from me. I think he was spooked when I told him we were good friends. He looked confused and nervous. No doubt Wilfred perceived me as threatening and perhaps unhinged. I finally left him alone.

No matter how irrational, part of me wanted to believe that everyone around me was lying, that this was a grand conspiracy. There is a saying by the great Jewish sage Hillel, my namesake: "If I am not for myself, who will be for me?" If I was for myself, how could I believe what people were telling me, what inquiries on Google showed or didn't show? There were times when I felt certain about who I was. Just as René Descartes asserts that at each time anyone thinks "I think, therefore I am," it is impossible to be mistaken, so it seemed to me that each time I thought "I am Nathan Feldman," this was also a self-evident truth. If I was correct about who I really was, then that meant everyone else was lying, engaged in deception. Such persecutory feelings often gripped me. But I knew that I needed to return to reality. This paranoia would not entirely go away until I finally discovered the disillusioning truth about my condition, a truth that made my paranoid episodes vaguely prescient. I will say more about these episodes later, and what they foreshadowed.

When not feeling paranoid, I wanted to find a rational explanation of my condition. Since I was now alone and unknown, who could I possibly turn to? There must be somewhere I could go for help. It occurred to me, when I was thinking clearly and rationally, that the best explanation of my condition was that I was a missing person suffering from an odd form of amnesia. But I never discovered information online about any person fitting my description. Still, I thought this would be a good place to start: to search the country, with help from law enforcement, for evidence of a missing person who matched my description. I had read online about the case of a man in Georgia who suffered from amnesia for eleven years but finally, through the use of his DNA, discovered who he was and reconnected with his family in another state. He had somehow ended up in a place far from his home, his family. He had no memory of who he was and his past.

I concluded—not sure why I didn't think of this sooner—that if I really was a missing person, the best way to confirm this was go to the police and ask for help. So, I walked to the police station. This is the advantage of living in a small town: you can reach many important places by foot in a matter of minutes. I knew where the police station was, just as I knew the location of what I thought was my place of employment. I wondered: How could I know these things if I was a missing person from another city or state? I entered the Winterville Police Department and told the officer at the front desk that I wanted to report a missing person.

"I'll need some basic information. Male or female? What's the name of this person?"

"Male. I don't know his name."

"How do you know this nameless person is missing."

"Trust me, I know. He's a homeless person."

"How long has this homeless person been missing?"

"I don't know."

"Are you kidding me?" He seemed genuinely puzzled, not hostile.

"No."

"A few months? Years?"

"I don't have a clue."

"Although I'm not sure whether I should take you seriously, I'll proceed. Where was this homeless person last seen when you discovered that he was missing—in a shelter, a tent, on the street, or somewhere else?

"He was spending the night in Red River Park."

"Do you have a description of this person? Age? Height? What's your relationship, if any, to this person?"

"Description? White. Probably forty-one. Probably six-two. I'm this person."

"Again, you're not making any sense. You're reporting yourself as a missing person?"

"Yes. I thought my name was Nathan Feldman until yesterday morning at 9:12 a.m. when I walked into what I mistakenly believed was my place of residence, the moment people stopped recognizing me. When I researched missing persons online, I didn't find my name; and I found nothing about a missing person fitting my description. I seem to be confused about where I thought I lived and worked. Even about my entire past. So, if I gave you his age or any other personal information, it might not be correct. As incredible as this still appears to me, I suspect that Nathan Feldman is a fictional character. I left my condo yesterday morning for a walk as Nathan Feldman, but when I returned from my walk that name was no longer on what I believed was my mailbox. And my name and face didn't seem to ring any bells when I came into contact with people who I believed knew me. Apparently, the Nathan Feldman who I thought I was doesn't exist."

"This may seem like an unnecessary question, but I'll ask it anyway. Do you have any form of identification?"

"Unfortunately, I didn't take my wallet with me when I went on my walk yesterday. I left it in my condo—or what I thought was my condo."

"Just to be clear: you can provide no information that would confirm your identity as Nathan Feldman?"

"None."

"Not even a Social Security number?"

"I can give you the number I remember, but I can also tell you that it will not bring up my name or probably anyone's."

"So, you're a homeless person with no way of proving your identity."

"Yes, as it turns out."

"We could do a nationwide search if we had your correct name. Since you're telling me that you're mentally confused, confused about who you are, your immediate problem seems one of unreliable memory or even a complete loss of memory. You seem to be a missing person suffering from amnesia. Did you have a recent head injury—for example, when you went on your walk yesterday? Did you fall and hit your head, or did someone assault you, strike you on the head?"

"Not that I am aware of."

"Please take off your cap and turn around. With your head shaved, it would be easy to see evidence of a serious head injury: swelling or a bruise. No sign of that. I do see what appear to be cuts, now small scars, on each side of the crown of your head and a smaller one behind your left ear. I see that you have a long scar on your left wrist, and what seem to be cuts on your left upper arm. Did someone attack you?"

"Not that I can recall. I was puzzled by those cuts on my arms that I saw for the first time after my walk on Saturday morning. And I saw the cuts on my head when I looked at myself in a mirror in a park restroom. I don't think I have a head injury."

"Your memory loss could also be caused by something internal, such as a brain aneurysm. Have you experienced nausea and vomiting, blurred or double vision, a severe headache?"

"No." I didn't want to tell him about experiencing what I called *existential nausea*. He would have thought me loony—or loonier than I already seemed. The truth is that *loony* might have been a good description of my mental state at that time. Or, more precisely, I could have been described as a *lunatic* because that's what I was feeling like. A crude nonmedical term, but still a word that I was coming to think was a perfect label for what I'd become.

"Would you mind if I fingerprinted you and got your DNA?"

"Not at all. That's what I expected you to request. Yes, please."

"And if we could get a photograph, we can immediately send that out nationally through various media with the question: 'Do you know this man? If so, please contact the Winterville Minnesota Police Department.'

That's all I know to do. That way we can do a national, and even international, search to try find out who you are."

"How long will it take to get the fingerprint and DNA results?"

"Our process is bit slow: two weeks. But distributing a photo of you could bring results before that. I don't suppose you have an email or a cell number I could use to inform you when we get the results?"

"No. While I was in the public library, I should have created a new email account, but neglected to do that. Not sure why I didn't think of that. I couldn't access any of what I thought were my email accounts. Yahoo doesn't recognize my password or username. It's the same with my university email. You see, I thought I was a professor of philosophy at Winterville State University. But that job appears to exist only in my head."

"Please be patient. If you can return two weeks from now, we may know something. Please call before you come to make sure we have the results. Maybe you can borrow someone's cell phone to do that. Save you a trip. Do you have a safe place to stay?"

"Yes. Thank you for doing this, even though I suspect you think I'm not in my right mind."

"If you will please step into Room A to your right, I'll have someone in there in a short while to take your picture, get your fingerprints, and do a DNA swab."

I waited a few minutes. A female police officer swabbed my mouth, got my fingerprints, and took a photo. Since I couldn't give her an address, email, or cell phone to notify me of the results, she also told me that I would need to return to the station in a couple of weeks. I left, wondering if there was some other way that I could continue the process of trying to identify myself, of finding my true identity.

I decided to return to the public library to continue my research, my attempt to discover something helpful about my identity. I had already searched for actual people named Nathan Feldman, and in fact found a real person with my exact name: Nathan Hillel Feldman, a PhD candidate in chemistry at Northwestern University. He was not a missing person. I even saw his photograph. He didn't look like me.

Although it seemed like a crazy idea, I decided to take a leap and google "fictional professor of philosophy named Nathan Feldman." This was, after all, one of my more implausible explanations: that I was a character in a work of fiction. Again, no matter how preposterous, I was wondering if a writer of fiction had invented my name and described my character in a draft of a work of fiction, something not yet published but posted online by the writer. Maybe I was a character in a work of fiction in process, something in draft form—and that's where I came up with my fictional name and history. If so, I thought it was possible that this writer discussed this character online and I saw this many years ago and maybe forgot. That it was lodged in my memory. I of course realized that this line of inquiry—namely, that I was a literary character—made no rational sense. But neither did my life. My past, as I remembered it, seemed to be nothing more than fiction, and my very "character"—Nathan Feldman, professor of philosophy—was clearly an invention, a product of someone's imagination. I think most people would agree that, given the evidence, it is beyond question that the Nathan Hillel Feldman, professor of philosophy and resident of Winterville, Minnesota is a fictional person, whether a literary character or not.

My wild hypothesis was not original. There was a movie that may have inspired it: *Stranger than Fiction*. In this 2006 film, the central character, Harold Crick—an unstable IRS auditor played by Will Ferrell in his first dramatic role—hears background narration that leads him to believe he is a character in a novel. When it becomes clear that the author-narrator is about to kill him—that is, have this character die—he panics and seeks to save his life by finding this author in order to persuade her to change her mind about how to end the novel. Although I heard no such background narration, I could say without fear of contradiction that my life seemed to be like something out of novel, maybe a work of science fiction. How could my life, as I remembered it prior to my return from that Saturday morning walk, be anything other than an invented story—if, as seemed to be the case, my name, Social Security number, past experiences, and my present life as a professor and resident of 413 10th Street South, Red River Park Condominiums, Unit 301, did not correspond to the facts?

If my autobiography—my life as *I* narrated it to myself—was not factual, someone must have created it, made it up, imagined it. Could that someone be me, in the hidden form of my subconscious mind? How could I misremember so much? One simple answer: because I had an imagination—and sometimes imagination and what we call memory cannot be distinguished. Philosophers who study epistemology are aware of this. And psychologists and psychiatrists also know this. I was well aware that what some people sincerely claim to remember are events and places their brain has manufactured. It happens all the time.

Honest and intelligent human beings can sometimes mistake the one for the other: imagined memory for actual memory. Perhaps my brain, for whatever reason, had shifted from genuine recollection to invented recollection—that I had subconsciously, spontaneously, and creatively composed a false narrative of my life, a pseudo-narrative that replaced my actual memories. A subconsciously invented narrative that I came consciously to believe. This is called confabulation. In my research I discovered that confabulation is a neuropsychiatric disorder wherein a person with memory loss subconsciously generates a false memory or a story without the intention of deceit. It was just one more hypothesis to explain what otherwise seemed inexplicable. This conjecture was at least more plausible than the idea that I was a character in a work of fiction—a wild explanation that I never completely left behind.

4. Analyze This

Days passed. As I wandered around Winterville, I was also wondered how I could make sense of what had become a very mysterious life, continuing to entertain all kinds of crazy hypotheses that might explain my mental confusion. I decided that I needed to stop all of this fanciful speculation about my mental condition and begin to seek answers that were empirically grounded. Based on facts, not fanciful conjectures. Other than the police, who else could I turn to for help? Perhaps I should have waited for the fingerprint, DNA, and photo results, but I was too impatient for that. It struck me that the most plausible explanation of my condition was that I suffered from a radical form of confabulation and therefore should seek the services of a psychiatrist. Such a professional might also help me overcome my recurring suicidal ideation.

It was, however, unlikely I could get an appointment with a psychiatrist at any of the local hospitals or a psychiatrist in private practice nearby. What psychiatrist would agree to see a man who had no health insurance, Social Security number, or any source of income? Fortunately, I knew a psychiatrist who taught a course in Winterville State University's Psychology Department. Or I thought knew her. According to my recollection, she was both a neurologist and psychiatrist—thus a neuropsychiatrist. I also recalled that Dr. Elizabeth Leah Cohen was a member of a neuroscience research team that was working on a special memory experiment. So, maybe I was in luck since memory was one of her areas of research. I knew that she had published a number of articles in prestigious medical and neuroscience journals on the nature of memory, memory loss, memory replacement, and traumatic memory. She had a psychiatric practice Monday/Wednesday/Friday, worked Tuesday/Thursday as a researcher for the Neuroscience Institute for the Study of Memory, and taught her WSU three-hour seminar class, Introduction to Psychiatry, on Wednesday evenings, starting at 6 p.m.

When I say that I knew this neuropsychiatrist, I mean not only that I knew of her, but also that I personally knew her. That was my recollection. It was, however, improbable that she would remember me, given what I had experienced since my Saturday morning walk. So, I didn't expect her to recognize me.

Nevertheless, I had detailed memories of her personal and professional life that turned out to be accurate. I would soon discover that my memory of our close relationship was another false memory. My recollection was this: since the WSU Psychology Department was next door to the WSU Philosophy Department, and I often worked evenings in my office, preparing for the next day's classes, I met her one evening after she finished teaching her seminar. I recalled—even if only in imagination—that at that first meeting I had a long conversation with Elizabeth and then, in short order, how we quickly became friends and then much more than friends.

I also recalled that during our first conversation she told me she was a distant relative of Leonard Cohen, my favorite singer-poet. We talked about his music, which she also loved. We had both enjoyed his last album—*You Want It Darker*—finished just before cancer took his life. The song after which the album was named resonated with me—and Elizabeth. If there is a God, a plausible case can be made—and Leonard Cohen was making it in song—that, given all the pain and evil in the world, this God must sanction darkness, evil, maybe even welcomes it. My world had become very dark, and I was well aware that countless others on the planet were experiencing their own forms of darkness—in many cases, much more horrible than mine. For example, victims of brutal warfare. Since the doctor did not believe in God, a divine explanation of all the darkness in the world made no sense to her. But she admired the willingness of Leonard Cohen, obviously a very spiritual but also questioning Jew, to call God out.

A Jew by birth, Elizabeth had left religious Judaism behind, probably because, growing up in a Haredi community in New York City, the Borough Park neighborhood of Brooklyn, she was exposed only to an ultra-Orthodox form of the faith. She rebelled at a young age against what she found to be an oppressive religious culture. Becoming a feminist at sixteen, she secretly studied science, especially psychology and biology. She could not abide her community's view of the place of women and its anti-scientific worldview. It was her community's reckless behavior during the coronavirus outbreak that became for her the final straw. At seventeen she ran away from her family and what she perceived to be a religious prison to take up residence in the home of an aunt who lived in Manhattan, a wealthy single woman, a poet who was a secular Jew.

Incredibly intelligent, Elizabeth went to Yale on a full scholarship as an undergraduate, with a double major: neuroscience and music—graduating early, in two years. Her natural skepticism and acceptance of Freud's idea that religion is a world of illusions led her to abandon Judaism altogether. I was unable to convince her to give Reform Judaism a try. I summed up for her the Reform version of Judaism: *Belief in God, optional. Working for social justice, required.* Such again is my memory, even if imaginary, of our first conversation. The first of many—and the beginning of what I recalled as an intimate and loving relationship. Now a very painful memory because it was, in all probability, false. Still, I could not let go of that memory.

Since it was Wednesday, I hoped to catch Elizabeth after her class. But I needed to look presentable. At the Winterville Salvation Army Thrift Store, which carried used clothing, I found a well-fitting, new-looking, white long-sleeve dress shirt with a minor tear in one of the shirt tails which I could tuck in. I also found a pair of presentable men's black cords that fit, black socks, and an attractive plastic gray belt. I also discovered a pair of black Adidas athletic shoes that sort of fit, maybe just a tad too large, but still comfortable, actually dressy looking. I left behind my tattered Nikes. I also picked up an old backpack to carry my new belongings. Although broke, I felt free to choose all of these items, as well as needed toilet articles, because the elderly woman who had given me the sleeping bag told me I could have them on the promise to pay for them later. A generous IOU.

I filled out a promissory note and signed it. Evidently this was her common practice, something she apparently did on her own. I wondered how many people actually followed through, paying what they owed. When I asked her about this, she responded: "I am guided by Deuteronomy 15:8 where the Lord commands this: 'You must open your hand to your brother and lend him what is sufficient for his needs.'" I appreciated the fact that she took seriously a *mitzvah* in the Jewish Bible, which she of course called the Old Testament. Given her generosity, I suspected that she made good when those who signed promissory notes did not keep their word. I was determined to eventually pay up. I remember her name: Doris Anderson.

It's strange how your needs can radically change when your world radically changes. In my previous life—the apparently illusory life I so well remembered—I would have felt deprived if I didn't get my daily hit of a $10.00 small espresso at a high-end coffee shop, and I felt proud of myself for always adding a 25 percent tip. This day I was ecstatic to receive gratis—well, really on credit—used clothes, toilet supplies, and an ancient backpack. I put my new possessions in the tattered carryall, put it over one shoulder, and walked toward my new home: Red River Park. I changed into the pre-owned clothes in a bathroom stall in the park restroom and put my old clothes in the backpack, now containing my few worldly possessions. Making sure no one in the park saw me, I hid this bag in the same thickly wooded area where I had stashed my sleeping bag. I, feeling like a new man in my more presentable attire, walked more confidently toward the university campus, what I remembered as my decade-long place of employment where neither students nor faculty recognized me. On the way to the university, I recalled that last year I won an award for excellence in teaching at that institution. Fame is fleeting.

I waited in the small lobby area of the WSU Psychology Department, just outside the seminar room where Elizabeth was teaching a class of twelve students. It was a senior psychology seminar: only seniors in psychology could register for this course. I remembered that some of our philosophy majors interested in psychiatry wanted to sign up for the class, but were not allowed to do so. It was 8:43 p.m. The class was supposed to end at 9:00. I was wondering: Should I tell Elizabeth that I remembered knowing her intimately? As I was rehearsing what to say, the class ended and students started leaving.

Finally, after answering questions raised by three students about next week's assignment, Elizabeth was alone and walking back to her office, very close to the seminar room, an office occupied during weekdays and other weekday nights by a psychology professor who taught Statistics in Psychological Research and Experimental Psychology. I knew him well, even if he no longer knew me. He had an interest in the psychology of religion which made for interesting conversations. I recalled that we had talked about teaching together an interdisciplinary course on religion. But that never happened, even in my memory—now, I had to keep reminding myself, more like imagined memory.

"Dr. Cohen."

"Yes."

"I'm Nathan Feldman, a professor of philosophy. Could I talk to you for a few minutes?" I knew of course that a few minutes would not be enough. Clearly, from her response, she didn't recognize me.

"What about?" Not unfriendly, but professionally cool. She was probably worn out from a day of practice at her clinic and then this long class. I recalled that three-hour seminars in the evening always took a lot out of me. I even had trouble getting to sleep following these classes. My brain was so stimulated by the give-and-take of the seminar discussion that usually I didn't fall asleep until about two in the morning. Most other nights I was usually asleep by eleven. Or so I misremembered.

"I once had an office close to yours—next door in the WSU Philosophy Department."

"You once taught here?"

"Yes."

"How long ago."

"Not too long ago. Obviously, it was before you started teaching your Wednesday evening class. I lost my position, even though I had tenure." Not sure why I had to add that last piece of information, especially given what appears to be a fact: I never taught at this university.

"So, despite tenure, you were terminated. Sorry to hear that."

"Yes. It's a long story."

"You don't have to explain. Without meaning to be rude, I need tell you that I'm winding down from a very long day and need to go home soon so I can get much needed rest and sleep."

"I completely understand. But my situation is desperate. I cannot wait weeks to get an appointment with a psychiatrist. I need to know tonight why I shouldn't kill myself." (There it was: the young Camus's fundamental philosophical question coming out of my mouth.)

Looking startled, but also trying to convey calmness, she immediately gave me a friendly look and motioned for me to step into her office and take a seat. The doctor could see that I was truly despondent and possibly a danger to myself. Elizabeth shut the door, but remained standing. It was astonishing that she was just thirty, having received from Harvard in record time an MD, with a specialty in psychiatry, and also a PhD in neuroscience. She completed her residency at Massachusetts General Hospital. A relatively tall (five-foot-ten), very attractive woman, with a dark complexion, black curly hair cut very short, she was always fashionably dressed. Her white pants were probably top of the line. On this summer evening, her light-brown stylish sleeveless top revealed very healthy-looking arms, not the model-thin appearance many women aspire to. Her arms were more on the athletic side, like those of a gymnast—which she in fact was as an undergraduate at Yale, someone who was very competitive in the sport, almost qualifying for the Olympics. She looked just as I remembered her— from a week ago! A very pleasant, even if untrue, memory.

"Let's see if we can get you some help immediately." Though obviously exhausted, she appeared very compassionate and acutely interested in what I had to say. Indeed, at the time, she struck me as extraordinarily kind, practicing what I then perceived to be an intelligent compassion that was not overwhelmed by the suffering of the other but oriented toward therapeutically treating it. In addition, in my memory she was not only a trusted close friend but my lover. My recollection of facts about other people had so far been spot on, even if they had no memory of me. As already indicated, my memory of her bio was in fact accurate, even if my recollection of our intimate relationship was untrustworthy. I asked myself: Should I strengthen my case by informing her of my detailed knowledge about her, detailed information that very few would know, that in fact only a lover or very good friend would know? I needed to be careful. I didn't want to alienate the only person who at that time could help me.

"Tell me what's going on, what makes you so disturbed that you are thinking about ending your life."

"It started last Saturday morning." That's how I began and then explained my story of loss, confusion about my identity, of not being recognized by anyone I thought knew me well while knowing a great deal about the lives of these individuals who treated me as a complete stranger. A story of apparently false memories about my entire past. I even shared my various wild speculations about what had happened to my mind and who I was. Then, I asked: "Have you ever encountered a patient like me? Do you know of a single case study that matches my mental condition?"

"Have you been using cannabis in any form?"

"No. Not that I can remember, but then again that's my problem: an inaccurate memory."

"Research has shown that the use of cannabis can contribute to spontaneous false memories. That's why legal testimony, witness accounts, by people who have used cannabis, are suspect. But there are no cases of which I am aware where this causes false memories covering an entire lifetime. That is not even possible, as far as I know. And the puzzle is that, although your memories of your past are false, they also contain information that is accurate, such as your memories about people who claim not to know you—where your memories about them, even of a very personal nature, are accurate from the point of view of these individuals who treat you as a stranger."

"Yes. That's what also profoundly puzzles me. And, to be honest, I still often feel certain that I'm Nathan Feldman and that my memories are true, memories of relationships with people who fail to recognize me."

"There is something called False Memory Syndrome. This refers to a condition in which a person's identity and relationships are affected by false memories, recollections that are factually incorrect yet strongly believed. The brilliant University of Pennsylvania mathematician Peter Freyd originated the term. I should emphasize that this is not considered a psychiatric illness in any of the standard medical manuals, including ICD-10 and DSM-5. I should also tell you that the Freyds—Peter and his wife, Pamela—founded the False Memory Syndrome Foundation in 1992 after their daughter accused Peter of sexually abusing her. They labeled this a false memory. This daughter, Jennifer Freyd, went on to become a professor of psychology and psychiatry who, unsurprisingly, specialized in childhood trauma, recovered memories, and parental betrayal."

"That of course raises questions about the Freyds's motivation for their work."

"Maybe their personal situation—what they claimed was their daughter's false memories—was the impetus to create the Foundation which, by the way, was dissolved in 2019. For those who are skeptical about their work because of the Freyds's personal history, it would be questionable *ad hominem* reasoning to discount their research findings solely on the basis of their daughter's claim, even if that claim was true. On the other hand, I think that the danger of the so-called False Memory Syndrome is that it can be used to discredit individuals who were actually molested as children. Whether or not there is such a syndrome, and whatever one might think of the motives of those who named it, there are clearly some cases of significant false memories, including cases where people" (here she made air quotes) "'remember' committing crimes they did not in fact commit."

"Do any studies include cases that involve people whose entire past recollections are false memories?"

"The so-called False Memory Syndrome, even if valid, is probably not relevant to your case because this disorder applies only to some of a person's memories, not to their totality. Usually, this syndrome has to do with memories of a traumatic episode."

"I hesitate to tell you this, but you are part of what I supposedly falsely recollect."

"What do you mean?"

"I remember that we were very good friends. Actually, more than good friends. My recollection is that I had an office down the hall and that is how we met, one evening after your class. My memory is not only that we hit it off, but that we became intimate partners."

"You have a memory that we were lovers!"

"Yes. I can even provide proof of that, but I'm not sure you will want me to verify this. I'm not sure you really want to go there."

"You cannot really verify what never happened. Maybe you saw a news story about me, accompanied by a photo, an article informing you that I taught here, and you then fantasized a relationship. That would fit with your pattern of false memories. The truth is that we've never met. That's a simple fact."

"It seems like only a week ago that we were together intimately and not a fantasy to me. That appears to me to be a simple fact. This is what I find so disturbing—namely that individuals who I thought cared about me, and even loved me, do not recognize or remember me."

"I can see how that would be disturbing, but you need to know, in our case, what you call a memory is really a fantasy—and not a true memory. I am flattered, but—"

"I don't mean to embarrass you, Dr. Cohen—but please explain this to me: How do I know that you have a mole on your right breast near your nipple, a one-inch scar on your left buttock, and on your right upper thigh, close to your pubic area, a tattoo of the Hebrew letters for 'To life: l'chaim'—which I thought was something very appropriate next your vagina, which I could also precisely describe, if you wish."

"Stop!"

She seemed shocked and embarrassed. Her strong emotional reaction confirmed that I was right about the three marks on her body. A long silence. She looked disturbed and her face became flush, but she recovered surprisingly quickly.

"I'm sorry. But that's a strong and apparently accurate memory."

"I'm not sure I can deal with this in my current state of fatigue. I need time to rest, sleep, and process this. I also need you to promise me that you will not do anything to harm yourself before we meet again. I can see you tomorrow evening at my clinic. I need your assurance that you will make

39

no attempt to take your life during this time. Or better, would you be willing to enter a residential behavioral health facility, a place that can keep you safe with professionals who can care for you and examine you? Possibly treat you."

"No. At this moment, in my current state of what you would probably call paranoia, I don't trust those I don't know, maybe not even those I thought I knew. Right now, at this moment, I mistrust everyone and suspect that people all around me are deceiving me, attempting to make me think I'm crazy. For some reason—probably because of warm memories—I trust you and am willing to suspend my plan to commit suicide for twenty-four hours. So that you have time to rest, sleep, and to try to figure out what you think is happening to me."

"Do you have a safe place to spend the night?"

"Yes."

"Okay, I will see you at seven tomorrow evening, at my clinic office, only a few blocks away, where we will have more privacy. I'm writing down the address."

She handed me an index card with the address of the clinic in her beautiful script.

"Thank you. I might just be able to sleep tonight, knowing that you'll try to help me, knowing that the world has not completely abandoned me, knowing that I have a brilliant neuropsychiatrist on my side."

I regretted describing the three marks on her body. I didn't need to do that. Still, it gave my claim about intimately knowing her a credibility it otherwise would not have had. When we met again, she did not mention this. Neither did I. I think my knowledge of these marks on her flesh provided her with shocking evidence to support my startling assertion that I knew intimate details about individuals who denied they knew me. Otherwise, she might have dismissed this claim as bogus, incredible. At the time, I thought that sharing this personal information about the three marks would make my case immensely interesting to her—and, on a personal level, I guessed that she would want to find an explanation of how I could have such intimate knowledge of her body. And of course I too wanted to know how I could have acquired this knowledge if we had not been together in a very personal way.

5. Stranger than Fiction

WHEN I FIRST EXPLAINED my condition to her, I told Elizabeth about my wild literary idea of who I might be. I informed her that there were times when I couldn't seem to rid myself of the idea that I was a fictional character in a novel. I know. I know. It was foolish to continue to take seriously the idea that I was the product of a writer's imagination. Elizabeth, interestingly and oddly, didn't think this was such a wild idea. Again, maybe the idea would have not entered my mind if I had never seen the movie *Stranger than Fiction*. During the time that passed, while I was waiting to see Elizabeth again, I became obsessed with this film. Since I didn't have access to a DVD player or to a streaming service, I looked for and found, to my surprise, in the Winterville Public Library a script of the movie. I studied the screenplay carefully to get a better understanding of the film and the background behind making it.

There were short introductory commentaries on the movie by the screenwriter, director, and producer. Since it was an original screenplay—and not a film based on a novel—the only way you could read *Stranger than Fiction* was in script form. Actually, this published version of the script was an earlier draft of the screenplay, slightly different than the finished movie. I spent a couple of hours in the library poring over the script. I couldn't check it out because I didn't have a library card—and without an ID of some kind, couldn't get one. So, I had to finish it in the library.

A character in a work of fiction? Why did I keep coming back to that? The rationalist philosopher in me wanted to absolutely reject this as preposterous, but the existentialist philosopher in me couldn't dismiss this on the basis of its absurdity because existentialism saw life itself as absurd. In Sartre's first novel, *Nausea*, the fictional narrator—despite being a seemingly level-headed historian—one day begins to think: "Anything can happen. Everything is terrifyingly possible." He imagines that the laws of nature could suddenly collapse. One image: birds peck at birch trees with their beaks and blood flows from them. Maybe Sartre had accepted David Hume's powerful critique of belief in causality and the laws of nature—raising questions about the justification of our belief in a necessary connection between cause and effect, suggesting it might be nothing more than a habit of mind. We repeatedly observe event B following event A—and so we assume the two are necessarily connected when in fact the connection is only an association in our minds, a mental connection. For all we know, there are no absolute laws in the cosmos and what now seems to be a fixed order can (re?)turn to chaos at any moment. Sartre's narrator in *Nausea* comes to feel that the so-called immutable laws of nature might one day break down partially or completely—and then even the seemingly impossible might occur.

The idea that a fictional character in a novel could begin to think for himself and one day recognize that he is a fictional character is of course absurd. Even if you dismiss the idea that this is a world where anything is possible, I would propose, simply as a thought experiment, that you imagine a fictional character reflecting on the possibility that he is only a fictional character. I, however, did not need to perform this thought experiment because I was obviously, in some sense, a fictional character! And, no matter how absurd, I couldn't altogether shake the idea that I was a fictional character in a novel. Why can't a fictional character in a novel ask if he is a fictional character? We simply need to imagine that a fictional character can transcend himself to contemplate such meta-questions. What if I was the kind of fictional character in a novel who did this? What if that was how my character was written—to be so self-conscious—and part of the author's plot? This kind of self-reflection on the part of the protagonist might be central to the fictional narrative I was in.

I kept returning to this thought: if my mind did not invent Nathan Feldman, then Nathan Feldman must be the invention of another mind—namely, the author who is making up my story. That also means that when this fabricated story ends, I will be no more. Did I want that? More often than not, I had to say: yes. When my desire to end my life resurged, I in fact welcomed death. I even sometimes prayed the following: May this story end soon, especially if that means the end of my nightmarish life as Nathan Feldman. A fictional death wish?

Although a fictional character owes his, her, or their life to the author, it's not necessarily a life to be thankful for any more than a real person who feels he owes his life to God necessarily feels gratitude to God—if, for example, it is a Job-like life. A believer who sees his life as a gift of God may wish, if his life is horrible, that he had never received this gift, had never been born—created. Maybe this person wishes to return the divine gift of life, saying politely to the Creator, "No thank you." Similarly, I could wish that the author who created Nathan Feldman had not done so. What if I want out, want to end this narrative? What if, within this fictional tale, I decide to commit suicide? Wouldn't that be the end of Nathan Feldman and his suffering? Fictional suffering. Maybe that's what I will do. What if, however, the author does not allow me to do that?

Can characters in a work of fiction really be independent of the author—exist on their own, think on their own, even in defiance of the author? In my now absurd world, the answer was *of course*. Writers often talk about their novel and its characters as having a life of their own, even about a novel writing itself. So, I reasoned, even if I was a character in a work of fiction, that did not mean I couldn't think for myself, go my own way, and even protest being this character, protest being thrown into the situation the writer has invented. For example, I can imagine Meursault in Camus's *The Stranger* having a life of his own. I can imagine Meursault protesting being made the mindless agent of a thoughtless murder of a nameless Arab on a steamy beach in Algiers. A scene in which the trigger of Meursault's gun seemed to pull itself, several times, the murder happening simply because the blazing sun reflected from an Arab's knife pierced Meursault's eyes. Meursault might not appreciate having his life, as he had innocently lived it in Part One of the novel, put on trial in Part Two and made a guilty life.

It was an unintentional homicide that the prosecutor, in Part Two, made to appear very calculated by retelling unconnected episodes in Meursault's life, prior to his act of taking the Arab's life, as if they were connected, as if they were events in the culpable life of a cold-blooded murderer-to-be. At the trial, Meursault was scathingly described by the prosecutor as a heartless person who could not even remember his mother's age and did not cry at her funeral, as if these were grave sins—the personal traits of a criminal. Even apart from the prosecutor's indictment of his life in Part Two of the novel, Meursault in Part One seems superficial, shallow, living only for the moment in the worst sense: completely self-centered, without real human emotion, incapable of love. While enjoying sex with his "lover," he is depicted as unable to utter the word "love" to the woman he is intimate with. Meursault might feel bitter at being depicted as a man who was thoughtless and who kills another human being for no good reason. Who would want to be remembered as that kind of character?

I too wanted to protest. If I, like Meursault, was only a character in a work of fiction, what happened? What went wrong? Why was my narrative—the story of my life as I remembered it—abruptly ended as soon as it began, by having all the other characters deny that they ever knew Nathan Feldman, the Nathan Feldman that I knew so well? Why thrust him—me—suddenly into this state of confusion? How did this advance any plot? It made no sense. Is that the point? Was the idea to throw Nathan Feldman into a state of confusion so that the life he had lived was not one that even his closest friends—even his lover—any longer remembered? So that I, Nathan Feldman, became a nonperson, someone completely lost—lost to himself and others? That seemed cruel—to me.

How is the author going to advance the story from here? Hasn't the writer trapped himself in a scenario from which there is no way out, no way forward? If no one recognizes Nathan Feldman and yet Nathan Feldman has a detailed knowledge of the lives of those who claim not to know him, where can the writer go with this? It would appear to me that the author has written himself into a corner. How can there be any plausible explanation of the mental condition of the protagonist? Any attempt to explain this will probably strike the reader as contrived. Hasn't the writer reached a dead end? I would think so. Still, all of a sudden, I wanted to see where this was going—where, even if only as a literary character, my life was headed. All of a sudden, I was no longer interested, at least for the time being, in committing suicide, even fictional suicide. These extreme mood shifts—for example, from despondency to curiosity—seemed to characterize my confused mental life at the time.

In a radical change of attitude, I was now in an expectant mood, wanting to live long enough to find out what would happen next—whether as fiction or reality. I especially wanted to see *how* Dr. Elizabeth Cohen—maybe she too was only a character in this work of fiction—*would* help Nathan Feldman. Or whether she *could* help me at all. I was still, with memories of our close relationship fresh on my mind, madly in love with this woman. *Mad* can of course mean insane. Was I madly in love in some pathological sense? Was I a fool for love? Plato insightfully describes erotic love as a form of madness, of losing one's mind. Perhaps my love for Elizabeth was indeed a kind of madness in the sense that my will to believe we had been lovers, and could be again, was completely irrational, crazy. Elizabeth had in fact called my memory our intimate relationship a fantasy. I didn't want to accept that.

How could I let go of my love for her? And I couldn't stop asking another question that seemed to me reasonable, anything but a sign of madness: If we were never lovers, what possible explanation could there be for my knowledge that the Hebrew letters for "to life" were tattooed near her vagina. This was something that clearly showed she had rejected her Haredi heritage because frum Judaism prohibits tattoos. That would confirm the accuracy of my memory of her as a woman who rejected religious restrictions. And I vividly remembered being physically up close and personal to that tattoo, many times! One simple explanation, the one I desperately wanted to believe: we were in fact once lovers. And if we had been lovers—whether in a novel or real life—why was she, or the literary character with her name, lying about this, denying it?

If I was trapped in a novel, I wanted to ask the reader: Do you understand the power of eros, sexual love? Can you understand why these questions about my relationship with Elizabeth Cohen were torturing me more than anything else? I couldn't simply stop loving a person I felt such passion for, forget that a week ago Elizabeth and I were intimate—and that we deeply cared for each other. That was my recollection. How could I be expected to forget this or write it off? Could you, dear reader, if you were in my place, forget about such an all-consuming relationship? You know the answer. I had a powerful wish: let every other memory be false, but please not this one. That wish was part of my (actual or fictional) character.

So, fiction or not, I wanted to see where this was headed, and my greatest desire was, to reiterate, that my relationship with Elizabeth be restored, no matter what else happened. In case this was a fictional work in progress, with the ending yet to be written, I also wanted to say, if anyone out there knows who is writing this story—assuming it is a work of fiction that is not yet finished—please urge the author to end it in a way that makes it possible for Elizabeth and Nathan to get back together. Yes, please urge the writer to make it a Hollywood ending. That was the very irrational and deeply romantic way I was thinking at one time—before I found out what was actually going on. Before I saw who Elizabeth Cohen really was. Before I discovered the awful truth.

6. Land of Dreams

IN MY INITIAL CONVERSATION with her, I also told Elizabeth that there was another explanation of my condition that I entertained, and even though it was also highly improbable, it was not as improbable as my sense that I was a character in a work of fiction. That other explanation was that I was dreaming. (I am, for the moment, putting aside a third, even wilder explanation, the conspiracy hypothesis. More on that later.) Elizabeth said that she could understand why, given how irrational things appeared to be in my life, I would think I was lost in a dream. I even told her that at times her failure to recognize me seemed to be part of a terrible nightmare in which those you love treat you as a complete stranger. Sometimes, when I was talking to Elizabeth, answering questions and asking questions, I couldn't get over my feeling that this was only a bad dream.

I simply needed to wake up and become again the Nathan Feldman whose memories were reliable and whose life in Winterville was in fact the life I so well remembered. And, most important, I told her that I wanted to wake up to be again the Nathan Feldman recognized by Elizabeth as her dear friend and lover. I didn't conceal from her how important our relationship was to me and how badly I wanted to restore what we had. She said she understood, but in fact this desire was, she again reminded me, only a fantasy, and thus itself very much like a dream. What I continued to want was for my present experience, a life in which we did not intimately know each other, to be a dream. And I was thinking that it really could be.

I had to ask the same question about my dream self that I asked when I suspected that I was a fictional character: Is it possible for someone in a dream to ask whether he is in a dream? Wouldn't such meta-thinking be evidence that one is really awake? Not necessarily. The idea that I was dreaming was a way of making sense of a world that otherwise didn't make sense—because what I was experiencing seemed to be precisely the kind of absurdity one experiences only in a dream. That's why this world seemed so absurd—to wit, because it really was only a nightmare. And there is no law of dreaming that says we can never be aware that we are dreaming. On the contrary.

Since this dream hypothesis kept entering my mind, I wondered if there was some way that I could objectively determine whether I was dreaming or awake. My first question became the one I started with: Could I really be aware that I was dreaming if I was really in a dream? The literature on dreaming says yes. In what are called lucid dreams, which can occur during REM sleep, the dreamer is conscious that he is dreaming and can even shape the narrative of his dream. The phenomenon of lucid dreaming, which has been scientifically verified, was recognized long ago by Aristotle in his treatise *On Dreams* where he states that such dreams occur when "the dreamer perceives that he is asleep and is conscious he is sleeping during which this perception comes before his mind." The difference was that while in lucid dreaming a dreamer *knows* that he is dreaming, I did not. I was only speculating that I was dreaming. I was in a state of uncertainty about whether I was dwelling in the land of dreams.

Such uncertainty wouldn't occur if I were in the midst of a lucid dream. I thought, however, that my experience might be a hybrid. Maybe I was in an in-between state: a state between complete immersion in a dream and a lucid state where the dreamer knows he is dreaming. Even our so-called waking state is not unambiguous. Can we, for example, really *know* that we are *truly* awake when we *think* we are awake? Philosophers such as René Descartes have been able to create doubts in the minds of those who were, before reading his *Meditations—Meditation 1*, to be precise—sure they were awake. Descartes argues that dreams and waking life *can* have the same content—that there can be sufficient similarity between the two states of mind that people can be deceived into believing they are awake when they are asleep. So, the divide between dreaming and being wake is not as clear as we often think it is. If I believe I am awake, how can I be sure this belief is justified? If I believe I am dreaming, can I sometimes be mistaken about this? In either case—with the exception of lucid dreaming—we lack certitude.

Despite its dream-like nature, I had to admit that everything I was experiencing seemed very real to me. My experiences didn't defy logic or science, which happens in dreams. I was doing normal things—eating, walking, conversing, even sleeping—that appeared actually to be happening. Days were passing. Let me repeat: my experiences since that transformative Saturday morning didn't violate the rules of logic or any naturals laws. There was, after all, no contradiction in asserting that people you thought knew you claim to have never met you. And having those who you thought were close to you fail to recognize you is of course bizarre, but it doesn't violate any law of nature. My body wasn't floating above the world, and the people I was in conversation with didn't suddenly turn into horses or pigs—the sort of weird events that occur only while dreaming. Wouldn't this be evidence that I wasn't dreaming since dreams supposedly contain occurrences that are absolutely illogical or scientifically impossible? Not necessarily.

There were two things in my dream history that I saw as relevant to trying to figure out whether I was dreaming or awake. First, I could recall having dreams in which I did normal things—whether eating my breakfast, having a conversation with a friend, or lecturing to a philosophy class. What occurred in these dreams did not defy principles of logic or natural laws. On the contrary, I remember having dreams in which I was developing an argument in a philosophy class (for example, about how personal identity depends on memory)—and upon waking I could recall the logical reasoning I used to make my case. So, the logic test wasn't always reliable as a test of whether I was dreaming. And I had many dreams that never violated the laws of nature.

Second, I could remember having dreams in which people who I considered my friends didn't recognize me, in which I had become a stranger to everyone. That is, in the past I had, even if rare, dreams in which people I knew well claimed not to know me. Then I woke up. So, this could simply be one of those dreams. Thus, what I was experiencing was not alien to my own dream history. The fact that I had experienced dreams in which I knew people who claimed not to know me seemed to count as evidence that my life as I was experiencing it, since that special Saturday morning, could very well be a dream.

My memory of dreams that were similar to my present state of mind did not, however, constitute proof that I was now dreaming. And my memory was the very thing that was in question. But I did read about other people with similar dream experiences: so, I wasn't alone in this. Unless this very act of reading was itself a part of my dream! This was my point to myself: if dream experiences can be consistent with the laws of logic, the laws of nature, and involve the experience of not being recognized by people we in fact know, then my dream hypothesis was not necessarily false. This, however, I had to concede, still did not prove that I was immersed in a dream. It only established the *possibility* that I was dreaming. Thus, I needed a more reliable dream test, something fool-proof, if possible. Even though my experiences since that shocking Saturday morning were consistent with my own dream history, I could, for all I knew, still be awake.

I discovered in the vast literature on dreaming that there were many dream tests. Here are some of them: You are dreaming if you look at a text on a page, look away, and the words suddenly change when you look back; you push a finger into the opposite palm and it passes through; you look at the time on a clock, quickly look away, then quickly look back, and the time substantially changes; you pinch your nose tightly with your mouth also closed tightly and you can still breathe; you try to fly and you can; you attempt to lift a very heavy object and you are able to do so without effort; you decide to walk through a wall and you do—and so forth. I had to admit to myself that I couldn't do any of these things.

I remembered, however, as I was testing my dream hypothesis, that a number of years ago, when I was teaching a class examining Descartes's dream argument, I told students about my own attempts to find a reliable way to decide the dream question. I informed them that I thought I'd discovered a reliable test to determine, with certainty, whether I was awake or dreaming. At first, I believed I had discovered two dream tests. I called these the pain and death tests. If it was a dream in which I faced the possibility of physical pain and/or death, I would deliberately court danger. My assumption was that, if I was dreaming, I could not experience pain and could not die. If I it looked like I was about to experience pain and/or die, either I would wake up or the scene would change. I told my students that I had repeatedly performed these tests only in lucid dreams.

I remember telling them about a recent lucid dream that took place in a wooded area where I faced great danger: a group of archers were about to shoot arrows at me. Believing that, because it was a dream, I would not be able to feel pain or to die—I invited the bowmen to bring it on. Without a shield, feeling like Superman, I walked toward the archers, virtually committing suicide. I told myself that because I knew I was dreaming—again, I was in a lucid dream—nothing could hurt or kill me. I was only half right. Unfortunately, when the arrows hit me, although I did not die, the arrows hurt like hell. I had falsely assumed that I couldn't feel pain in a dream. So, I dropped that criterion. But, although I could feel pain in dreams, I was never able to kill myself or die in a lucid dream. When it appeared that I was about to be die, I always awoke or the scene changed. Thus, I concluded that this provided all the proof needed that I was dreaming. So, my foolproof way to demonstrate to myself that I was dreaming became the suicide test. Some of my students expressed their doubts about the wisdom of this test and said they would never try this because it seemed risky and reckless—or words to that effect.

For me, the self-destruction test worked without fail. When in a lucid dream, I felt it was risk-free. I had survived countless suicide attempts in my dreams. And, if someone questioned my memory on this, I could point out that this test also worked for others. You can find a version of my dream test in an interesting movie that has dreaming as its theme: the 2010 film *Inception* starring Leonardo DiCaprio. The complicated plot of *Inception* has to do with entering the dreams of people to take control of their subconscious minds for nefarious purposes. In this film, what I had assumed to be my two original dream tests were, to my surprise and fascination, being tested by some of the film's characters. Dream researchers in the movie reach the same conclusion I did: the pain test is not reliable but the suicide test can be. One dream researcher in the movie, however, discovers that there are exceptions to the death test. In some cases, the person, instead of waking up or finding himself in another setting, in fact drops into infinite limbo, or, in some cases, actually dies. That's where the movie is just a movie, deviating from what I think is a truly reliable test—again a test that many others, not just me, have found reliable.

Although interesting and visually stunning, *Inception* is also in many ways a silly movie—and it is filled with gratuitous violence. In this movie, I should also point out, there was another test to determine whether one is dreaming or awake: spinning a top. If a top spins indefinitely, one is dreaming, if it stops spinning you are awake. I was never able to verify this test, but the suicide test remained for me absolutely reliable. In my lucid dream experiences, there were no exceptions to this test—after all, I am alive—and thus it remained a solid way to prove to myself that I was dreaming. This was the gold standard for me when I was having a lucid dream, a way of proving to myself I was dreaming.

Of course, one obvious drawback to the suicide test is that if you are mistaken, you may die. This was what skeptical students repeatedly said about this test. But I never thought I was risking actually killing myself because I had performed this test only during lucid dreams in which I *knew* that I was dreaming. These are, after all, dreams in which you are not only aware that you are dreaming but in which you can in fact even shape the dream narrative. If, however, I really knew I was dreaming, one might reasonably ask the question: Why even perform the test? My answer: performing the suicide test in such dreams was simply a way of showing my confidence in the claim that I was dreaming. It was a way to prove what I claimed to know: to prove my truth claim. It was a way of demonstrating that I was veridically aware that I was in a lucid dream—that I had no doubt about this. And I knew that others who performed this test said the same thing—that in lucid dreams it was a way to confirm what they clearly perceived, namely that they were asleep. In lucid dreams I was also aware that, even though my experiences felt vivid and real, they were not in fact real. The ultimate proof that it was a lucid dream was the suicide test. I never thought that when I attempted suicide in a lucid dream I was endangering my life.

The problem, however, was that in my confused state of mind, the one that emerged after that life-changing Saturday morning walk, I didn't feel the same certainty about being in a dream. In truth, I wasn't sure whether I was awake or asleep. Obviously, if I was dreaming, it wasn't a lucid dream. Still, my experiences were so bizarre—even if not illogical or inconsistent with the laws of nature—that I could reasonably doubt that I was actually awake. I thought the suicide test was the one way I could prove to myself that Nathan Feldman and his memories were real, meaning that what I had been experiencing—a Nathan Feldman who was self-deceived about his identity and who was stranger to all those he thought knew him well—was in fact only a very bad dream. After all, it was not that different from dreams that I and other dreamers reported having many times. At the public library, I went on dream chat sites to confirm this.

The important question for me then became this: Given my uncertainty about whether I was dreaming, should I still try the suicide test? Because I could not assert beyond a reasonable doubt that I was dreaming—because it was obviously not a lucid dream—maybe the suicide test was too risky. In fact, I had to admit that there were indicators that I was actually awake. After all, I had failed the other tests that would supposedly show I was dreaming: pushing a finger through my palm, flying, walking through a wall, etc. I couldn't do any of these things—which meant that I might be awake. So, the suicide test could prove fatal. Did I want to take the chance that I might actually die?

In truth, a desire to kill myself was reasserting itself. So, again another abrupt change in mood. Given how miserable I was feeling, I again welcomed death as a release from what seemed like a nightmare, even if it was really only a daymare. I was ready to die. If this was my actual life, then I really didn't want to continue it. I had, after all, lost everyone and everything I loved. I had lost my reasons for living. Despite my promise to Elizabeth Cohen not to kill myself, I decided to risk death, to do something that could end my life. But my hope was that I would in fact wake up and recover the life I remembered and wanted back. If this was a dream, I desperately wanted to wake up. I was ready to try what had always worked in the past to wake myself or at least change the dream narrative.

Would this decision amount to breaking my promise to Elizabeth Cohen—the promise not to harm myself. Yes, but that was less important than ending my misery. And if it was a dream, waking up would mean that I would have Elizabeth back; it would mean that her failure to recognize me was only part of dreadful dream. More important than keeping my word to what was probably a dream version of Elizabeth, attempting to kill myself was my best bet for recovering my life with her. And, at that moment, I decided I would rather die than live without her love.

When people who feel suicidal promise their psychiatrist that they will not try to kill themselves, they are often just telling their doctor what they think she wants to hear. In my case, however, when I made a promise not to take my life, I wasn't necessary lying to Elizabeth. It is what I believed at the time. But, once I left her, I again fell into despair and couldn't stop thinking: if this was really my life, death would be preferable. At that point, I wanted either to wake up or to die. If I was trapped in a nightmare, then attempting to kill myself would restore me to the life I so well remembered. And if I was awake and it ended a life that was itself like a nightmare—so much the better. It then became only a question of means. How should I try to end my life? I didn't have a loaded pistol whose barrel I could put in my mouth or any pills to take for a lethal overdose. I was, however, close to railroad tracks where trains ran frequently.

So, I walked to the tracks. In Winterville, there are actually three train tracks close together. That's why, if driving, you sometimes have to wait for what seems like forever for all the trains to pass. One train passes and, as you drive toward the next track, a new train may appear. I can even remember many times having to wait for a third train to go by. It seemed that on some days that the trains were timed to delay drivers indefinitely. In any event, I knew that I would not have to wait long for a train to come: either a dream train or a real one. When I was close to the tracks, I sat down on a bench only a few yards away from where a train would soon be approaching. No one was around. I waited.

When I heard the faint sound of a train whistle, I was ready to make my move. Yes, it seems like a horrible way to die. But I had read that if you step quickly right in front of an approaching train, so that hits you square, you're dead before you know it. Instantly. Of course, there could be no proof of this because those who succeeded had not lived to tell. If, however, you are hit by a train and don't die, that could be a very painful experience—and you might be completely disabled, mentally and physically, for the rest of your life—a nightmare itself. And, dream or no dream, I would feel the horrible impact of the train, even if it didn't kill me. I now knew that I could experience pain in a dream. And this pain would be truly awful. But I couldn't let that stop me.

I wrote my name and that of Elizabeth Cohen on the index card that she had given me, the one with her clinic's address, and put the card in a back pocket, so that if I in fact died whoever found my body and searched me would see a name for the deceased. They would then of course have a corpse that probably couldn't be identified, despite my name on the index card. But they would also have the name of someone who knew me, if only in passing. I was of course wagering that stepping in front of the train would wake me up—wake me up to the familiar life I had once known and enjoyed. Suddenly I heard and then saw an approaching train. Since I was only a few yards from the track, I could quickly stand and dash in front of the speeding locomotive that was pulling a very long line of cars. I was ready. To my puzzlement, I noticed what looked like a drone just above me as the train approached.

But I lost my nerve. At the last moment, I got cold feet and decided not to take the risk, the risk that I was awake. As the train moved closer, my life felt too real to be a dream, and I experienced the need, even if I was still despondent, to stay alive to see if Elizabeth could help me. The will to live and the will to die were struggling within me, but at the very second that I needed to make a decision about whether to jump in front of the train, my will to live appeared to win out. Or maybe I really wanted to die but simply didn't have the guts to throw myself on the railroad track.

7. A Beautiful Mind

AFTER MY INITIAL MEETING with Elizabeth, twenty-four hours would pass before I saw her again—the twenty-four-hour period I had pledged to stay alive. I was able, after all, to keep my promise not to commit suicide. Just barely. Prior to walking to the railroad track and then not making my move to end things—whether because I truly wanted to live or because I lost my nerve—I had kept myself occupied. Before I decided to walk to the tracks, I had been very busy. That morning, the morning after my meeting with Elizabeth at the university, I, feeling hungry, enjoyed a free breakfast at a Catholic church that served the homeless and then lunch at the Salvation Army. Christians of various denominations were keeping me from starving. Despite my continuing distress and despair, hunger had made itself felt, demanding I eat something. Following a long-established Buddhist tradition, I decided that, in my homeless state, I would only eat two meals a day—breakfast and lunch.

It is not unusual for those dependent on alms in a Buddhist community of monks or nuns to eat only twice a day or even have only one meal. People often mindlessly assume that they must have three meals a day or more. In what I remember as my former life, in addition to three meals a day, I recall that I usually had a midafternoon snack, and often a post-dinner treat, maybe a banana and yogurt a couple of hours before I went to bed. So, actually more than three meals a day. Buddhism is identified with a middle way between excess and self-mortification. To keep hunger away, I adopted a modest twice-a-day eating routine. Many places in Winterville fed the unhoused. Thus, I had a rational plan for how to nourish myself if—and, again, it was always, in those days, a big *if*—I decided to stay alive.

After breakfast, I wasted the morning indulging my deep nostalgia for what I had lost. Having lost all of my most important relationships, I was experiencing a profound loneliness. And I was obsessively ruminating on suicide as a way to stop the pain. Before deciding on suicide by locomotive, I had been trying to avoid making a decision about my fate by doing research in the public library that afternoon. An incurable academic, I had always believed that reading was the ultimate solution to any problem. One just had to find the right book, the right article, or maybe even the right screenplay.

The afternoon before my walk to the railroad tracks was when I carefully read the script of the movie that had inspired one of my crazier, seemingly absurd, speculations about my condition—that I was a fictional character. Off and on, I kept thinking that I was the creation of some unknown author who appeared indifferent to the terrible suffering he or she was putting me through, like the novelist in *Stranger than Fiction* who was planning to kill off Harold Crick. This writer was causing Crick to feel extreme existential anxiety because she was narrating a story that described his death as imminent. As it would turn out, Harold Crick's shocking discovery that the author of this novel was plotting his demise foreshadowed what I, Nathan Feldman, would face in the not-too-distant future. I would soon discover that my life was all too similar to that of Harold Crick.

That afternoon in the library was also when I did research on the science of dreaming so that I could better evaluate the possibility that my bizarre experiences were simply events in a bad dream—that I was lost in a nightmare. If dreaming, I wanted to wake up. Before I decided to try what had always worked for me—the suicide test—I read about the already mentioned alternative tests that supposedly would allow me to determine whether I was dreaming or awake. Any and all of these tests would have of course been safer than my own: attempting to kill myself. But, after thinking this through while researching dreams in the library, I finally decided to wake myself up or perish by jumping in front of a train. And of course, when push came to shove, I decided not perform that test.

Given how implausible the fictional character and dream hypotheses were, maybe this library research was really only a way of killing time while I eagerly waited to meet again with the woman who might provide me with a truly scientific explanation of my condition, who might even be able to cure my disorder. Perhaps my speculation about being a fictional character and about my life as a dream were at that time mere idle ways to distract myself before seeing Elizabeth again. My dream hypothesis had, however, motivated me to try something that could have proved fatal, something that might have resulted in my never seeing this woman again. But even if

I saw her again, I reminded myself, she would not truly see me. After all, Elizabeth appeared to have no idea who I was and who we had been as a couple—because, from all the objective evidence I'd been forced to accept, our intimate relationship was a figment of my imagination.

So, I might as well have been dreaming about the two of us. By now it should be clear that it was for me pure torture that this woman who I thought deeply loved me no longer even recognized me. Apparently, I was to her a complete stranger. Leaving the library, I had been ready to die on a railroad track—until I no longer wanted to. Or lacked the courage to do so. Different explanations of my puzzling condition had appeared before my mind and then disappeared; and feelings of desperation, some inclining me to self-destruction, left as soon as they came. After I decided not to step in front of a train, I actually felt at peace. I was now more than ready to get the opinion of a professional and felt fortunate I would have that opportunity. And, in the back of my mind, no matter how irrational, was the recurring hope that I could somehow reestablish a relationship with Elizabeth; win her over a second time. I had lot of confused feelings about Elizabeth and our relationship.

Having had time to think things over after deciding not to step in front of a train, I was trying to be *philosophical* about my condition, in the lay sense of that word—meaning that I was attempting to stay detached and serene in the face of my identity crisis. I was almost feeling hopeful. Maybe that's a bit hyperbolic as a description of my changed mood, but when Elizabeth asked me, when I saw her again, if I was still feeling suicidal, I said I was not. At that moment, this was the honest truth.

The truth about my emotions had become elusive, a moving target. Buddhism had taught me that emotions, like everything else, arise and pass away. This applies to both positive and negative emotions. Positive emotions such as hope can, however, be seductive, making one want to cling to them as if they could be permanent, as if one had the power to make them endure. By the time I saw Elizabeth the second time, my mood had changed significantly since our first conversation. Curiosity had again, at least temporarily, replaced despair. I was interested, as mentioned repeatedly, in seeing where all of this was headed, and whether I could discover my true identity.

Yes, that is precisely what I was feeling: curiosity, even philosophical curiosity. I recalled, even if misremembering, that one of my strong philosophical interests had been the problem of personal identity and the role of memory as a crucial marker that distinguishes one person from another. I tried to positively view my situation as an opportunity to explore objectively the question of my own personal identity, of who I really was. And Elizabeth would be assisting me in this investigation. That also gave me hope. My change in mood was, I have to admit, probably largely due to Elizabeth's willingness to work with me, to help me figure out what had happened to my brain. When I saw her again, it was difficult to take seriously the idea that she was a fictional character, or that I was one. And I couldn't believe, once I saw her that Thursday evening, that she and I were interacting only in a dream. She seemed very real. Her intelligence and beauty still took my breath away—as they had the first time we met, that apparently false memory of when I was a professor down the hall from her. My memory of that first (imagined) meeting was that she was not only physically beautiful but also had an extraordinarily brilliant and exceptionally creative mind. A beautiful mind.

My objective became, putting all wild speculation aside, with Elizabeth's guidance, to discover the medical truth about my confused mental condition, and I was ready to embrace the idea that I was suffering from a serious mental illness. My very willingness to entertain the fictional character and dream hypotheses, not to mention my paranoid episodes, seemed to be evidence that I needed professional help, the help of a neuropsychiatrist who could provide a medical explanation of my strange psychological condition. Thus I, in a mood of great optimism, was hoping that "Dr. Cohen"—or should I address her as "Elizabeth" since I could not let go of the memory that we were very close—would in time provide a correct diagnosis and a way back to sanity. Out of respect for her as a psychiatrist, and the recognition that I was now her patient, I kept things formal. I would address her by her title.

I entered what was a recently built three-story clinic for behavioral health, looked at the list of providers on the wall, and walked to an office complex on the first floor. The letters on the door: NISM. Within this door there were a large number of office suites, all occupied by neuroscientists, psychiatrists, and neuropsychiatrists who were employed by the Neuroscience Institute for the Study of Memory. Elizabeth's door was open and I walked in. She was sitting behind her desk—looking beautiful and brilliant. You could see her sharp intelligence simply by looking into her dark brown eyes, as if those lovely ocular globes somehow mirrored the extraordinary mind behind them, before she even said one word. Or so I felt at the time as someone still lovestruck and lovesick. I would learn all-too-soon how blind—and dumb—love can be. I came to understand how love can profoundly distort one's perception and obscure the truth about the beloved.

I walked into Elizabeth's office, wearing the same pants, shirt, and shoes I had on when I last saw her. I had washed the shirt in the park restroom sink the night before—at least the parts under my armpits. Couldn't bring myself to take more clothes from the Salvation Army without payment. I did, however, acquire from SA deodorant so I wouldn't smell-up my only dress shirt. I certainly didn't want to reek of body odor when I met again with the woman who I perceived to be—who I remembered as—my intimate partner. Initially there was some awkwardness between us as we obviously both remembered what had become, for now, a taboo topic, namely how I had described three marks on private parts of her body. We didn't talk about this when we met the first time at her clinic office. That would be a subject for the second and what would turn out to be a very sobering final conversation at the clinic.

Getting right to the point: "Dr. Cohen, after having time to think about my case, do you have any opinion about what happened to my memory, to my sense of who I am?"

"Please sit down. Your case is complex—and I have to tell you, professionally interesting. I was thinking that you might be suffering from dissociative identity disorder, what used to be called multiple personality disorder. A person suffering from this has at least two distinct personalities, each with a unique name, personal history, even a different voice, mannerisms, and different memories. There can also be differences in how familiar the different personalities are with each other. If this is what you are suffering from, you clearly don't know your other identity or identities. There are cases where an individual with dissociative identity disorder, living out an alternative personality, wanders off or travels elsewhere. So, you may have left your home in another city or even another state."

"I could be living out one of my personalities, far from home?"

"Yes. We will need to schedule some extended sessions one-on-one in order to see if we can bring out the other identity or identities, to see if this is what you have: dissociative identity disorder. This is a very rare condition, occurring in anywhere from one half to 2 percent of the population, and it occurs more frequently in women than men. Your condition also has some features of what is called dissociative amnesia. Both disorders can occur together. I should point out that dissociative amnesia is also very rare, only affecting about 1 percent of men and a bit under 3 percent of women in the general population."

"How does my condition resemble dissociative amnesia?"

"Those who suffer from this cannot remember important information about themselves, such as their name, personal history, family, or friends. In your case, although you cannot remember these things about yourself, you seem to have, in place of these, false memories. Your mind may have somehow invented all the memories you are now experiencing—and, yes, we could even call what your mind has created a fictional person, although not a literary character. You appear to be remembering someone else's life—and, to repeat, a completely imagined life. If you also have dissociative identity disorder, you may be living out the fabricated life of one of your personalities. If you have dissociative amnesia by itself, there are features of your condition that don't fit the typical profile. Memories of another life are not something that characterizes dissociative amnesia as it is typically presents itself. But you could have a special, even anomalous, form of dissociative amnesia. It may be amnesia combined with confabulation."

"I know about confabulation. But what's the cause of dissociative amnesia?"

"A stressful or traumatic event: being in combat or being a victim of a crime can be the trigger. At this point, I really don't know enough about you to say whether a traumatic event has caused your condition. There may have been such an event, one we will have to try to uncover, discover. Again, you could have a form of dissociative amnesia that has triggered confabulation, the unconscious creation of false memories that are filling in the blanks of your lost true memories. If we can cure your amnesia, the confabulation will probably cease."

"If that's what I have, how long does dissociative amnesia last?"

"It usually occurs suddenly, and in many cases lasts for only a few minutes. This clearly is not true in your case. Sometimes, it lasts for hours or days. In rare cases, it can last for months and even years. But, to reiterate something important: if you have dissociative amnesia, it is not presenting in the usual way because your brain seems to have replaced actual memories of your past with invented ones. If you have dissociative amnesia, and your mind is generating substitute false memories, then some form of confabulation seems to also be operating. But we still need to explore the possibility that you suffer from some form of dissociative identity disorder. If it makes you feel any better, I want you to know it is my provisional medical opinion that we are not dealing with a psychosis. We are, I believe, dealing with an anomalous memory problem."

"Yes, in fact that does make me feel better, since I have been thinking that I was crazy, that I was suffering from a serious mental illness. Assuming that I have a memory disorder, is there any treatment?"

"Psychotherapy is one treatment. As I practice it, this means talk therapy involving cognitive-behavioral techniques. Hypnosis may also help. I don't know of any medications that are effective in treating dissociative amnesia, but there are medications to help treat anxiety and depression, if you are suffering from either of those. We can start treatment soon. Since your suicidal ideation seems to have ceased, we don't have to worry about getting you out of that. That would prolong the treatment."

"I want to get started."

"Good."

"And to be completely honest with you, I firmly believe, at this moment, that I know who I am, despite evidence to the contrary. I have a strong sense that I am a single personality: Nathan Feldman. And I feel that my memories are genuine. Will that pose an obstacle?"

"Yes. It would be helpful, if you wish to recover, for you to accept the idea that you have, at the very least, a serious memory disorder—that your memories of your life as Nathan Feldman are false and that your actual identity is unknown. A refusal to give up the conviction that you are Nathan Feldman, with the specific memories you have reported, will make my job more difficult. Our aim is to recover your true self and your actual memories. For that I need your cooperation and openness to rethinking your identity."

"My sense of who I am is not something I've chosen, or see a way to easily change. I'm well aware that the evidence counts against my belief that I'm Nathan Feldman. Although I sometimes entertain the hypothesis that I'm a fictional character, or sometimes doubt that I'm Nathan Feldman, you need to know that most of the time I naturally and automatically see myself as Nathan Feldman. The idea that I am someone other than Nathan Feldman—or that Nathan Feldman is an alternate personality—is not an idea that I can fully comprehend or easily embrace. What I'm telling you is that I don't have a sense that I've forgotten who I really am or that I have more than one personality. I feel that I know who I am. I am singularly and truly Nathan Feldman: that's what I honestly believe. It may surprise you that— although I'm a philosopher, a professional skeptic—I'm not experiencing any doubts about my identity, despite the overwhelming evidence to the contrary."

"We will have to work on your resistance. Since you remember yourself as a philosopher not only trained to be skeptical, but also a philosopher who claims personal identity theory as his special area of research, that is something we can use to help overcome your resistance. It means that you're probably open to exploring conflicting ideas about human identity, including your own, and not being dogmatic in your thinking about who you actually are."

"Yes, that's true. My philosophical position, as I remember it, is that personal identity is defined in terms of both physical and psychological markers. These include such physical elements as your body, biological gender, distinctive voice, distinctive face, distinctive walk, and other physically observable characteristics. The psychological factors include such things as personality traits, concrete plans for the future, a peculiar sense of humor, belief system, value system, psychological gender identity, and, most important, if one is an adult, memories that include recollections about one's childhood, adolescence, and adulthood to the present. I have a long history of memories that are distinctively mine—a detailed autobiography, even if false. Thus, I have a clear sense of my own identity, and that's why I find it difficult to doubt my sense of who I am. Again, I'm just being honest."

"Fair enough. Even though you strongly identify as Nathan Hillel Feldman, a professor at a state university in Winterville, Minnesota who grew up in Bryan, Texas, was raised by Jewish parents, Ted and Sarah Feldman, you must, as someone trained in epistemology, recognize the unreliability of memory and the fallibility of self-certainty: that you could be mistaken about these things—about who you are."

"Yes, I agree. I recognize that, because it is an empirical matter, my feeling of certainty about who I am is questionable. Although I would assert that while we are thinking of the meaning of the symbols $2 + 2 = 4$ we cannot be mistaken about the truth of this simple mathematical formula, the same is not true for factual claims, including claims about who we are and our own past. Memory claims are fallible empirical claims. Claims of a factual nature, no matter how confident we feel, are subject to falsification. Thus, even though I now feel certain that I'm Nathan Feldman, with the history I've described, I am well aware, given the evidence that contradicts this, it is probable that I'm in error—that my beliefs about myself are false. Thus, I know, empirically speaking, that I should admit that I am mistaken about who I believe I am. My reason tells me this—so I am open to working to change what I strongly believe. And, yes, as someone trained in epistemology, I don't confuse a feeling of self-certainty with objective truth—even though the subjective self-certainty is there."

"That works in your favor. That helps a lot. Would you be willing to come back tomorrow afternoon at 2:30 p.m. so we can get started? I assure you that I'll do my best to correctly analyze your condition and bring you back to who you really are."

"Yes. But you do realize I cannot pay you anything. I'm completely broke. And I don't have a Social Security number, or any information that might be useful in getting some kind of compensation for your efforts."

"Yes. I understand. Just as lawyers sometimes work pro bono, so do I. To be honest, I have a professional research interest in your case. And I believe I can get to the bottom of your memory problem and solve the mystery that is Nathan Feldman."

"That gives me hope. I'll see you tomorrow. And thanks for being willing to treat me gratis."

"My pleasure."

I left Elizabeth's office, once again feeling optimistic. And I knew I needed to work to weaken, indeed overcome, my dogmatic belief about who I was. I needed to practice the epistemological humility that I recall telling my students they should cultivate—to remember what I repeatedly told them: that philosophy calls for the courage to be willing to challenge, to question, even our most cherished beliefs about the world and ourselves. I thought that this philosophical posture, if I could sustain it, would help me overcome my resistance as I worked with Elizabeth to discover my true identity. The problem, however, was that my resistance quickly reasserted itself.

8. Conspiracy Theory

AFTER LEAVING THE DOCTOR's office, although feeling hopeful for a short period, I found myself falling into a state of full-blown panic and paralyzing fear. There was again that sudden change in mood that Buddhism warned me to keep in mind: how emotions can change in an instant, for no good reason. Although my conversation with Elizabeth was momentarily reassuring, and I felt optimistic when I was with her, after I left her office, I began to feel deep skepticism about Elizabeth's ability to help me. Despair about my condition, hopelessness, resurged. That night in the park I didn't sleep well; the high humidity didn't help. I was feeling both angry and sad. And there were times, before and after my visits with Elizabeth, when I became completely disconnected from reality.

During what I'm calling paranoid episodes my mind went far beyond freely embracing wild conjectures about what was happening to me. During these times, I was not calmly entertaining over-the-top explanations of my condition, as I had in the case of my thoughts about being a fictional character or in my speculation about being lost in a dream. When I experienced a paranoid episode, I involuntarily saw all people as menacing—as working together to destroy me. This was something that imposed itself on my psyche; it invaded and took over my mind, infected my thinking so that I could no longer think straight. When I experienced such persecutory feelings, I perceived the world as toxic and threatening.

I've come to sympathize with those who embrace irrational conspiracy theories and also those who suffer from paranoia. Although during these episodes, there were moments that I knew, rationally speaking, that it was more likely that I was self-deceived than that I was deceived by others—most of the time, during these periods, which could last for hours, I couldn't let go of the thought that people around me were conspiring to make me think I was crazy. Consider, for example, Juliette Prowess, the woman I remembered as my neighbor across the hall in the Red River Park Condominiums. My memory told me that Juliette and I had, during the four years I was a resident of the condo complex, long conversations about love and life as we consumed one of her fine wines, usually late on a Friday afternoon. We were both winding down from a week of classes—and often complaining about the college administration or disinterested students. She was ten years younger, but we became fast Platonic pals. The Juliette I so well knew was a lesbian who preferred staying in the closet because of her fundamentalist parents. She was open with me about a lot of things, and she knew I could be trusted to keep her secrets.

If she would have let me, I could have told Juliette—who now denied knowing me—not only about her hidden passion for women, but about her religiously backward parents; her position as a specialist on the Russian Orthodox Church, teaching at a relatively liberal Lutheran college in the area; her research on twentieth-century Russian theologians, such as Sergei Bulgakov and Nikolai Berdyaev; her five summer trips to Russia; her favorite restaurants, and much more. Sometimes we ate out together: so, if Juliette who denied knowing me allowed me to talk to her, I could also have told her about her favorite dishes and favorite restaurants. It was again one of many cases where I knew intimate details about the life of a person who claimed to have never met me. There is no way I could know these things unless these people also knew me well. Or so I reasoned. When I was captured by a paranoid mood, I became convinced that people like Juliette were part of a large community of individuals who were ostracizing me, who were freezing me out. Juliette had become my enemy: I could not perceive her otherwise. She, like the others, was determined to drive me to the edge of a cliff where I would fall into an abyss, the abyss of insanity.

Since this group of coconspirators included everyone who denied knowing me—people I in fact knew well and who I believed, despite their protests, also knew me well—I had to include in this community of deceivers Elizabeth Cohen, the woman I was supposed to trust to diagnose and cure me. I wanted to believe she was on my side—but, after initially being comforted by her presence, I, during these episodes, couldn't shake the feeling that she was lying to me, that she really knew who I was—and, indeed, that we had actually been lovers. What was her motive? At first, I wasn't sure. Although she told me that she thought my condition was not a mental illness, I believed, when I was experiencing paranoia, that stealthily she was trying to make me think I was psychotic, that I had lost my mind, not just my memory but my grip on reality, my sanity. She never said that, but she didn't have to. This at least was my perception of her during my persecutory periods. These paranoid episodes were so disturbing that they contributed to my recurring suicidal ideation.

During these all-too-long stretches of time when I believed in this conspiracy of all against one, I couldn't explain how so many people were able to meet and organize this mass lie, but I was convinced that they had. Even the secretary of the WSU Philosophy Department. I was shocked that Marge would enter into such a conspiracy to harm me. Had I somehow offended her or alienated her? At first, let me repeat, I could not understand why so many people like her were out to get me, but I knew that they were. One thing I could not deny: I was Nathan Feldman and my memories of my life before that Saturday morning walk were accurate memories. That could mean only one thing: everyone was lying to me. People did not wish me well: they wanted to destroy me by destroying my sanity. Maybe they were trying to drive me to suicide. Again and again, my question was of course: Why? My ultimate paranoid conclusion, already indicated: it was simply because I was a Jew. They, I was convinced, were all closet antisemites. They were trying to get me to kill myself so there would be one less Jew in the world. They almost succeeded. I, however, became determined during these confusing periods of paranoia, even while feeling suicidal, not to let these people drive me insane and drive me to destroy myself.

Thus, I had a twisted way of justifying my suspicion of others and my trust in my own sense of who I really was. I thought that if I could speak to an impartial observer, someone who would truly listen to me—who was not a part of the community bent on destroying me—I would say to this person the following. Put yourself in my place. You know who you are and who you have been. Would you really doubt your own mind if people you knew well suddenly claimed not to know you? How easily would you give up the conviction that you are who you think you are? If you dismissed the idea that you were a fictional character or were in a bad dream, then where would that lead you? It would lead you to trust yourself and no one else.

After all, you know best who you are. You know yourself in a way no one else can know you. You cannot let others take that away from you. No matter what the evidence there is to the contrary, your very dignity and integrity as a human being with your name and your memories demand that you never succumb to their lies, never stop believing in yourself. That was how I was thinking during these periods when I was feeling that I was a target for elimination. I couldn't stop thinking that there was a well-organized antisemitic plot to destroy me. My perception was distorted in the same way it was that day when I could have sworn that twigs blown from a tree fell onto the sidewalk in front of me to form a swastika.

And there was a day when I chanced upon a gathering in a building on what I knew was my campus. At that gathering at Winterville State University, I saw Marge Cook, Juliette Prowess, Elizabeth Cohen, Wilfred James, and others—friends, colleagues, and acquaintances—who had denied knowing me. When I entered the room, they suddenly stopped talking. So, I knew that they had been talking about me. And I suspected that they all hated Jews. I could not forget that in Nazi Germany, people who were highly educated, and otherwise good people, had joined in the persecution and the murder of Jews or were willing to look the other way when this happened to Jews who had once supposedly been their friends and neighbors. Maybe those neighbors who looked the other way secretly celebrated the removal of Jews. During these periods of deep paranoia, I was convinced that Elizabeth was only pretending to be a Jew to win me over. She had seduced me, enticed me to become her lover, to get her hooks into me. Was her name really Elizabeth Leah Cohen? When caught up in paranoia, I was convinced she was lying about her Jewish heritage.

When earlier I shared with Elizabeth my recurring persecutory feelings and observation of that gathering, she tried to convince me that my perception that people had gathered to talk about me was probably only a dream and pointed out that in some cases we mistake dreams for real experiences or actual memories. She reminded me of my own speculation that all of this was only a dream. She said that irrational feelings of persecution are not unusual when everything and everyone in your world appear to be conspiring against you, when you feel that you know who you are and cannot accept the idea that something has gone wrong with your mind. And, when I was caught up in paranoia, this was what I would expect her to say to keep me ignorant of what was actually happening. Although I didn't openly challenge her, I came to feel that, when I was experiencing one of these dark moods, that she was lying about everything, that I should never trust her. I had, during these paranoid episodes, the strong impression that she was behind this conspiracy against me—indeed, that she had orchestrated this entire project of deception.

I may have lost my ability to reason logically during these paranoid periods, seeing Elizabeth as part of a plot to destroy my mental health—but, as things turned out, my suspicions about the doctor, my unwanted but continuing skepticism about Elizabeth's trustworthiness, her truthfulness, were not entirely mistaken. I was of course mistaken about there being an antisemitic conspiracy led by Elizabeth, but I was not mistaken about her role in organizing people to deceive me. This became clear when I returned to see her at the clinic. Before I discovered the truth, and despite my lingering skepticism about her motives, part of me was hoping that I was wrong about her and that she truly wanted to help me. I told myself repeatedly that I needed to get past feelings of persecution, put myself in her capable hands, and trust that she genuinely wanted the best for me. And I did have that warm memory, however fantastic, of us as lovers. I was deeply torn in my perception of her—but my ambiguous feelings about her were about to be resolved.

9. Web of Deception

WHEN I ARRIVED FOR what I was told would be my first therapy session—which would in fact turn out to be our last conversation—Elizabeth said she had something very important to reveal to me that would explain everything, that would explain my confused state of mind, false memories, and how she could restore me to my true self. That's when I discovered that my paranoid feelings about her were, even if not entirely accurate, still very insightful.

"You wanted to tell me what?" She could probably hear the suspicion in my voice.

"This may come as a shock. We decided it was time to inform you about our experiment."

"What experiment?"

"The one that created your fictional identity, that of Nathan Feldman and the memories that you, as Nathan Feldman, have been wrestling with. We wanted to explain the origin of these false memories."

"Who is the 'we' you're referring to?"

"The research team at the Neuroscience Institute for the Study of Memory. Our complex is a branch of that national research organization based in Minneapolis. I'm the lead researcher on this project, the person who will write up the results."

"So, you're saying I've been the involuntary subject of an experiment?"

"No, Aaron Levitt, your true self, has been our subject, and he gave us permission to implant temporary artificial memories in his brain—the memories that you, Nathan Feldman, have. We were able to submerge Aaron's actual memories and to create an impermanent substitute memory stream. You have mentioned to me more than once the film *Stranger than Fiction* and how you identified with the central character because you, at least sometimes, saw your life as a work of fiction. You were in fact very perceptive in thinking this. I want to inform you that you weren't far off. My role in this experiment was similar to the novelist in that movie, the woman who is narrating Harold Crick's life."

"This sounds like a very bad sci-fi movie. Implanted memories! You've got to be kidding."

"I assure you I'm not. We had to put Aaron under for days. After suppressing Aaron's actual memories, we were able to replace them with a transient synthetic memory stream. By manipulating specific neuronal circuits in Aaron Levitt's brain, making his mind receptive to our new input, the narrative of your life was created in the complete absence of real experience. Aaron's brain circuits that would normally respond to actual experiences and events were artificially stimulated and linked together to form artificial memories. Using electrodes to stimulate and record the activity of nerve cells, we created a lifetime of synthetic memories that persisted when we awakened you on that special summer Saturday morning. On what we temporarily turned into a *tabula rasa*, a blank mental slate, we created a panorama of Nathan Feldman's life, from childhood to adulthood. Manipulating memories by tinkering with brain cells in mice had become routine in many neuroscience labs. Our team drew from successful MIT experiments with mice that submerged actual memories and then implanted temporary false memories in these animals. We did the same thing with your brain. Since impermanent false memories had already been successfully implanted in the brains of sleeping mice, we believed we could achieve the same result with Aaron's sleeping brain. Of course, working with a human brain was much more complicated and challenging.

"Our ambitious aim was to create an entire lifetime of artificial memories that would temporarily override Aaron's memories. We weren't sure that what we learned about the implantation of temporary false memories in mice would work with a human brain. We had repeatedly failed in earlier experiments and had to constantly go back to the drawing board. Now our team is very pleased with the results. Let me repeat what we achieved: we were able to submerge and preserve memories in Aaron's brain while provisionally replacing them with your invented memories. We plan to publish our results in a forthcoming issue of *The Journal of Neuroscience*."

"So, you're telling me that I have been your lab rat."

"That's crude language to describe our successful experiment. To use your language, it would be more accurate to say that Aaron Levitt was our lab rat. A better metaphor would be to say that he was our lab mouse, since our work was modeled on research done with mice, not rats. As I just said, we were able to capitalize on the successful memory experiments done with mice and use that knowledge to construct our much more complicated experiment, using Aaron as our subject. It was AI technology that really made this experiment work. Your firm belief that you are Nathan Feldman made it clear to me that we had successfully infused Aaron's brain with the fictional narrative of Feldman's life. By implanting temporary artificial memories, we created a different human being—indeed a person distinct from Aaron. Intravenous feeding was required because, using a recently developed long-lasting general anesthesia, we had to put Aaron under for several days in a sleeping brain state that was completely receptive to our AI stream of virtual memory. By doing this in an accelerated way, in a matter of days we were able to create Nathan Feldman's lifetime of memories, like a movie sped up."

"Forty-one years of memories!?"

"We didn't need to give you total recall. Most people have huge gaps in their memories, only partially remembering their past. The ability to totally recall almost all of one's past experiences in great detail, including detailed memories of each day of one's life—called hyperthymesia—is rare and can be a curse to those who have this ability. Most people who write autobiographies and memoirs lack this rare mnemonic ability, and so face the problem of selective, limited, and even unreliable memory as they attempt to recollect a whole life. Giving you normal partial recall made our job much easier. Thus, we didn't have to create forty-one years of false memories. We gave you relative recall of the past that probably feels very natural to you, a limited recollection of your past but one filled with details of particular events in your invented life."

"AI technology that gives me relative recall that feels natural! I would call this sci-fi bullshit, but, unfortunately for me, too much is falling into place—including cuts on each side of the top of my skull. Incision scars of course. I'm beginning to comprehend my bogus life. Things are starting to make sense, disturbing sense. This explains how I know so much about individuals who claim to have never met me and how I can have memories about such things as my life in Bryan, Texas, my life as a college student, my knowledge of the University of Houston, doctoral study at A & M, an accurate memory of the house I lived in while working on my PhD, my knowledge of the Winterville Philosophy Department, including details about the department secretary's work habits, and a detailed knowledge of the layout of what I thought was my place of residence."

"Yes. Since I taught at the university, I knew a lot about the philosophy department, including the faculty and even the secretary, including her habit of working on Saturdays. She was usually still there when I arrived early to prepare for my Wednesday evening seminar: so, we got to know each other well. She was full of information, maybe some of it gossip, about faculty members and the administration. And Juliette Prowess is a friend of mine. To be accurate, contrary to your fabricated memory, she is in fact very open about her life as a same-gender-loving woman. I have spent evenings in long conversations with her. Because of her, I knew the names of all the other residents living at Red River Park Condominiums."

"Thus, my knowledge of this place and who lived there.

"Yes. Once we thought that we had successfully completed the process of implanting a lifetime of artificial memories, we were ready to test this by placing you in the proper setting, a block from the Red River Park Condos. That's where we brought you to consciousness—literally woke you up—on that beautiful Saturday morning of June 10, 2023. At the moment you confidently walked up the steps of the condo complex and buzzed Juliette to let you in, it looked like our experiment was successful. Juliette confirmed that you said you were Nathan Feldman and asked her to let you in. From that moment to the present, all of your behavior seemed to confirm the success of memory implantation. We believed that we implanted memories not only of the location and layout of your condo, but also of the state university, public library, Red River Park, police station, Salvation Army, and so forth. We observed that you found these places without having to ask anyone for directions, confirming for us that the virtual map we implanted in your brain was retained and experienced as memory."

"And I have in my brain false memories of a whole lifetime—well, to be accurate, the partial recall of events in my invented life."

"Yes. Drawing from information that Aaron provided us before we put him under, we created a plausible story of your life, a stream of synthetic memories that we believed we were implanting in your brain while you slept. With Aaron Levitt's input, we created memories of your childhood, adolescence, and your adult life to the present, indeed all of your false memories."

"So, using own Aaron's memories, creatively altered and embellished, you filled the details of a fabricated life?"

"Yes. Aaron Levitt helped us more fully invent your character and experiences as we worked to create an entire life and a distinctive identity. It would be more accurate to say that Aaron Levitt and I coauthored Feldman's life story—creating memories that seemed natural to you. Aaron drew from his own experience as a professor of philosophy in Duluth and his own past to help us create a rich narrative, filled with many memories from his childhood, adolescence, and his undergraduate and graduate education. Our special project was to implant temporary artificial memories, but we believe we could have made these memories permanent if that had been our aim. We also believe that we could have permanently deleted certain memories in Aaron's brain, but we didn't do that. We did, however, following Aaron's request, perform a procedure on his amygdala that eliminated his excessive reactivity (in ordinary language, his anger problem). That was a permanent change, a benefit of our experiment for Aaron. Aaron did not want you to experience his tendency to feel rage, to be plagued by that. Aaron's contribution to the narrative of your life was very helpful. He provided us with details of the life of someone who ended up teaching philosophy in a way that was politically radical. Thus, loosely based on his life."

"You're telling me that you, with Aaron's help, were my Kay Eiffel, the novelist played by Emma Thompson in *Stranger than Fiction*, who is narrating Harold Crick's fictional life."

"Yes, I've already said that's a good comparison. Since the experiment was obviously a great success, we are now ready to dissolve these fictional memories and recover your authentic memories, those of Aaron Levitt. It's time to restore you to a consciousness of your actual identity, to return you to who you really are, just as I promised you when we last met."

"So, you're blithely telling me that these memories of my life that have been torturing me were invented—that Nathan Feldman doesn't really exist, that my memories are indeed lies, your lies. Which means that you have been deceiving me all along. This also means that, even during my paranoid periods, I was sensing the truth about you—that you were untrustworthy. Remember, Elizabeth—by the way, I no longer consider you my doctor— you led me to believe you were interested in curing me, even suggesting that I might be suffering from dissociative amnesia combined with confabulation, or dissociative identity disorder, or all of the above. You weren't really exploring these possibilities at all. You were putting on an act. Your promise to diagnose and cure my disorder was itself a lie."

"I was trying to determine, with certainty, that our experiment had succeeded, to make sure that you really thought you were Nathan Feldman, thereby confirming that our attempt to implant synthetic memories had worked. That you were not pretending, putting on an act. As I have already said, our observation of your behavior that Saturday morning when you confidently walked up the steps of the Red River Park Condos—and everything since then—appeared to confirm that our experiment was a success, but I needed to make sure. Now I'm certain. I've reported this to our NISM team. Until we saw success with you, implanting false memories on such a large scale had never been done before. Your strong reaction to what I am telling you is further confirmation that the experiment worked."

"Still, you've been lying to me."

"Again, what you need to recognize is that I didn't lie to Aaron Levitt, the person you really are. I did deceive Nathan Feldman, an invented person. As I've now repeatedly said, you were right when you speculated early on that your life, as you remembered it, must be a work of fiction. But it was not literary fiction. In a special sense, it was science fiction. Aaron Levitt gave us permission to create Nathan Feldman. And let me remind you of something else: he helped us write the story of Nathan's life, with parallels to his own. In coauthoring your fictional life, Aaron took full responsibility for this project. I can show you a legal binder containing the signed consent and release forms, with the terms of the agreement, giving us his fully informed permission to be the subject of what turned out to be a breakthrough experimental study."

"But don't you see the problem, Elizabeth? As you have said in so many words, you invented a person, a distinctive individual with a unique consciousness and personality, with feelings and longings: Nathan Feldman. Now you're saying, as if it were no big deal, 'to hell with Nathan Feldman.' Your plan now is to kill Nathan Feldman. To kill me, even though I continue to identify as Nathan Feldman. This is all-too-close to the darker dimension of the plot of the movie *Stranger than Fiction* in which the clueless protagonist, Harold Crick, hears a female novelist not only narrating his life but also announcing his impending death. No wonder I was drawn to this movie, its script. I sensed that it was also my story. As it turns out, my story is more similar to that of Crick than I could have ever imagined. I too am a fictional character being told he will have to die soon. Only, in my case, you as the coauthor of my fictional life are telling me to my face that you plan to kill me—and, unlike the movie, I cannot change your mind about murdering me."

"You are being needlessly dramatic. I cannot murder someone who isn't real, a fabricated character. I'm surprised that you're not more interested in learning more about who you really are. Don't you want to return to your true self and be done with these memories that you have admitted haunt and torture you?"

"Yes, please do tell me more about the person you are calling my true self."

"Aaron Levitt, also Jewish, is a former professor of philosophy who lost his position at the University of St. Mary in Duluth because COVID caused a substantial drop in enrollment, leading to severe budget cuts. He read about our research project and actually contacted us, asking if he could volunteer for this experiment. Of course, it didn't hurt that he would be generously compensated for his participation."

"How much did you promise him?"

"The exact amount was $100,000. That is what the contract states. This is what you—or, to be accurate, Aaron—will receive once we perform the reversal procedure."

"Wow! So, you made Aaron an offer he couldn't refuse. Don't you think this could be construed as blatantly opportunistic and economically coercive in the case of a man who was out of work and desperate for money?"

"Not at all. Aaron told us he could easily find a well-paying job, just not one in philosophy. He assured us that he had other skills and lucrative job options. One reason he was interested in our project was that personal identity theory, especially the role of memory in creating a person's unique identity, was a strong research interest. He believed that he would benefit not only financially from participating in this research, but also academically and professionally. He told us that he was working on a book on the problem of personal identity and thus felt fortunate that he could be our first experimental subject. To reiterate something you need to understand: Aaron's eagerness to be an experimental subject qualifies as informed consent in the fullest sense. His understanding was that, at the end of this experiment, if it was successful, we would restore his actual memories. To respect that agreement, we need you to undergo the reversal procedure. I would like to schedule this as soon as possible so that we can honor the contract we made with Aaron."

"So, you need my permission to do this?"

"Actually, we don't. We need Aaron's permission and we have that. Do you really still think you are Nathan Feldman? You seem to have a resistance problem."

"Yes, as a matter of fact I do. That is the same language you used when, in our last conversation, I insisted that I was Nathan Feldman and you deceptively suggested I might be suffering from a dissociative identity disorder or dissociative amnesia, or both. Fuck what you call a resistance problem. Fuck you and fuck your fellow deceivers. I'm telling you in no uncertain terms that I refuse your request to undergo a procedure that would lead to my extinction. I see my refusal as an act of self-preservation."

Unfazed by my blunt language, Elizabeth calmly continued to defend her project.

"That, as I already said, is testimony to the success of our project: your continuing belief, despite all the objective evidence, that you are Nathan Feldman. Let me show you our documentation, including information about your actual childhood, your education, your academic career prior to termination (again, due to budget exigencies), your publications, your family history, etc. We have a video interview with Aaron Levitt that we would like you to watch."

"Nathan Feldman now has very little dignity and respect. I need to stand up for myself. From my perspective, the reversal procedure is a plan to kill me. Even though he may not be a real person to you, Nathan is very real to me. I am Nathan Hillel Feldman. And you cannot erase me unless I give you permission. Without my consent, you cannot hook me up to anything. Any attempt to physically force me to undergo a reversal procedure would be viewed by the police as kidnapping and probably battery."

"We of course want you to do this voluntarily. We do not want to coerce you in any way or harm you. From the beginning, we did everything we could do to keep you safe."

"What does that mean?"

"When you first came to the university to talk to me after my class, you threatened to commit suicide. Keeping that from happening was our priority. We had informed Aaron Levitt that this experiment carried risks, including the risk of death—in this case self-caused because of the predictable despair and depression we knew that Nathan would probably experience, at least at first. Aaron signed on in full knowledge of that."

"You, however, seemed to take a risk with my life—with Aaron's life—when you told me, after I informed you that I was suicidal, to please wait twenty-four hours, basically not to harm myself during that period of time. I agreed not to harm myself and to meet you at your clinic office a day later. But how could you know that I wouldn't kill myself during that time? How could you know I would keep my word, given how despondent I was? Didn't you put my life at risk by doing that? In fact, I came close to ending my life."

"We knew how to keep you safe during that time—and even after that."

"Explain that to me. Exactly how did you keep me safe?"

"We had you followed—and, while he was unconscious and with his prior permission, we inserted a tracking device into Aaron's left groin. It also quickly detects any form of poison or overdose you might imbibe or inject—sending this information to our lab that would have immediately sent a paramedic unit to your exact location. We also had a drone above you day and night, with precise thermal imaging. So, we monitored you—externally and internally—around the clock."

"I wondered about that: what I thought was a drone. So much for my right to privacy. And what about *our* relationship? My memory of our intimate relationship is obviously false, another implanted memory. Does that include my recollection of three marks on your body, something that seemed to embarrass you when I informed you that I had this intimate knowledge? Were you faking embarrassment? Did you implant in my brain a memory of our intimate relationship, with details about your body, whether true or not?"

"Yes."

"That was rather cruel."

"I wanted you to have someone that you felt you could trust, a mental health professional—who you also fondly remembered as your lover, some-one you thought, even if your memories were false, might actually become your lover in the future—someone you could turn to if you became de-spondent. Creating memories of a close relationship with me, and a strong attachment to me, was another way to keep you safe."

"Safe but deceived and secretly watched day and night. I did so want to trust you, but my instincts told me not to. I remembered you as my lover and was still in love with you—a memory and a feeling that you implanted in my brain. That wasn't just deceptive; it was heartless. You deceived me in more ways than one. Indeed, I would say that you created a web of decep-tion. Keep in mind that, despite what my heart told me, my viscera told me something else—and now I see that, even if my heart was fooled, my gut instincts about you were right."

"You need to accept the fact that Nathan Feldman is not a real person. And you also need to keep in mind that the success of this experiment means that we will eventually be able to help countless people who suffer from disabling traumatic memories—by replacing them or deleting them. And for people who, for whatever reason, suffer from serious memory gaps, we can, with the help of family and friends, create a narrative that then becomes synthetic memory, filling in the blanks with recollections that will feel natural and normal to the patient. You have made possible one of the great breakthroughs in memory deletion and replacement. It is a breakthrough that will restore an untold number of disturbed individuals to mental health, to a normal life, to a life without mentally disabling traumatic memories. It will also help amnesiacs who suffer permanent memory loss."

"That's all well and good. Now that you know this can be done, that will have to suffice, because I will not submit to the reversal procedure. I'm leaving now, and don't expect me to return. We're done."

"You need to understand that you really don't have a choice. You will revert to Aaron, one way or the other."

Before I turned and walked out the door, I could see her disappointment and surprise. But did she really think that the person she created, the one who, because of the experiment's great success, was absolutely convinced he was Nathan Feldman, would effortlessly comply with her request to have himself extinguished? Deleted? I'm not sure what term to use to describe a procedure that would end my life as I knew and remembered it. If she thought it would be easy to persuade me to consent to my erasure, she was surprisingly naïve. Did those who organized this experiment really believe that the artificial person they created would happily agree to be uncreated, that he would somehow welcome oblivion? If so, despite their expertise as neuroscientists, they were stupid in not thinking this through. I wanted to get as far away from these researchers as I could. And never to see Elizabeth again as long as I lived.

I would of course need to recreate myself. Thinking quickly and drawing from the academic knowledge I possessed—thanks to Aaron—I believed that the best plan was to create false transcripts of academic work and to produce an impressive CV that included made-up publications in leading professional philosophy journals, with also a list of papers delivered at various important conferences. Those reviewing credentials in academic job applications tend not to do the work of tracking down scholarly articles to read them. Most academics are too preoccupied with their own work and research to bother to do that, even if they are on a search committee for a new professor. Who has the time? This would allow me to find employment at some school, in some department—maybe in another country. Canada? My plan was to disappear from Winterville and find my way to a distant place where I could begin again, to recreate my academic self. Since I had no money for travel, I would hop a freight train if necessary. Or hitchhike out of Winterville and travel far away. Or maybe I could gain possession of Aaron's vehicle, assuming he had one. If I could find his car keys, and locate his vehicle, I would be on my way to a new life. And I might have to rob someone or some place to get the money needed to recreate myself, to invent yet another false identity, to start a new life beyond Winterville.

It could be argued that in making this decision I—who accused Elizabeth of planning to murder me—was in effect murdering Aaron Levitt. As cold as it sounds, I'm willing to admit that. What the researchers had apparently never anticipated—and, again, this is surprising—was that the fictitious character they created would fall in love with his fabricated self to the point of seeing Nathan Feldman as his true self—and that he would aggressively resist any attempt to obliterate him. To be honest, I surprised myself in not wanting to become again my actual self. But this is the only identity Nathan ever knew; Nathan's memories seemed real to him; Nathan obviously experienced them as making him who he was. This was, as Elizabeth said more than once, testimony to the success of their memory project. They were so thorough in creating Nathan's memories—of effectively implanting them in Aaron's brain—that Nathan could do nothing other than claim this narrative as his own, even if it was as fictional as a narrative found in a novel. He owned this autobiography: the artificial past he remembered, the parents he loved, the person he called Nathan. Here I am describing Nathan in a third-person voice when what feels most natural is first person.

I never knew Aaron Levitt. I discovered that we did have many things in common. This was no surprise, since Aaron had helped fashion my life to resemble his: my memory of where I was educated, a strong interest in personal identity questions, a dual religious life, a commitment to neo-Marxism, a love of travel and good food, the guilty pleasure of living a bourgeois life. But I felt no obligation to restore Aaron's life, especially at my own expense. What did I owe Aaron? It came down to my life versus his. All of a sudden, after I was informed about the experiment, my refusal to have my memories erased was nothing more or less to me than an act of rational self-defense. I was Nathan Feldman, not Aaron Levitt, and I planned to be Nathan for the duration. Despite all of those powerful and persistent suicidal thoughts that I had been experiencing, now, when faced with possible destruction, I wanted to live more than ever. Somehow—and this surprised me—Elizabeth's plan to erase me revived, indeed strengthened, my will to live.

If Elizabeth had been in my place—had she become, say, Miryam Rothenberg with false memories of a whole lifetime—would she be willing to have her new life extinguished? I have my doubts that this fictional Miryam, even if she were shown the terms of the experiment, would consent to being erased. Even if she were shown documentation that she was really Elizabeth Cohen. Even if she were shown signed legal forms that said Elizabeth Cohen had consented to the implantation of false memories with the understanding that at the end of this experiment she would have her native memories restored.

Once you create a person with a different identity, with a firm sense of who she or he is—or, if nonbinary, who they are—all the facts and signed documents in the world will not faze this artificial person if this newborn adult has a powerful desire to survive. In the face of this threat to erase me, to erase my memories, let me repeat: my will to live was actually stronger than ever. I desperately wanted to save the only self I could remember being. But I needed to figure out a way to make my life viable, indeed successful. This became my challenge. And, it would shortly become clear to me that the Aaron Levitt I did not allow to be resurrected might not be worth restoring to life. There was apparently a very dark side to this man.

10. Suspect

BEFORE I SET OUT to create a new life and a new identity in a new place far from Winterville, I was curious about what, if anything, the fingerprints and DNA I provided the police would tell me about Aaron Moshe Levitt. Would it reveal something Elizabeth had not told me, since she had concealed so much? Did I know everything I needed to know about Aaron? I was even wondering if Aaron Moshe Levitt was the actual name of their experimental subject, whether Elizabeth had also lied about this. Maybe this was also a fictious name. My DNA was the key. I knew that DNA could help someone with long-term amnesia find his family.

In the public library, as already mentioned, I read online how DNA enabled a man who was suffering from complete memory loss discover who he was—after not knowing this for eleven years! In 2004, this amnesiac was found lying unconscious by a dumpster behind a Georgia Burger King—naked, bloodied, and covered in ant bites. He had no identification. Because of where they found him, the police gave him the moniker B. K. He turned that into Benjamin Kyle. He had zero memories about his life up to that point. Like me, Benjamin Kyle, legally speaking, didn't exist. But, finally, through DNA analysis, this man discovered in 2015 who he was: William Burgess Powell. He was ultimately reunited with his family who lived in Indiana. It was his case I had in mind when I first went to the Winterville Police Department. I thought at the time they could do the same for me.

Powell would of course be someone who might benefit from the knowledge gained through the successful memory experiment that I had made possible. With the help of Powell's family, NISM could reconstruct his past and implant memories that, although synthetic, would feel natural and real to Powell. I can testify to that. Thus, Powell's memories of his life could be restored—artificially. If Powell had not shared his DNA, he probably would have never discovered who he was. I was happy that the experiment which created me could be used to help people like Powell. And I was hoping that, like Powell, I could discover who I really was. If I wasn't Nathan Feldman, was I really Aaron Levitt?

I went to the police station to confirm or disprove Cohen's claim about my true identity. I was hoping to learn something about my actual family, my heritage. As it turned out, what I learned had more to do with crime than family—which of course is what you should expect when a police department has access to your DNA and decides to send it to a crime lab. When I found out what the police discovered, it became clear that I had made two very unwise decisions: first, providing the police with my genetic information, and, second, actually showing up to get the results. But, in fairness to myself, how could I have anticipated what I was about to be told? After all, I had been informed by Elizabeth that Aaron was a respected professor who taught ethics and was known for his commitment to social justice. She told me that while living in Duluth, he had, working with different progressive faith communities and human rights groups, organized pro LGBTQIA2S+, anti-racist, and pro-immigrant educational forums, seeming to want to make his community a morally better place, striving to reduce hatred and prejudice. He appeared to be a *mensch*.

Two weeks had passed since I walked into the front office of the police department and reported myself as a missing person, giving the police access to my biological self. If they confirmed I was Aaron Levitt, I was hoping to discover something new and revealing about this man. I was not, however, prepared for what I learned that day. I innocently informed the officer at the front desk—not the same cop I had talked to two weeks ago—that, having reported myself as a missing person with amnesia, I came to get my DNA results. I explained to this officer that I was there in the hope of discovering my true identity. He asked my name, and I informed him that I had mistakenly thought I was Nathan Feldman, telling him this was the name I gave the police when I reported myself as a missing person. The officer appeared startled. He quickly consulted with another cop, both speaking in whispers. He then immediately asked me to put my hands behind my back while the other officer handcuffed me and led me to an interrogation room.

They addressed me as Aaron Levitt. An anonymous caller had told the police that the missing person photo they sent out was of Aaron Levitt. The police, I think, perhaps with good reason, arrived at the conclusion that when I walked into the station two weeks prior, I had, for some reason, deliberately given them a false name. Two detectives questioned me. When—after reading me my Miranda rights, which I found puzzling and confusing—they started questioning me about the murder of someone I had never heard of, I hesitated to continue speaking. Having watched enough *Dateline* episodes to know to ask for a lawyer, I stopped the interrogation and did precisely that. They then told me I was being arrested for murder, which so shocked me that I didn't hear anything they said after that. My brain shut down.

Since I had no money for a private attorney, a public defender was assigned to my case. I was taken to the Madison County Jail where I sat nervously waiting for my lawyer to arrive. Twenty-four hours later I was walked from my cell to a conference room where a young woman was waiting to see me. She turned out to be my public defender: Sue Bradley. They had put me in ankle shackles and handcuffs, as befits someone accused of murder. For all the authorities knew, I was a dangerous person, a violent man. The murder had apparently been very brutal. An armed female deputy stood inside the room while I talked to my attorney. Although my public defender looked very young, was only five-foot-four, and very thin, I would later discover that Sue was a force to reckon with and a person prosecutors never treated as a lightweight. She informed me, to my shock and horror, that my DNA and one of my fingerprints were found at a murder scene two months ago. Although they had this forensic evidence from the crime scene, they had no way of matching this to anyone until I gave them what they needed.

"If you had not provided the police with this identifying information, you probably wouldn't have been arrested so quickly. And you let them take your photograph which they started distributing. With that additional identifier, once they got the incriminating results of your DNA and fingerprints, they could give the public a face and create a wanted poster with the phrase 'person of interest in a murder case.' With your picture out there, they probably would have arrested you sooner than later. Clearly, if you committed this murder, you were sloppy, leaving a lot of evidence that you were at the scene of the crime. It looks like there was an attempt to clean up and remove evidence of your presence, but if you attempted this, you failed. You gave the police all the forensic information they needed to arrest you."

"I don't remember killing anyone and cleaning up a murder scene."

"Let me start with two questions. First, why did you voluntarily give the police your DNA, have them take your fingerprints, and sit for a photo?

They're looking at this as a request to be caught. Second, and very important to your defense, if you are going to plead not guilty, why would your fingerprints and DNA be at the scene of this murder. That evidence, plus what looks like a motive—something we will discuss later—will make it extremely difficult to create reasonable doubt."

"But I didn't commit this crime. I'm not guilty of murder."

"Really? As your attorney, I will of course defend a plea of not guilty, if that is your wish. But the problem for you is that we have a murder scene where, on the body, under the fingernails, and on the clothes of the victim, is your DNA. Clearly there was a struggle: it looks like the victim fought back and took some of you with him before he died. Only your DNA is on his body, clothes, and under his nails. And there is a single clear fingerprint on a bathroom mirror at the victim's home that matches yours. It looked like other fingerprints had been cleaned off the mirror with handwashing soap. But one was missed—and that, along with the DNA on the victim and your blood at the scene of the crime will be more than enough to nail you. So, again, a careless job of erasing the evidence of your presence at the crime scene."

"In response to your first question, I was confused about who I was. That's why I went to the police: I was there to discover my true identity. When I innocently allowed the police to acquire this identifying information, I thought that I might be suffering from a form of amnesia, amnesia combined with false memories. When I reported my confusion to the police, they requested that I provide my genetic information and sit for a photo. They said it might help me discover my true identity. I treated myself—as did the officer at the front desk—as a missing person, a missing person suffering from memory loss. I had nothing to hide. I wanted the police to have my fingerprints, DNA, and picture so that they could discover my true identity. In response to your second question, I can only repeat that I don't remember cleaning up a crime scene because I have no memory of committing a crime."

"Yes, I have been told about this, about forgetting your actual name while possessing apparently false memories of Nathan Feldman's entire past. The police were generous enough to give me details about your helpful first visit to the station that has now resulted in your arrest. How you had so generously provided them with inculpatory personal information. They are now suspicious about that visit, as I will explain in a minute. After they published your photograph, they received an anonymous call from a woman who recognized this as a picture of Aaron Levitt. She, as it turns out, will be a key witness for the prosecution. Then, after they received the data from the Bemidji Crime Lab that incriminated you, they sent out an all-points bulletin—two days before you visited the police station the second time. Every local police officer had your photo with the information that you were a person of interest in a homicide. This was about to be released to the FBI and the Madison County Sheriff's Department as well as other police and sheriff departments everywhere—and to local and national media. Given all the evidence of your presence at the murder scene, I need to ask what defense attorneys usually don't: Do you really want to claim that you are completely ignorant of this crime?"

"How often do I have to say that I was genuinely confused about my identity and have no memory of committing this crime. I didn't know anything about Aaron Levitt until recently. The only memories I have are those of Nathan Feldman."

"So, an amnesia defense with a twist: your memory of the murder has disappeared and now you remember being someone else. Let me play devil's advocate. Speaking impartially, I need to tell that this is a highly problematic defense. Not credible at all. The prosecutor will argue that you are faking it, pretending that you lost your memory. He will argue that, fearing you would be caught, you, in a preemptive strike, went to the police department in order to create an amnesia defense, a ruse that you thought could exonerate you when you were finally arrested. How convenient that you now identify as Nathan Feldman, not Aaron Levitt, and that you have no memory of what Aaron did."

"But that's the truth."

"Let me be honest. Your situation will be perceived as similar to that of a person accused of murder, for which there is compelling evidence of guilt, who says he was drunk at the time of the homicide, blacked out, cannot remember doing it—and so should not be held accountable and punished. In response to a claim of not remembering a murder due to intoxication, eyes usually roll because many people hearing this defense will reasonably suspect that this person is lying, faking amnesia. And even if jurors believe that this person blacked out because he was drunk, do you think that would lead them to declare the offender not guilty? If you plead amnesia—that you somehow, after the crime, lost any memory that you committed the murder, and have come to think you are someone else—you will probably be laughed out of the courtroom, with jurors, if you choose a jury trial, having a good laugh along with the prosecutor."

"My claim about losing my memory—and having false memories—is not as weak as you seem to think it is. You haven't heard the whole story. The memories that I have as Nathan Feldman were created in a memory experiment, an experiment to implant artificial memories, sufficient to provide me with a complete life history. The actual memories of Aaron Levitt were temporarily submerged so that I would have only the synthetic memories of Nathan Feldman, the person I believed I was. Still do. You probably aren't aware that neuroscience can now replace a person's actual memories with false memories. I don't have access to any of Aaron Levitt's memories: zero, zilch."

"Implanted false memories? So, you still don't acknowledge that you are Aaron Levitt?"

"Correct. That's a question the head researcher, Dr. Elizabeth Cohen, the one who directed this memory project, kept asking me, after she informed me about the experiment. She was asking this to confirm for herself that the experiment worked. And, wasting no time, she wanted me to agree to a reversal procedure so that I could return to my true self. I refused."

"A scientifically based false memory plea. This is still a questionable defense. Can you provide documentation of this experiment? Can you verify that this occurred?"

"Yes. You need to contact Dr. Cohen, a neuropsychiatrist and lead local researcher at the Neuroscience Institute for the Study of Memory. She has an office at the Winterville Behavioral Health Clinic on South Oak Street. She also teaches a class at the state university."

"This gives me some hope. So, Dr. Cohen and her fellow researchers will testify that this experiment was successfully performed and that you have only the pseudo-memories of Nathan Feldman and none of the real memories of Aaron Levitt?"

"Yes. You can get the sworn testimony from Dr. Cohen and her research team at the Institute. She can provide evidence, scientific evidence, that I'm not faking it. I should probably also tell you that when she asked me to undergo the reversal procedure I basically told her to go fuck herself. But I'm sure she would be more than happy to present the findings of her research. She seemed very proud of the success of this cruel experiment."

"So, you parted on bad terms?"

"Yes."

"That doesn't matter. Her testimony, along with that of her colleagues, will be very helpful. But you need to keep in mind that this testimony—even if it's credible—will not necessarily exonerate you. We are in murky legal waters, and the law may not be on your side. It will not be easy to use this extraordinary amnesia argument to get a not guilty verdict."

"You strike me as very young. How many murder cases have you had? Sorry to express doubts about your credentials—but my freedom is on the line."

"Although I may seem young, I'm older than I look and am in fact a very experienced defense attorney. I graduated in the top of my class at the University of Minnesota Law School. I have defended a variety of individuals charged with a wide range of offenses, including murder, with an impressive record of success. I know what I'm doing, but this will be a very challenging case, even for me. And let me say, selfishly, a challenge like this is something I would have killed for. Maybe that's a bad figure of speech in your case. What I want you to realize is that all the evidence in the world that you suffer from a special kind of amnesia may not be enough to exonerate you. But I will do my best to successfully get a not-guilty verdict. An uphill battle. For some jurors, once they see the compelling evidence showing that Aaron Levitt committed this murder, and that, at the time, knew what he was doing, you will be, in their minds, guilty of murder, even if they believe you now suffer from amnesia."

"How can I be guilty of a crime I don't remember committing?"

"I'll get to that. But here is something else we cannot rule out. The DA may ask that Dr. Cohen and her colleagues restore you to your real self: Aaron Levitt. In that case, with the forensics they have, it may be a slam-dunk for the prosecution. If this procedure is performed, and the memories of Aaron Levitt are restored, out goes the amnesia defense."

"And that would also mean the end of my life. Can they perform the reversal procedure without my consent? As I've already told you, I rejected Elizabeth's request that I undergo this. I so identify as Nathan Feldman that, even before my legal troubles due to Aaron Levitt, I had refused to undergo the procedure, although I stood to gain $100,000. That's what they promised Aaron for his participation in this experiment. Of course, I as Nathan Feldman would not be receiving that amount of money because, if I underwent the reversal procedure, I would be no more."

"Interesting. I'm not sure where the law will end up on this question: that is, whether you can be forced to undergo the reversal procedure. From what you've told me, I assume that you also want me to fight for your right to refuse this?"

"Yes. Absolutely. Even if Aaron is my true self, as the neuroscientists keep saying, I don't identify as Aaron. I am not now Aaron Moshe Levitt and have no plans to ever become him. I'm more convinced than ever about this because of what I've now learned about Aaron's dark side. From what I've been told, it was a very brutal murder. Why should I allow Aaron to have another chance at life, especially at my expense?"

"Assuming that you are not required to undergo the procedure, here's something we need to prepare for: the prosecution may argue that, after the crime, Aaron volunteered for the memory replacement experiment so he could plead ignorance of the crime. In other words, they could argue that Aaron deliberately chose to do something that would cause him to lose his memory of the crime. He did so with the intent of denying responsibility for his criminal behavior. This was, therefore, premeditated amnesia or a voluntary act of becoming an amnesiac. This is an argument they might successfully make to hold you accountable for the murder—if we don't find a good way to rebut it. What complicates things is that this may have very well have been Aaron's actual intention in volunteering for the experiment."

"So, this would mean, if the prosecution is successful, that, despite the fact that I don't remember committing the crime, I can still be found guilty of murder."

"Yes, the prosecution could persuasively make a case for your culpability in spite of your memory loss. As you may know, there are two requirements for criminal culpability: *actus reus* and *mens rea*. Are you familiar with these terms?"

"Of course. But remind me of their exact meaning."

"At the time of the crime, the first question is: Did Aaron Levitt voluntarily commit an act of murder? That's *actus reus*. The second question is: Was Aaron aware of what he was doing? That is *mens rea*, referring to a guilty mental state. In other words, the court will be asking whether Aaron Levitt was, at the time of the crime, in control of his behavior and whether he acted purposely to end a life. Within the domain of a guilty mind there is a great range, a continuum of guilt, with punishment proportioned to the degree of mental culpability. Was this a carefully planned act or a crime of passion? Either would make Aaron guilty of criminal homicide, but, if the latter, not first-degree murder. If we could show it was a spontaneous act of blind rage, we then have an unpremeditated homicide and thus a crime that would be punished less severely."

"I am at the disadvantage of not knowing Aaron Levitt's state of mind at the time of the crime."

"In Aaron's case, given the evidence I've seen, a crime of passion argument does not look promising. The homicide looks well-planned. Even if, contrary to the evidence, we could show that the homicide was not planned, you can still be found culpable for murder. It appears that the prosecution can probably prove beyond a reasonable doubt that, whatever the level of your culpability, you should be held criminally responsible for the homicide. *Mens rea* can be established. And there is no reason to believe that, at the time of the crime, Aaron's behavior was involuntary: thus, the *actus reus* requirement can also be satisfied. Given all the evidence, and what can be established about Aaron's state of mind at the time of the crime, prosecutors can probably demonstrate, beyond a reasonable doubt, that you are guilty of premeditated murder. You need to understand that from the standpoint of the law, as the prosecution will interpret it, you and Aaron are legally the same person."

"Which means, to repeat an important point, that even if you can persuasively make the case that I have only the memories of Nathan Feldman, I will still probably be convicted of murder."

"That's right. But they will not necessarily be successful in getting to a guilty verdict if we can use your current state of mind to keep you from ever going to trial. We may be able to use your peculiar form of amnesia, as documented by NISM, to raise questions about whether you are able to defend yourself in a court of law. If it can be scientifically demonstrated that, because of a medical procedure, you have no memory of the crime, we could then argue that this memory deficit is an obstacle to defending yourself against the charge of murder. We can make the case that you are not mentally competent to stand trial—not in the sense that you are mentally ill, but in the sense that your lack of a memory of the crime means that you are unable to competently assist in your own defense."

"So, my amnesia could be used to prevent a trial from happening?"

"Yes. We could argue that you cannot adequately defend yourself because you have no memory of what you did. If you have no recollection of the crime you are accused of committing, this raises a question about whether you should be prosecuted at all. The foundation of this legal strategy is the view that trying you for a crime you cannot recall committing is a violation of your constitutional right to a fair trial. Therefore, as long as you have only the memories of Nathan Feldman, and lack those of Aaron Levitt, I could argue that you lack the knowledge you need to legally defend yourself—or help me defend you."

"The argument would be that I shouldn't go to trial because of my inability to defend myself. That, mentally speaking, I am at a disadvantage in the courtroom because, lacking a memory that I committed the crime, I cannot fully understand what I am charged with."

"Yes, more or less. Let me be more precise: I would be arguing that your current state of mind—due to medically induced amnesia—undermines criminal responsibility *procedurally*, even if it does not undermine your criminal responsibility *substantively*, to use another legal term. This means that although we grant that at the time of the crime Aaron Levitt acted voluntarily and knew what he was doing—that's the notion of *substantive* responsibility—we can still argue that, procedurally, in a court of law, you are, in your current state of ignorance about the crime, incapable of assisting in your own defense. Our defense would be that the development of amnesia after the criminal act procedurally undermines your Sixth Amendment rights."

"So, if I understand what you are saying, there is a possible successful procedural defense based on my lack of memory that will occur in a pretrial hearing where you will attempt to persuade a judge that I am not mentally fit to stand trial."

"Yes. In *Wilson v. United States* (the District of Columbia, 1962), when the defendant alleged that he did not remember committing the crime he was accused of, the court recognized that amnesia might be relevant to the accused's ability to defend himself. But, if that's going to be our argument, we will need to discredit what I anticipate will be another move the prosecution might make—and that is attempting to show that you are malingering, that you are faking a loss of memory. It appears that we can persuasively rebut that by putting on the stand Dr. Elizabeth Cohen and at least some of her colleagues who worked on the memory experiment. They will have to do a good job of explaining the science and showing that you have only the implanted memories of a fictional Nathan Feldman. This might also require, in addition to the testimony of Dr. Cohen and company that you are not faking it, the absence of any nonverbal cues associated with lying, evidence from hypnosis if the judge allows it, and evidence from the results of personal integrity tests. Do you know if any of these tests were performed before they concluded that the experiment was a success?"

"As a matter of fact, they didn't perform any of these tests. They must have been able to confirm for themselves the success of their experiment once they started to observe my behavior after they drove me to their pre-planned location near the Red River Park Condominiums. They could immediately see that I believed I lived there. They observed me confidently walking up the steps to the condo and entering the outside door to the units. For the researchers, this was the initial evidence that the implantation of false memories had worked. After that, carefully observing me, day and night, everything I did confirmed for the researchers the success of their experiment. And in her recent meeting with me, Dr. Cohen apparently proved this to her satisfaction by the way I answered questions, always insisting that I was Nathan Feldman, and absolutely refusing to undergo the reversal procedure."

"These daily observations of you and Dr. Cohen's conversations with you may not, unfortunately, constitute sufficient evidence to rebut the claim that you are a malingerer. You could have been faking it from the beginning and throughout the period of observation. And you could have been faking it when Dr. Cohen recently interviewed you, pretending you were Nathan Feldman and that you knew nothing about Aaron Levitt. And faking it now, faking it with me. Here is what the prosecution's rebuttal will look like: If Aaron's plan was to avoid conviction for murder by taking part in this experiment to create false memories for the purpose of creating an amnesia defense, then he/you would play along with this experiment, acting as if it were successful, to provide a basis for amnesiac denial. When you went to the police station to report yourself as a missing person, this was your ploy. The prosecution may even put expert witnesses on the stand who will say that implanting a lifetime of false memories is not scientifically possible."

"How do we counter this?"

"The various tests I mentioned—and others—need to be performed by NISM to support the implanted memories claim. The combined weight of a battery of honesty tests and universal agreement by NISM researchers that you are an amnesiac might impress the judge and hopefully persuade her that you shouldn't go to trial."

"Does that seem the best legal strategy—that is, to claim that I suffer from a special form of amnesia and to use this to convince a judge in a pretrial hearing that I'm not able to defend myself and therefore should not be tried for murder?"

"This, at the least, should be our opening strategy, our first legal move. We have nothing to lose. The judge, however, may not be persuaded that you are unable to defend yourself, even if we present strong medical and psychological evidence that you have no memory of the crime. Unfortunately, despite *Wilson v. United States*, most courts have found amnesiacs competent to stand trial. In *United States v. Andrews*, the defendant accused of a bank robbery claimed to have no memory of the crime due to a history of alcohol and drug abuse. The Seventh Circuit refused to follow Wilson, stating that no other circuit has adopted Wilson's comprehensive approach. There is also *United States v. Stevens*, which held that amnesia is not a bar to prosecution of an otherwise mentally competent defendant. The judge will probably declare you to be mentally fit to stand trial."

"So, even if we can persuade the judge that I suffer from amnesia, this might not be sufficient to protect me from prosecution, from going to trial?"

"Correct. A finding of amnesia will not automatically achieve this. You can be sure that the prosecutors will, even if the judge accepts NISM's claim that you have no memory of the crime, argue that this alone does not exonerate you from being guilty of murder—that in fact you still should be held responsible for the homicide that they will argue you in fact committed. And, as I have also already said, even if the judge were to accept NISM's findings and conclude at the pretrial hearing that your mental state makes going to trial a violation of your right to a fair trial, the prosecution will then probably do everything possible to have your amnesia cured, to restore Aaron's actual memories and bring him, not you, to trial."

"Until this first legal proceeding, the one where we make the case that I should not go to trial, I assume I'm stuck in jail."

"Yes, unless you can make bail, assuming that you are given that option and you can raise the amount required. Aaron was an only child whose parents recently died in a car wreck: that much of your autobiography is the same as his. But there never was an inheritance, a fictional detail he added to the narrative of your life. His parents were heavily in debt, and creditors seized all assets. No relatives or friends have come forward. As I understand it, Aaron, although once well-to-do, now has very little income to draw from—income which is yours. The $100,000 for the experiment will only be available if Aaron is restored to himself. But even if you were rich, I'm not sure it would make a difference. Since this is a murder case, indeed a vicious homicide, the district attorney's office will probably argue successfully that you are not only too dangerous to be released but that you are also a flight risk—and thus bail will be denied."

Those were Sue's sobering words before she had to leave me to be in court for another case. I would see her again at the pretrial hearing where she would make the argument that this should never go to trial. After spending all too long behind bars, the pretrial hearing finally happened. Unfortunately, the judge ruled that I was competent to stand trial, especially since a plausible case could be made that I was malingering. Although the testimony of scientists from NISM, along with the results of various truth-tests, were presented, the prosecutors disputed the claims about my lack of memory and introduced their own experts who testified that, in their opinion, I was guilty of malingering and that implanting memories in a global way was not possible.

When we met again to discuss a defense strategy for my trial, Sue told me one possible defense would be to argue that Aaron and I are mentally different human beings. This would mean arguing that, legally speaking, Aaron and Nathan are legally distinct persons. Because of the overwhelming evidence of Aaron's guilt, Sue was not interested in denying that Aaron was responsible for the murder. Instead, she would argue that I wasn't responsible for what Aaron did, that I wasn't Aaron in any legally relevant sense. This would require that she do some of the work that interested me: talking to the jury about what constitutes a person's distinctive identity, including the unique memories of this person, whether veridical or not. It would be similar to a dissociative identity disorder defense. Sue would argue that my identity is distinct from Aaron's because of the implantation of false memories, creating a different person, a person who should not be held responsible for Aaron's actions. To make this case, we would have to convince a jury that I was not faking it: that I truly lacked Aaron's memories, that my memories were distinctive and completely different. NISM experts, who failed to convince the judge at the pretrial hearing, would, working to persuade a jury, have to be at the top of their game in making the argument that I was not Aaron Levitt—and be able to rebut the prosecution experts' claim that submerging real memories and implanting false ones was science fiction.

Thus, we would need to convince a jury of this—not a judge because we agreed that, although the judge might not be persuadable, we might be able to persuade twelve jurors I was not guilty or, at the very least, cause one of them to have reasonable doubt. Yes, a jury trial was our best bet. We would try to convince the jury that I, Nathan Feldman, have a memory bank different from that of Aaron Levitt. I mean literally that "we" would try to persuade the jury because I agreed to take the stand. I believed that I could convince a jury that NISM's claims about my memory were true. I—and this was a mistake—did not testify at the pretrial hearing. But that was water under the bridge. We now had to go to trial, and Sue thought I would make a compelling witness for the defense because it was unlikely the prosecution could shake me, or catch me in any lies—for the simple reason that I was not in fact a malingerer. My testimony might turn out to be my best defense if I were a credible witness, which we were convinced I would be.

If Sue adopted this Nathan-is-not-Aaron defense, a theory of personal identity would be central to her argument. And I could help Sue with that. But she warned me that since this was similar to a dissociative identity disorder defense, the chances of success were low. Historically, she wanted to emphasize, this defense has rarely been successful. Courts generally have found that although individuals may have distinct personalities that control their behavior, this condition does not preclude criminal responsibility. But Sue assured me that, if we decided that this legal strategy was too risky, there were a number of other possible lines of defense. She promised that at our next meeting she would lay out other legal options for my consideration.

11. Anatomy of a Murder

WHILE WAITING TO SEE Sue again, I had time to become knowledgeable about the crime committed by my other self. Alter ego? It would probably be more accurate to describe me as the alter ego. This murder was shockingly gruesome. Sue had left a bundle of thick documents about the murder, information gained in discovery, materials the prosecution was required to provide the defense, evidence the prosecution intended to use at trial. I learned that the murder victim, Samuel Shaw, was intimately—that is, sexually and romantically—involved with a woman Aaron evidently thought belonged to him. Margaret Newman was a thirty-five-year-old woman Aaron believed to be his devoted lover. Margaret had evidently concealed from Aaron her involvement with Shaw—a thirty-three-year-old, strikingly handsome, and very wealthy real estate agent. Like Margaret, Samuel was also a Jew in a community with so few of us.

When Aaron found out about this relationship—it was unclear how he discovered they were seeing each other—he obviously became very disturbed, as revealed in texts to Margaret that she shared with the prosecution. Once affluent, but now unemployed and just scraping by, Aaron was probably feeling insecure and clearly threatened by Margaret's attractive and rich suitor. Rather than target Margaret, Aaron's wrath seemed to have been directed solely at Samuel.

There was evidence that Aaron often followed the two lovers when they were together. He had even parked outside of Samuel's house several evenings when Margaret spent the night there. A house security camera caught this, showing a vehicle that was clearly Aaron's. And a few weeks before the murder Aaron, finding the real estate agent's cell number online, texted him several times, asking Samuel to stay away from the woman he claimed as his partner, threatening him if he didn't stop seeing Margaret. These were anonymous texts—Aaron never identified himself. But

Margaret probably told Samuel who was sending these messages. Samuel, for some reason, did not notify the police about these threats. Aaron had evidently tried to permanently delete these texts, but failed in that effort. The police IT department was able to recover them.

On the night of the murder, Aaron was able to enter the back door of Samuel's house before he arrived home from work. Aaron wore a ski mask as he entered the house—so his face could not be caught on camera. Although the real estate agent had cameras all around the outside of his home, his alarm system was not working that night, something that would have, as Aaron was using a tension wrench with a rake to pick the backdoor lock, triggered an alert to the security firm and also an alert to Samuel's cell phone, with a video of the person breaking into his house.

Was breaking and entering a house with an inoperative alarm system just dumb luck? Probably not. It was later discovered that a service worker from the alarm company was scheduled to repair the malfunctioning system the next day. Did Aaron somehow discover this and decide that he needed to execute his plan before the repair? The discovery documents revealed that he had been following Samuel, trying to find out everything he could about this man. He had been playing private detective, carefully investigating every aspect of Samuel's life. Aaron in fact posed as a private investigator, handing out a phony PI card with a phony name to those he questioned about Samuel. By asking questions that created doubts about Samuel's good character, Aaron wanted to make his rival's friends, acquaintances, and business associates suspicious of him, to besmirch Samuel's good name if possible. Unemployed, Aaron had plenty of time to snoop. He appeared to be in a state of moral decline, consumed with jealousy and determined to hurt Samuel's reputation.

Apparently, Aaron, in the end, wanted to do more than tarnish Samuel's good name. He ultimately decided on a drastic action that seemed completely out of character, namely murdering Margaret's new lover. With the alarm system not working, Aaron's only challenge was getting into a locked house. One of Aaron's odd skills was apparently picking locks, something he had mastered during a wayward adolescence in Houston during which he was arrested for several thefts of unusual items: for example, breaking in and stealing a signed first edition of Jean Paul Sartre's *Etre et Neant* (*Being and Nothingness*) from the home of a retired Rice University professor of philosophy who had befriended Aaron and showed him his library. Aaron was caught and arrested but the professor decided not to press charges on the understanding that Aaron would return the book, which he did.

There were other similar thefts, not your standard break-ins, often rare collector's editions or original manuscripts of works by Sartre, one taken while visiting Paris with his parents. Amazingly, Aaron managed to steal the original manuscript of Sartre's *War Diaries* housed temporarily, for a traveling exhibit, in a then-prominent Parisian bookstore—La Hune (now permanently closed), located in a quiet corner of the city at 16 Rue de l'Abbaye in Saint Germain-des-Pres. The store, surprisingly, did not have an alarm system. As Aaron picked the lock to the bookstore's back door, an outside camera caught his masked image.

The police did not need to search for this sixteen-year-old Sartre-obsessed thief because Aaron returned to the store a few days later, bringing with him this valuable manuscript. The bookstore owner, although relieved to have Sartre's *War Diaries* returned undamaged, was not in a forgiving mood and so called the police. Aaron waited patiently for the gendarmes to arrive. He was taken away and placed in a juvenile detention facility, to the embarrassment of his parents. Aaron explained to his parents and the authorities that he just wanted time to examine Sartre's actual war journals carefully—including crossed out words and whole paragraphs, that did not appear in published editions—in the privacy of his hotel room while his parents were enjoying Parisian nightlife. Fluent in French and already well-read in French existentialist philosophy, Aaron was clearly a precocious teenager and a very unusual thief. My recollection of discovering Camus's *The Myth of Sisyphus* in the Bryan High School library and stealing it was no doubt one of Aaron's memories that was imported into my memory stream.

Aaron was never locked up for any length of time for these literary thefts because his family's high-priced lawyers were able to work out plea deals—and ultimately have all of these strange juvenile crimes expunged from the record. Consequently, there was no legal trail of his youthful biblio-thefts. All the books and manuscripts he stole were eventually recovered or returned—again, often returned by Aaron himself. Although there was no legal record of any of his thefts, the Winterville DA somehow found out about these youthful crimes, perhaps planning to use this information to document Aaron's break-in skills. They found in his cheap, run-down, and cluttered Winterville apartment a break-in tool kit (ordered from Amazon): different-sized tension wrenches and a triple hump rake. A small wrench was used to apply tension to the lock, as the rake was used to scrape over the individual pins and force them into place for the lock to be unlatched. This was disclosed in the discovery documents.

Back to the murder. A security camera caught the image of someone Aaron's height and build entering and leaving the back door of Samuel Shaw's home during the time the murder occurred. Given the genetic evidence of his presence at the scene of the crime, this person, despite the ski mask, could only be Aaron Levitt. Aaron knew that his entrance and exit would be captured on video. But he also knew, because he was wearing a ski mask, that his face would never be on camera. And he looked down so that his eyes could not be seen. But that precaution was trivial compared to his carelessness at the scene of the crime. After entering the house, Aaron apparently hid somewhere inside, waiting to kill the man who had stolen Margaret from him.

Why his weapon of choice was a knife rather than a gun is unclear. Maybe he thought he could better express his anger with a blade rather than a bullet. And the sound of a blade repeatedly penetrating flesh was relatively quiet compared to the sound of gunshots: no neighbor would hear his knife thrusts. It appears that Aaron attacked his victim from behind—that he first knifed Samuel in the back of the neck. Then, when Samuel turned around, Aaron stabbed him thirty-one times all over his upper torso—finishing the job by cutting his throat, almost severing Samuel's head. Aaron was obviously enraged. When Samuel turned to face his attacker, there was clearly a struggle because Samuel's palms showed multiple defensive wounds.

Aaron, right-handed, in missing his mark several times, slashed his own left wrist and inflicted cuts on his upper left arm, as he continued to stab Samuel. Stabbing one's own body is not unusual in homicides where there are multiple angry knife thrusts. When an assailant with a knife is enraged, he tends not to be completely in control of his weapon. Rage causes a knife-wielding attacker to become careless as he repeatedly stabs his victim. It was clear that, despite the severe wound to the back of his neck, Samuel, once he turned around, was able to fight back and knew he was he in the fight of his life that he, unfortunately, lost. The one fingerprint the police lifted was probably the result of Aaron taking his gloves off in Samuel's bathroom to wash the wrist that was severely cut and badly bleeding—and to find something to stop the flow of blood. Compared to his wrist wound, the cuts on Aaron's upper left arm were minor, even though they too left scars. A single fingerprint was left on the mirror that opened to a cabinet containing bandages that Aaron was apparently looking for to cover the gash on his wrist.

Aaron obviously tried to remove evidence of his presence at the scene of the crime, but had not done a good job. He failed to fully clean up all the blood seeping from his wrist wound. The police used Fluorescein to detect traces of Aaron's blood. This was accomplished by using a fine-mist spray bottle containing this chemical: spraying Samuel's clothing, the floor, and the wall near where the body was found in the living room. It was also used in the bathroom where Aaron shed a lot of blood that he evidently tried to clean up. In a darkened room, Fluorescein can reveal blood evidence not visible to the human eye. It can detect blood even after multiple cleanings. Leaving his blood was like leaving one more DNA calling card. And Aaron's fingerprint on the mirror was simply icing on the cake for the prosecution, adding one more piece of evidence to their powerful circumstantial case against Aaron. Although he had evidently carefully planned this murder days ahead of time, what ultimately did him in was the fury he felt when he saw Samuel. It seemed to get the best of him once he saw his handsome, wealthy rival enter the house: he clearly lost control while knifing Samuel. The murder weapon, probably a serrated knife, was never found. A serrated knife was in fact missing from Levitt's kitchen-knife set. Another nail in his coffin of guilt.

Elizabeth Cohen must have noticed that the subject for her grand experiment had injuries on his upper body. Of course she did. After I completed my walk on that beautiful Saturday morning, the day Nathan was born, I was puzzled by the scar on my left wrist and the still visible cut marks on my left upper left arm. I had no memory of how they got there. It looked like I had been in a fight—because in fact Aaron had. Now these marks on my body made sense. In the person of Aaron Levitt, I had been in a struggle with the man Margaret loved more than Aaron. Did Elizabeth ever ask Aaron why he had a scar from a long, deep gash on his left wrist and other cuts on his upper left arm? In addition to the electrodes implanted through small openings in Aaron's skull into certain areas of his brain, they had also placed electrodes on Aaron's bare chest during the procedure, in order to monitor his heart. So, in overseeing the experiment, Elizabeth obviously saw that Aaron's upper torso showed signs of injury.

Again, I doubt that Elizabeth asked Aaron about what had happened to him. She was probably so happy to get a subject for her experiment that her policy was to ask few questions and proceed ahead at full speed. Something like this: I will ask no questions about these wounds so Aaron will not have to tell me any lies. She was good to go as long as Aaron could provide his fully informed consent to be her guinea pig. Although Elizabeth had a beautiful mind, an extraordinary intellect, her professional integrity and emotional intelligence may have been less than I had originally judged them to be. Elizabeth may have, in order to get on with her grand experiment, self-censored questions she knew she should ask Aaron about his injuries. And, clearly, she felt little compassion for the person she had invented: me. After seeing the success of her experiment, Elizabeth was ready to erase Nathan Feldman: to quickly destroy the new human being she had created. She was ruthlessly cold and clinical in creating a person whose life meant nothing to her once she was scientifically done with him. Evidently, to Elizabeth, Nathan Hillel Feldman was expendable and his feelings were irrelevant. This woman I had once so passionately loved suddenly became someone I now passionately hated. The Buddha was right: not only can our emotions change in a flash, but a new emotion can be the opposite of the one it replaces.

The truth was that the subject of Elizabeth's experiment—Aaron Moshe Levitt—had fallen into her hands because he had fallen on very hard times, in more ways than one. Aaron had taught at a private Catholic college in Duluth, Minnesota, the University of St. Mary, but had recently moved to Winterville after he lost his job because, as indicated already, of cutbacks due to the college's COVID-inflicted financial losses: a drop in enrollment that made budget cuts necessary. Because of low enrollment in philosophy courses, that department became one of the primary targets for downsizing faculty. They would need to cut it before they touched their highly prized USM Theology Department, although course enrollment there was not much better than philosophy classes. They were after all a Catholic institution that encouraged students to take courses in church doctrine. It, however, said a lot that they had hired a Jew and even allowed him to teach a course called Introduction to Judaism—a course that, unfortunately, disappeared with Aaron's termination.

Aaron did not, despite what he told the people at NISM, have any good job prospects. He moved to Winterville because the woman he loved lived there. It had been a long commuter relationship, with many ups and downs—and he probably thought that his relationship with Margaret would improve once they lived in the same city. Aaron had no friends in Winterville. Margaret was the only person he knew in the city. And, when, after he told her he was moving to Winterville, she did not invite him to move in with her, that should have been a sign to Aaron that all was not well with them.

He had cashed out his retirement funds and savings to have enough money to pay for a place to live and other necessities while he looked for work. None of the colleges in Winterville were hiring, and Aaron seemed to have a difficult time finding a nonacademic position he thought was appropriate to his level of education. In the meantime, he discovered that the woman he had assumed to be totally devoted to him had found someone else, something she had not been open about. Again, I'm surprised that she was not his murder victim. My guess is that Aaron deluded himself into thinking that with Samuel Shaw out of the way he could win Margaret back and have her all to himself. Margaret knew, of course—even before the evidence came in—that Aaron had murdered Samuel. If anything, this act permanently alienated her from Aaron and made her fearful for her own life. In taking Samuel's life, Aaron had actually made himself the last person Margaret would ever want to see again.

After the murder of Shaw, Margaret refused to take Aaron's calls or answer his texts. She changed her cell number and moved to another city. Maybe, fearing for her life, she decided not to immediately contact the police to share her suspicion. But after I was arrested, and it was all over the news that Aaron Levitt was in custody, charged with the murder of Samuel Shaw, and denied bail, she came forward to express her willingness to testify against Aaron. She was the anonymous caller who, early on, had told the police Aaron Levitt was the man in their photo. Once she discovered that "Aaron" was locked up, she must have felt it was safe to become an important prosecution witness. She was surprised to learn that I, a man who looked exactly like Aaron, claimed to have no memory of her, that I denied ever knowing her. She probably suspected that this was Aaron putting on an act, pretending not to know her and to have any memory of the crime.

And it's possible that, after the murder, Aaron, desperate, saw the invitation to be the subject of a major memory experiment as a way to get much needed money and to disappear for a while—in this case, into a laboratory bed for an experiment that would at least temporarily erase his memory of the crime and provide him with the defense that he was no longer Aaron Levitt. He probably thought along the same lines that Sue and I did: namely that proof of the success of the memory experiment would either prevent his prosecution or it would allow him to plead amnesia if put on trial. That is, as already suggested, he may have had his own amnesia defense. Aaron might have mistakenly thought, as did I, that he would be safe from conviction as long as it could be demonstrated that he suffered from amnesia.

Aaron was in fact trapped in a catch-22. If Aaron, in participating in the memory experiment, was betting on an amnesia defense and, if against the odds, this defense was successful, he, Aaron Levitt, would not be aware that he benefited from this legal strategy. Aaron would not be cognizant of the success of this amnesia defense, and he would not receive money for participating in the experiment. He would remain Nathan Feldman. But if Aaron was restored to himself by NISM, although he would receive a large sum of money, an amnesia defense would no longer be possible. Aaron would then face a charge of murder with no exculpatory condition. He would of course have $100,000 to hire the best lawyer he could find, but even with a really good criminal defense attorney, the evidence against him was so strong that he would probably be sent to prison for life.

12. Executioner's Song

FACING A CHARGE OF murder and defending himself against that charge was not Aaron Levitt's challenge. It was mine. And, whatever the consequences, I wanted it to remain my challenge, not his. When I met with Sue Bradley again, she informed me of two other legal options. She, however, first reviewed the weakness of any argument based on an unorthodox amnesia defense. Since she knew that I was attracted to a defense that made a case for my distinct identity as Nathan Feldman, Sue wanted to emphasize what she had already told me: that it was unlikely I could legally distinguish myself from Levitt, even if we could demonstrate that I had none of Aaron's memories. The prosecution's important legal rebuttal would be that I am Aaron Moshe Levitt and, at the time of the crime, Aaron appears to have satisfied both the *mens rea* and *actus reus* requirements. There was overwhelming evidence that he planned the murder, indeed many days in advance—that it was not a crime of passion in the sense of being an act of spontaneous homicide—although, as already noted, Aaron probably surprised himself by his own rage as he started to stab Samuel Shaw. After all, it was clearly overkill, not unusual when the motive is jealousy. In any event, despite the strong emotion involved in killing Samuel, it looked like a powerful case for first degree murder could be successfully made.

Even if we could convince the jury that I had no memory of the crime, amnesia had proved to be a weak defense in most courtrooms. Sue bluntly reminded me that the defense *I cannot remember committing the crime* would probably not impress most judges and juries. To the question of whether a special amnesia argument—based on a medically induced temporary suppression of Aaron's memories and the implantation of Nathan's false memories—could be a convincing defense, she said that the answer was, in a courtroom in Winterville, Minnesota, more than likely an emphatic "No!" Sue pointed out that, from the perspective of criminal law, my inability to remember committing homicide doesn't mean that I, at the time of the crime, didn't intend to commit the murder. Legally, it will be argued, I am Aaron Moshe Levitt, and any claim that I am not would be hard to defend. As already noted, if Aaron himself was really counting on this line of defense, he was overestimating its chance of success.

Since there was strong evidence that Aaron knew what he was doing at the time of the crime, it was unlikely that my current mental state could be used to exonerate me. From a legal perspective, it is the defendant's mental state at the time he commits an offense that is important. That's why the courts have generally upheld a defendant's murder conviction despite his failure to remember killing the victim. I couldn't seem to leave behind Aaron's obvious culpability for the murder of Samuel Shaw—which attached itself to me, memory or no memory of what I did. The criminal justice system, despite what might seem to be its unfairness, continues to punish defendants who cannot remember the crime. Thus, our chances of success in trying to separate me from Aaron were not good.

"But if that's what you want me to argue—that you are not Aaron, have none of his memories, and thus should not be held accountable for what he did—that's what I will do. This case, at its strongest, would be based on making a persuasive argument that you suffer from anomalous forms of both dissociative amnesia and dissociative identity disorder: the diagnoses you told me that Dr. Cohen came up with when she was deceiving you! If that is the defense you want me to mount, just keep in mind the low probability of success."

"What are other possible defense strategies?"

"There is a legal move we could make if you are willing to plead guilty."

"And that is?"

"A Norgaard Plea where you plead guilty but say you cannot remember the crime due to amnesia."

"What's the advantage?"

"You avoid a trial and, given your confession of guilt, the penalty may be less severe. But you'll probably still spend a long time in prison. Of course, prosecutors and the judge will have to agree to this plea deal and its terms."

"What's in it for the prosecution?"

"They avoid a trial where there is always the chance that a jury will not convict you. Juries are notoriously unpredictable. If I make a powerful case for reasonable doubt based on medically induced dissociative amnesia and dissociative identity disorder, it's possible we could win. Not likely, but possible. And the prosecutors know that I can be a very persuasive defense attorney. I think I am the public defender that they least like to face. I work very hard and often surprise them with what I come up with. Still, I think, despite my legal skills, if we go to trial, making the case that you are not guilty because you are not Aaron Levitt, have no memory of being him, and have no memory of the crime, his crime, the probability of winning is not great. So, a Norgaard Plea is worth considering."

"But I'm not guilty and so I don't want to plead guilty."

"Okay. There is another possible option: an Alford Plea."

"I have seen (or falsely remember seeing) enough real-life crime shows to have a rough idea of what that involves. But it has never made sense to me."

"That's because it doesn't pass the commonsense test. It's the paradoxical move of pleading guilty even while not admitting guilt, while denying that you committed the crime! Basically, it means you register a formal admission of guilt, but you do not admit committing the criminal act and assert your innocence. It is sometimes described as 'a plea of guilty containing a protestation of innocence.' You simply acknowledge that the evidence presented by the prosecution is likely to persuade a judge or jury that you are guilty. Just thoughtfully consider the Alford Plea as well as the Norgaard Plea—in addition to the Nathan-is-not-Aaron argument. There may be other legal strategies we can explore, but these three are enough for you to think about for now."

"Okay. I'll seriously weigh these options—and, if you come up with other legal strategies, I would like to hear them."

"See you in a few days. I'm working on another case that should be done soon."

Despite its low probability of success, I eventually decided to go with what I thought was the most honest defense strategy, one based on anomalous forms of dissociative amnesia and dissociative identity disorders—again, to repeat what Sue said, the very diagnoses that a deceptive Elizabeth Cohen had suggested. That meant persuasively making the case that Nathan Feldman and Aaron Levitt are, legally speaking, two different persons. I repeated my offer to take the stand and answer all the questions the prosecution had to throw at me. I agreed with Sue that they would not catch me in any lies because I would not be lying; they would not be able to show that I was putting on an act because I wouldn't be. Sue was obviously convinced that I wasn't faking amnesia and so had confidence in the persuasive power of my testimony.

Our central claim would be that I have a completely different identity. Although Aaron and I are genetically identical, we are not the same person. Sue would argue that we are analogous to identical twins. To hold me accountable for Aaron's actions would be like holding an identical twin responsible for what his sibling did. As I was sitting in jail thinking about how I could help Sue make a case for my distinctive identity and thus different responsibility, waiting to go to trial using the Nathan-is-not-Aaron defense, I was told that the prosecutors planned to push hard for the reversal procedure. Sue told me that she believed that the prosecuting attorneys were now doubtful that they could show I was guilty of malingering because NISM now had an impressive battery of psychological tests that showed my truthfulness. And every member of the research team would testify that, in their considered opinion, I was telling the truth.

In addition, the judge agreed to admit into evidence the results of a new very advanced functional magnetic resonance brain imaging (fMRI) procedure that tests for deception. Using this highly reliable test, NISM found no signs that I was guilty of deception. In addition to the documented reliability of this brain imaging test, I think the prosecution also feared that my own consistent testimony might be enough to persuade the jury that I was not a malingerer. So, from the prosecution's point of view, there was now substantial evidence that the experiment to implant false memories was a success. In a sudden change in strategy, the prosecutors submitted a request to the judge that I be required, as soon as possible, to undergo the reversal procedure. They obviously saw that they would have a much better chance of convincing a jury of the guilt of the accused if they could put on trial a man who was indisputably Aaron Moshe Levitt.

I wasn't worried about this because Sue thought she could defeat the request, and she didn't think that Judge Maureen Sullivan would approve an act of medical coercion, the imposition of a medical procedure without the consent of the patient. Sue argued, in a hearing about this, that forcing me to undergo the procedure—performing this operation without my consent— would be medical battery, the crime of inflicting physical harm on a person in a medical setting. It would be the violation of my right to decide what medical treatment I should receive or not receive. Sue told me that Judge Sullivan had a reputation for being fair. So, we were hopeful. Unfortunately, the judge's decision in my case was the opposite of what we expected.

The judge said in her decision that the research team of the Neuro-science Institute for the Study of Memory had now demonstrated to her satisfaction that the implantation of false memories had been successful. And she noted that the prosecution agreed. This changed everything. Judge Sullivan stated that it "was clear that Aaron Levitt had legally authorized that the reversal procedure must take place if the experiment was success-ful." The judge reasoned that the research team was obligated by law to perform this procedure "precisely because of documents signed by Aaron Levitt and Dr. Cohen." Elizabeth told the judge that Aaron had given his informed consent to the experiment with the explicit understanding that the reversal procedure would occur once the success of the experiment was confirmed. She had legal documentation that Aaron's participation in the experiment was based on that understanding.

According to Judge Sullivan, the facts were clear: Aaron Moshe Levitt was, legally speaking, a person whose legal rights needed to be respected; Nathan Hillel Feldman was not. I was a fictional character, with no legal rights—a nonperson, from the standpoint of the law. What was central to the judge's decision against me was the agreement that NISM made with Aaron—a legal contract—to restore him to his true self and to restore his actual memories. The reversal procedure was, Sullivan concluded, legally required, and my objection to this procedure based on the claim that it would be medically coercive, a violation of my rights as a patient, and thus constituted the crime of medical battery, was groundless.

The judge kept repeating the point that I was a fictional rather than an actual person—and that "Aaron Moshe Levitt was, from the perspective of the law, indisputably a real person." And he was the person who needed to stand trial for murder. In her decision, Judge Sullivan drove home the point—asserting it again and again—that failure to perform the reversal procedure would be a violation of a legally binding contract and a violation of Aaron's legal rights as an experimental subject. Supposedly, I did not have any rights that could be violated because, legally speaking, I did not exist. The irony is that, if the Aaron who was charged with murder could talk, he might want to challenge the reversal procedure, contract or not contract. But the judge had ruled, and a date was set for the procedure. The judge was, as I saw it, singing an executioner's song, Elizabeth's song. She in effect signed my death warrant.

Sue had argued forcefully and eloquently against the procedure, draw-ing on the notion of personal identity that she and I crafted, maintaining I was, legally speaking, a person with the right to refuse a coercive medical procedure. She pointed out that I had a unique consciousness, distinctive memories, and a different personality. The judge did not find this argument legally persuasive. To be honest, I could see the soundness of the judge's reasoning. From the perspective of the law, Aaron was a person whose rights would be violated if the procedure was not performed—and I was in fact Aaron's creation. Even I had to admit—if only silently to myself—that, legally speaking, I was an invented or fictional person and Aaron was a real person. Still, the decision of the judge was crushing. And I was not about submit to it. Even if, legally, I didn't exist, I still felt I had a moral right to life, indeed more of a moral right to life than Aaron! Given the fact that I would soon be transported to the Institute for a transformation back into Aaron, I needed to figure out how to save myself. I was desperate to come up with an escape plan. As extraordinary good luck would have it, I found myself suddenly sharing jail space with a man who would be my savior.

13. The Defiant Ones

WHEN I RETURNED TO jail after my last meeting with Sue Bradley, I encountered my cellmate, Martin Jackson. He was a fortyish coal-black African American charged with resisting arrest in a protest against police brutality inflicted on a young black man caught speeding. No doubt the long and dangerous chase made the police officers angry because the fleeing speeder had endangered many lives in running red lights and stop signs, going up to eighty in residential areas and then close to one hundred on the freeway. The cops clearly took out their anger on this reckless individual when they finally captured him after his car went into a ditch and turned over. Not wearing a seatbelt, he was thrown from his convertible—which probably saved his life. This young black man was driving drunk. But no matter how reckless the driver had been, Martin—who was sympathetic to the white police officers' anger in this case—said that "they crossed the line in beating the shit out of an intoxicated and defenseless man lying on the ground." He was hospitalized for serious injuries—not from the car turnover but from the assault by the cops.

One officer was reported to have screamed: "you fucking n***** ape." So, racism played a role in their attack. Martin was arrested the next day when he boldly entered the police station with others, all carrying signs to loudly protest this incident. The protest and the subsequent arrests were captured on video by local media—big news in this small town. Martin had refused to leave the station and did not submit quietly and cooperatively when they arrested him on the spot. They had a difficult time taking him down—indeed, had to tase him several times to get him under control. He was very strong and actually skilled in mixed martial arts, having once been an MMA competitor.

I had the cell to myself until Martin arrived. Why was Martin put in with me? There were other two-person cells in the jail complex occupied by only one inmate. Was it my good luck? After all, Martin turned out to be a perfect cellmate and partner in crime. We were close to the same age and, surprisingly, had much in common. We were ebony and ivory in the best Paul McCartney utopian sense of that metaphor. A chance pairing? Or were we put together because our jailers discovered we were both Jews? Since there was only one Tanakh in the jail library and I had borrowed it, maybe they thought we could share that. Also, maybe because we both demanded kosher food, even though neither of us was really a kosher Jew. We requested kosher meals because they were superior to standard jail cuisine. We were in fact progressive outlaw members of the tribe: "woke" Jews who thought the most important thing in Judaism was its strong commitment to social justice.

Or were we put together because they discovered we were both unemployed PhDs—Martin's in sociology—academics who deserved each other. That's what Aaron was, and I was, to my jailers, Aaron. Maybe they thought that this commonality would keep us from getting bored and keep us out of trouble as we talked about whatever entertains out-of-work professors. They also rightly assumed we were both lefties. Those responsible for pairing us were obviously unaware that incarcerated radical ex-profs can become very clever escape artists when they put their heads together to outwit their jailers. We became the defiant ones. We were Sydney Poitier and Tony Curtis, symbolically chained together, bound together religiously, politically, and professionally. Shouldn't the authorities have been wary of coupling criminal academics who they must have perceived to be serious menaces to society: I a homicidal jealous lover who brutally killed the other man, and Martin a cop-hater who could become a cop-killer? Wrong on both counts. In truth, we would be a menace to our jailers.

Let me repeat: they foolishly underestimated our ability to outsmart them. They never considered what devious and brilliant plans for deliverance socialist intellectuals, with time on their hands, are capable of. They obviously never anticipated our ability to defeat their plan for my future, the plan to transport me to NISM for obliteration. We cleverly put in its place a plot for my liberation. Maybe, in fairness, I should give Martin full credit for the scheme that would free me because he is the one who made it happen. I simply cooperated with his cunning ploy. After hearing and finally believing my bizarre story, Martin became committed to my liberation. In working to free me Martin would be fulfilling a great *mitzvah* in Judaism called in Hebrew *pidyon shvuyim* (literally, redemption of the captives): the obligation in Jewish law to free fellow Jews who have been unjustly imprisoned.

Yes, Martin was a black Jew of which there are all too few in the world. And he was very black—something he told me elicited prejudice not only from white people but even from some other blacks who were not so black, a bias called colorism: prejudice against very dark skin. So, Martin had to deal with multiple bigotries: racism, colorism, and antisemitism. Some of the latter was coming from his Black Lives Matter brothers and sisters who saw all Jews as fanatical lovers of the colonial state of Israel, and they saw Palestinians as their kin suffering from brutal Jewish oppression. Martin tried to tell them that there were Jews critical of Israel's decades-long mistreatment of Palestinians, working to stop it, but they seemed not to hear him.

There were of course a few days of mutual suspicion when Martin was first placed in my cell, but over time and long conversations, we were delighted and surprised to discover what we had in common: to wit, that we were both Jews, radicals, and out-of-work profs (well, Aaron was)—a special kind of brotherhood. We (I only in imagination) also had in common that we were transplanted Texans who had grown up as left-wing political freaks in that overwhelmingly right-wing state. And it also turned out that we shared an inclination to extravagant pleasures, he having a taste for expensive sports cars that he raced and I (in false memory) for costly trips to beautiful beaches throughout the world. Martin was not only a radical in theory: he was clearly one in practice, an organizer who was determined to thwart the dreams of Christian white nationalists.

Did our jailers know they were dealing with wealthy socialists, always a threat to those in power because wealth can be subversively used to undermine the status quo? Of course, my story of wealth was only semi-autobiographical—or should I say, to be more accurate, pseudo-autobiographical. It was, however, probably true of Aaron Levitt; he too was once an affluent socialist who spent extravagantly on material delights while wanting the same for every person. I was now in fact almost destitute because Aaron, although once well-to-do, had become unemployed and poor. After being terminated as a professor, he used up most of his remaining income simply to survive in Winterville. Any leftover income in his bank account would probably have to go the county to cover the costs of my public defender. And as long as I remained Nathan Feldman, I wouldn't get that generous

NISM check for being an experimental subject. My plan was of course to remain Nathan as long as humanly possible.

While I was in fact impoverished, my cellmate, fortunately, still had wealth and did use it for subversive ends. I discovered that Martin had published a number of sociology textbooks, left-leaning publications about class, race, gender, sex, and economic power, the kind of texts that many liberal and progressive sociology professors love to use. His *Introduction to Radical Sociology* was in its third edition and his many other sociology textbooks had been updated to reflect changing times. In fact, Martin was making so much from these publications that he didn't need to work for living. So, yes, he had been denied tenure despite his textbook success, but he could easily make it without his university salary. It did hurt, however, he told me, that his colleagues in the Winterville State University Sociology Department did not value what he published and were probably jealous of his success—including his significant earnings from these textbooks—and so were looking for a way to humble and get rid of him. Although they were all white, he didn't think race played a role. In his tenure review, a majority of his colleagues claimed that, because he had not published refereed articles in scholarly sociology journals, or published any genuinely scholarly books, he was not a real scholar.

Clearly, a majority of those in the WSU Sociology Department did not appreciate his textbook-writing skills—and so voted against tenure. Thus, despite awards for outstanding teaching and the fact that his textbooks were used in countless colleges and universities throughout the United States, his position was not renewed. That was my good luck because, with so much time on his hands, Martin was drawn to protest events, even to actions that carried with them the risk of arrest and jailtime. Yes, fortunate for me, Martin got arrested and thrown into jail precisely when I also found myself behind bars and condemned to death.

I told Martin my incredible story about being made the victim of a cruel experiment, of having false memories implanted in my brain, of identifying as Nathan Feldman, of legally fighting to keep alive a person with a constructed identity, but losing. Losing legally, although, I told Martin, my brilliant young female attorney did her damnedest to dissuade the judge from ordering the reversal procedure. I explained to him that Nathan Feldman was the only identity that I recognized and that I did not want let this identity, even if manufactured, be extinguished. I informed him that I was not just sitting in jail, but actually sitting on death row, waiting to be executed. Although incredulous at first about my claim of having in my brain implanted false memories covering a whole lifetime, I ultimately convinced him, referring to NISM's documentation of this experiment that could be found online. Martin seemed to understand and sympathize with my condition.

I pointed out that the man they wanted to resurrect at my expense was, from all the evidence—and it was compelling—a murderer, and a brutal one at that. Indeed, I argued that he is the one who should be executed. I told Martin that since there is no death penalty in Minnesota that if they revived Aaron, he would never have to pay the ultimate price. Instead, I would have to pay that price, in his place. I wanted Martin to know that I wasn't going down without a fight. As they tied me down in preparation for the reversal procedure and began to inject a general anesthetic, I would resist to my last moment of consciousness as Nathan Feldman. I would curse and fight them and make my execution as difficult as I could for Elizabeth and her coconspirators who were playing God with my life. I was of course hoping it would not come to that—hoping that I could avoid being erased.

I shared with Martin that one of my areas of research was personal identity theory. I told him that central to one's distinctive identity, from my perspective, are unique memories, a memory stream that constitutes a distinctive life narrative. We distinguish people from each other and identify people by a number of different physical and psychological traits, but one of the most important ways one person distinguishes himself, herself, or themself (if nonbinary) from another, and claims to have self-knowledge, is by having a unique set of memories. My memories are not the same as Aaron Levitt's. That makes us different persons.

Some critics of my view, I acknowledged to Martin, might argue that the important difference is that Aaron's memories are veridical and mine are not. Does this, I asked, make Aaron's life more valuable than mine? I wanted to challenge the view that Aaron is a person and I am not because his memories are true and mine are not by asking my critics this question: Do you really believe that all of your memories are objectively true? Your memories of your childhood or even what happened last year? We know how unreliable memory can be. How many people who write memoirs get things wrong? Our recollections are often notoriously imaginative and inaccurate.

Yet, however unreliable they are, you still call all of the memories you experience *your* memories, making you who you are. They are your personal memories, making you the distinctive person you are, even if many of these memories are—if you are honest—highly dubious, less than fully true, and some even completely untrue. A memory is still a memory even if it is not true. Memory does not carry with it a self-verification process. Indeed, there is no way for people to verify the truth of all of their memories. Even Facebook junkies don't post all of their experiences. The point I was making to Martin was this: even if you're not sure all of your memories correspond to the facts, you still call them *your* memories. I choose to do the same while recognizing that all of my memories are false! They remain, nonetheless, uniquely my memories.

And if anyone is not convinced by what I have to say about memory, I would also argue that, when it comes to personhood, memory isn't everything. I also have a firm set of beliefs and values—and a way of looking at the world that sets me apart from other persons, including Aaron. I also have a distinctive personality that others can recognize as such. Despite what the law says, I see myself as a real person with rights, including the right to continued life. Should my life be sacrificed to save Aaron's? Does Aaron deserve to live while I don't? Why? It could be argued that he forfeited his right to life when he took an innocent human life. That is what the Torah asserts, even if the rabbis of the Talmud made it very difficult to apply this law, making the evidential conditions required for applying the death penalty very difficult to satisfy. That's as it should be for capital punishment.

I pointed out that Aaron was a Jew who should have understood the value of innocent human life and that, as the sage Hillel said, whoever takes one life destroys the world. But what if it is life versus life? What if it is necessary to choose between two human lives? Then things become more complicated. Comparing our two lives, I reiterated my claim that I had more of a right to life than Aaron. I argued that all of those who loved Samuel Shaw—his family, friends, and Margaret Newman—would probably agree with me. Knowing the brutal way he died, the vicious nature of Aaron's act of murder, I told Martin that it was my firm belief that all of those who loved Samuel Shaw would agree that Aaron Levitt did not deserve to be restored to life. If they had to choose which of us should live, whom do you think they would choose? This was the line of reasoning I shared with Martin, and he seemed to be persuaded by the case I made for valuing my life over Aaron's. Clearly on my side, the challenge became for Martin how to save my life, how to free someone he believed to be unfairly imprisoned and unjustly sentenced to death.

14. Dead Man Walking

BECAUSE MARTIN FOUND MY case compelling—a just cause—he put off making bail, something he could have easily done. He wanted to hang around long enough to see how he could help me. Martin seemed to reflect deeply on what I told him. He was on my side, not only morally but practically, determined to do something to liberate me. Putting himself in my place, thinking like the good empathetic and critical sociologist he was, Martin could completely understand my point of view, why I identified as Nathan Feldman, even if I was an invented character. Martin believed that the reversal procedure should never happen. And, most important, he had a plan for me, a way to keep Nathan Feldman from being erased.

Martin said that he knew people who could free me. It would require intercepting the jail van that would be transporting me to the Institute, disarming the guards, tying them up, and then quickly taking me to a secure place, a place where no one could find me. It meant transporting me far from Winterville to some distant location and providing me with the credentials I would need—another name, a driver's license ID, a Social Security number, etc.—to start a new life. It would also involve changing my appearance. Martin assured me that all of this was possible; he just needed time to devise an escape plot and then fine-tune the details. My date with death was fast approaching, and I needed to tell him about a serious obstacle to his plan to free me.

"Martin, I appreciate your offer to help, but I don't want you to take any legal risks for me. Besides, there is a serious impediment to any escape plan. The deceptive psychiatrist who wants to turn me back into Aaron Levitt—the man I now consider my Hyde personality—informed me that before Aaron underwent the procedure to implant false memories a device was inserted into his left groin. They did this with his written legal consent. I did see a small scar there but thought that Aaron, in his rage while stabbing Samuel Shaw, had accidentally done that to himself. I learned otherwise. The NISM experimenters, fearing I might become suicidal because of suddenly becoming a stranger to everyone I thought knew me, inserted a device that detects dangerous substances or anything life-threatening I might put into my system. They wanted to be ready to rush me to an emergency room if I imbibed anything that could be lethal. Of course, this would not have prevented me from taking my life in the way I planned: stepping in front of a train. But that function of the device is not the problem. The problem is that it also serves as a tracking instrument. NISM and law enforcement will know immediately where I am wherever I go."

"Don't lose hope. Our objective now is to outsmart the authorities at every step on your way to freedom. It is fortunate for us that NISM revealed this to you—the hidden device. That was a serious mistake, just as serious as the error of assuming the new person they created would willingly go along with the reversal procedure. Our immediate objective is removal of the tracking device. After that, we will devise a plan to intercept the jail van on its way to NISM. Let me think. Let me think."

No cell phones were permitted in the jail. Martin made an outside call on a jail phone, inviting a friend to visit him. He told me that this man, also African American, was the key to removing the transmitter and then to my liberation. When his visitor arrived, they had to speak to each other on jail phones separated by a glass partition, conversations that were probably monitored and even recorded by jail authorities. Martin and his visitor apparently spoke in some kind of code. He was able to convey to his friend a request for specific items, communicating to him precisely what was needed to extract the transmitter. He requested a whole list of things without naming them explicitly. Later, he would also communicate in code to this comrade a plan for intercepting the van on the way to NISM.

The first order of business was, however, to acquire the tools needed to remove the device from my groin. Martin had to communicate to his visitor the surgical tools he required without revealing to anyone listening to this conversation what exactly he was requesting. From what Martin told me, it had to do with words spelled backwards, metaphors interpreted literally, and saying the opposite of what he meant. For example, Martin asked his interlocutor to contact a mutual friend, Pras Fink, who he described as a man with deep pockets, and ask him to come to the jail to discuss paying Martin's bail. He also asked his visitor to contact their old Norwegian friend Grus Sevolg who Martin said was a lawyer; he spelled out his name and gave his visitor two different phone numbers for the attorney. Then, Martin, expressing concern about how he should plead in court, told his visitor that he would need to "thread the needle between confessing guilt to the charge of resisting arrest and not actually apologizing for his actions." Finally, Martin said to his visitor that he wished he had some alcohol, laughing and saying, "I don't mean rubbing alcohol."

Not complicated for his friend in crime: he was asking for a sharp pocketknife, surgical gloves, needle and thread, and rubbing alcohol. There was also coded language for other items, including cotton balls, a flashlight, small forceps, and a local anesthetic. Apparently, each digit in the fictional Grus Sevolg's two fictional phone numbers corresponded to a letter: when the letters were spelled out, they named the other items needed for the surgery. Martin came back to the cell with details about what was afoot: namely, gathering the materials needed to extract the device from my groin. Execution of the plan was Martin's responsibility. In other words, he would perform the surgery.

In the middle of the night while no one was looking, Martin would have to find the entrance point in my left groin where the transmitter was inserted. Using the sharpened blade of a pocket knife, he would have to make a deep incision in my groin at the insertion point. He would then have to pull out the device with forceps. How Martin was able to get the knife, isopropyl alcohol, surgical gloves, cotton balls, forceps, and flashlight into our cell had everything to do with a cooperating overnight guard who was also an African American and a member of a radical black organization of which Martin was the leader. Martin's visitor, also part of the same organization, communicated what was needed to this guard when he was off-duty. Unfortunately for me, although this guard was able to bring in almost everything required for the surgery, he failed to bring any kind of anesthetic, any painkiller.

In addition to providing Martin with most of the requested items, on the night of the surgery, around three in the morning, this guard was supposed to loan Martin his cell phone so that its flashlight could be used to allow Martin to see what he was doing. Holding the flashlight steady was my assignment. I was supposed to keep the light focused on the surgery site, despite the terrible pain I would be experiencing while the surgery was being performed. The cotton balls soaked in alcohol and the surgical gloves were to be used to keep the process as sterile as possible. These alcohol-saturated cotton balls were needed to clean my groin area before Martin carefully made his incision. And the alcohol was also to be used to sterilize the knife blade, forceps, and the threaded needle. Martin, who once studied to be a surgeon, had learned the basics, including how to precisely make an incision and to effectively sew up a wound.

Flunking out of medical school because of an addiction problem, Martin later found his calling in sociology. He came to love this much more than medicine. But to return to the operation: as luck would have it, the surgery was a success, even if painful and bloody. During the surgery, my job, in addition to shining a light on the surgery location, was, absent an anesthetic, not to scream from the pain caused by the deep incision and the sting of alcohol in my wound. To keep from screaming, I, while holding the cellphone flashlight in my left hand, bit down on my right forefinger so hard that I was afraid I might actually sever it with my teeth. I almost passed out from the pain. Before the bleeding in my groin was out of control—and the blood did seem to be gushing—Martin, skillfully, using the needle and thread, did an impressive job of suturing my wound. He then wrapped one of my T-shirts around the sutured area. For all I knew, despite all the precautions, my wound might eventually become infected and life-threatening.

After all, it was not a hospital setting, and it was hard to keep my sutured wound clean. I wasn't able to take any antibiotics before the surgery to prevent infection. But it was worth the risk, the risk of possible death from infection. The alternative, after all, was the certain death that would occur if I underwent the reversal procedure. After the surgery, I knew that, if everything went according to plan, I would no longer be a dead man walking—walking from the jail van into NISM for my scheduled erasure. Instead, I would be a liberated prisoner walking away from the intercepted van toward a new life.

But none of this would have been possible without the inside man who risked a lot to make the surgery happen. This jail-guard-confederate, already mentioned, had, on different visits to our cell, when he was supposedly trying to break up altercations between Martin and me, provided the crude medical supplies we needed. Of course, our arguments were nothing more than theatre. We wanted to appear as anything but comrades in arms. In our undergraduate days we had both studied drama and performed in college plays—so we knew how to put on a good act. The guard, also play-acting, threatened to put us in different cells if we continued these arguments.

I felt grateful for the existence of this guard who was a member of Martin's radical black organization whose mission was to undermine the growing white nationalist movement while also working to free imprisoned blacks that Martin and company believed were victims of a grossly unjust legal system. His organization saw the so-called "justice system" as still very much dominated by a white racist ideology—the reason for the disproportionate number of blacks in US prisons. Martin's organization made generous donations to the Innocence Project because 58 percent of those who benefit from it are black. His organization also managed to place guards in different jails and prisons throughout the country to make possible—where there was no legal recourse—the liberation of blacks that his organization judged to be unjustly jailed or imprisoned. It orchestrated some ingenious and bold prison breaks in different states, freeing those it saw as unjustly imprisoned blacks to start a new life with a new identity, sometimes in another country. Or, as in my case, the organization occasionally freed unjustly jailed whites, if Martin thought this would serve his organization's mission. I would be, once freed, invited to join his organization to participate in their—often under the radar—battle against white nationalism and other forms of racism.

Martin's organization would not only be the agent of my liberation but also of my transformation into someone with a different identity. Although I didn't know this at the time Martin was planning my escape, he had elaborate plans for my post-jail life. Thus, as it turned out, I wasn't being freed purely out of the kindness of Martin's heart, although I have no doubt that he has a very kind heart. No, he had big things in mind for me, a role that he must have trusted—but could not know—that I would agree to fill. A *quid pro quo*? Maybe. Clearly, Martin knew what he was doing in more ways than one and how to bring off his various schemes. I was so desperate to be freed and untrackable that Martin's help seemed like a dream come true, even though the surgery was excruciating and bloody. I would soon discover how this operation and my liberation would serve Martin's larger mission—fighting white nationalism.

This part of my story, a tale of amateur surgery performed in jail in the dark of night, along with a later event—the interception of the van carrying me to NISM—may smell like a *deus ex machina*. If this were a novel, that's probably what some readers would call it: a literary move that is the equivalent of divine intervention? Or actual divine intervention? Although, as already indicated, I remained open to the possibility of God's existence, and—for a fleeting moment—thought that Martin was literally a godsend, I could not in all honesty believe that an omnipotent and good God was at work in my life or in the world in any way. There was too much injustice on the planet for that to be the case. And actual divine intervention would be an implausible plot twist in this already implausible story. But *deus ex machina* as a literary device does not really require a God character at all, but only some arbitrary fictional contrivance—for example, the good luck of having Martin as my cellmate—to solve what looks like an unsolvable problem that the writer has written himself into. A lazy solution to a plot dilemma?

Since I was, from time to time, still thinking of myself as *possibly* a character in a work of fiction, I was okay with what looked like an artificial literary solution to my date with death, a way to avoid execution now that my will to live was strong. At least that's what I felt during this time when, above all, I wanted to avoid being turned back into Aaron. I had never completely ruled out, even after I was told I was the subject of a memory experiment, that the narrative of my life, including the experiment, was part of a work of fiction, maybe a novel—perhaps a work of science fiction that included a fictional Elizabeth Cohen's invention of my fictional life. A little convoluted, I grant you.

What might seem like a *deus ex machina* in my case—Martin Jackson—would be par for the course in this story of an unreal life, a life in which I was told that my memories were not real and that the friends I knew so well were actually strangers who didn't have the faintest idea who I was. I seemed to be a character in a story with an implausible plot—perhaps, as already indicated, a work of science fiction about implanted memories. I appeared to be trapped in a narrative where anything was possible, where anything could happen. I remembered that as the theme of Sartre's novel *Nausea*. Suddenly, my luck in this absurd story had turned for the best when Martin entered my cell—just when I needed to get out of a very tight spot. A contrivance of the author writing my story? Maybe.

But sometimes what seems like an artificial plot device used to resolve what appears to be an unsolvable challenge—in this case, saving the jailed and otherwise doomed protagonist through the sudden introduction of a knife, sterilizing chemical, cotton balls, needle and thread, surgical gloves, forceps, flashlight, and a man who just happens to possess basic surgical skills—is a mirror of life itself. Serendipitous events do happen in real life, no matter how absurd and unlikely they may seem. Although rare, a remarkable confluence of favorable circumstances can occur. Or should I say that sometimes one gets very lucky. Most of my luck as Nathan Feldman had been bad. So why not, on rare occasions, the opposite? It should also be noted, however, that a serendipitous convergence of favorable facts can, in real life, often be followed by very bad luck, maybe even a disaster. So, if you are starting to think God or Good Fortune is on your side, just wait a little while and you will quickly be humbled and brought back to the reality of an indifferent, if not malign, universe.

Back to the surgery: I did worry about infection, but I didn't want the authorities to know about the removal of the tracking device. My wound, which had been sutured with black thread, didn't look healthy—in fact, it looked greenish-black. Would my good luck in having an amateur surgeon as a cellmate be undone by fatal gangrene? I had to take that chance. Any request for a nurse to check my wound, or any call for sheriff-assisted visit to the ER, would have brought attention to the suspicious location of my infection and the amateur suture job, revealing that the transmitter had been removed. I'm sure that law enforcement was informed by NISM that I could easily be located because of that device. Now, thanks to Martin's surgical work, his removal of the tracking device, the authorities would no longer be able to easily discover my location. This successful operation was a major achievement, something I wanted to remain my secret. I could only hope infection didn't set in.

15. The Great Escape

I'VE ALREADY REVEALED THAT the second phase of Martin's plan was successful. Have I taken the drama out of this event? Perhaps. Still, how this was accomplished is worth recalling. I was in a jail operated by the Madison County's Sheriff's Department. Madison County included Winterville and a few other smaller Minnesota cities. On that special afternoon when I was in a sheriff's van on the way to the Institute, not very far from the county jail, there wasn't much time to pull off my liberation. An armed guard was in the back of the van with me—and an armed guard was next to an unarmed driver. I was surprised that they had me only in handcuffs, with no leg shackles. Pleasantly surprised because this made me more mobile. With my ankles free, I was ready to run for it. Small-town carelessness? Maybe.

Their assumption that there was a tracking device hidden in my body may have caused the Madison County Sheriff's Department to relax their guard, believing that I could be quickly apprehended if I escaped. I kept the tracking device in my pocket so that the staff at NISM monitoring it would believe that I was on my way. Given that belief and the short distance from the jail to the Institute, I think those in charge felt that two armed guards could keep me secure and that once I reached NISM, I would be secured by medical means. I later learned that those transporting me were told that, as soon as they arrived at the Institute I would receive an injection, a sedative that would cause me to fall asleep. That injection, law-enforcement officials were assured, would keep me incapacitated until the reversal procedure was performed, scheduled for early that evening.

As the van was moving toward the Institute, about halfway there, on a lonely road between thickly wooded areas on both sides, it met what appeared to be a highway department roadblock with what looked like workers in brightly colored vests and hard hats, just ahead. Before the van driver knew it, another roadblock was also put up some distance behind the van so no cars could get through. All of my liberators were black, in sunglasses, and wearing what looked like COVID masks. So, neither their faces nor their heads could be seen. Two "workers" approached the van and stood at each van window. My rescuers immediately drew and pointed their weapons, disarming the front-seat guard and ordering him and the driver out of the van. The back of the van was a closed windowless compartment: those in this compartment could not see anything going on outside the vehicle, and they could not easily hear what was going on in the front. My emancipators ordered the deputy with the keys, the driver, to open the back door of the van and to tell the deputy guarding me that he should put his weapon on the floor. This guard complied, surrendered, and unlocked my handcuffs as ordered. The guns of both armed guards were thrown into the woods. The three men were then zip-tied, gagged, and locked in the back of the van. I threw the tracking device onto the van floor before the door was locked.

I was immediately taken away by my two rescuers; the third who had put up the rear roadblock joined us shortly. The three guided me through a densely wooded area to a highway rest stop where a black SUV with tinted windows was parked. We quickly entered the vehicle. The driver traveled slightly northeast on a long highway trip close to the Boundary Waters Canoe Area Wilderness in Minnesota, and turned off on a county road and drove about twenty miles through a secluded forest, very beautiful. Then he turned off on a dirt road, traveling another five miles. When we arrived at what I discovered was a very nice five-bedroom two-bathroom cabin in this remote area, Martin was already there. Sitting in front of the cabin was his expensive Czinger 21C hybrid sports car—3D printed, with a driver's seat in the central position—that can rocket to sixty miles per hour in 1.9 seconds, with a top speed of, incredibly, 253 miles per hour. At least that's what Martin told me when I inquired about this vehicle that I knew must be his.

Martin had made bail the morning I was being prepped for my afternoon trip to the Institute. He wanted to be able to welcome me to my new life as a free man. When I walked into the cabin, Martin greeted me with a huge smile. When those who rescued me took off their disguises, I noticed that the person who had set up the rear roadblock was a woman. She towered over all of us—basketball player tall and very athletic looking, with tattoos covering both arms: in beautiful cursive red script, the names of innocent unarmed young black individuals killed by the police. The two men looked equally fit. All in their early thirties. Each had the darkest of dark skin—like Martin's. It seemed that one needed to have very dark pigment to be a member of Martin's organization.

Martin looked very different without his orange jail garb. He wore a black three-piece suit. Under his black suit coat was a velvet black vest over a white shirt with a black tie in a half-Windsor knot—an outfit that he said was inspired by the way the radical black professor of philosophy Cornel West always dressed. West, a democratic socialist—whose radical political ideology was grounded in progressive Christianity—wanted to look his best when fighting the good fight; he called this his cemetery attire, a uniform that kept him ready for both battle and burial. Jackson liked this idea—namely to dress ready for both combat and death. Martin's battles, like Cornel's, were usually of the intellectual type, a battle of ideas and arguments. But their ideas and arguments made both of them possible targets of violence. No doubt both of their lives had been threatened more than once by the racists they relentlessly attacked—in speeches and in writings. I should point out that Martin never ruled out physically engaging the enemy, possessing the MMA skills necessary to successfully do so if someone, or even some group of men, physically attacked him. And, if it should appear that he needed more than martial arts skills to defend himself, Martin was armed, in a hidden waistband holster, with a top-of-the-line pocket pistol—a Ruger LCP II 380, a perfect, surprisingly accurate, concealed-carry firearm, very reliable for self-defense.

Martin quickly provided me with civilian clothes. When I removed my jail outfit in a bedroom with just the two of us present, Martin looked carefully at my left groin where he had performed surgery. He said it was looking good. Martin removed the thread—causing me to wince, even though he was trying to be gentle. He then cleaned and put a bandage over the healing wound. Earlier, when I had been worried about infection, my perception may have been distorted by the black thread that gave the sutured area a blackish look. Once the thread was removed, the wound appeared to be healing nicely. So, I no longer had to worry about gangrene. I quickly put on the new clothes that Martin requested I wear: Heritage slim-fit blue jeans, a Van Heusen pale blue long-sleeve shirt, dark blue Ferragamo socks, and Cole Haan gray sneakers. Everything fit perfectly because I had given Martin my precise measurements. He had also purchased other similarly styled shirts, pants, socks, and shoes—so that I would have a completely new wardrobe, clothes that apparently matched the attire worn by a man I would be asked to impersonate.

Those who liberated me were radical opponents of white nationalism—much more militant than people in Black Lives Matter, and, indeed, not opposed to lethal attacks on the enemy. They were targeting a specific white nationalist organization that my persona-to-be had been invited to join. They called themselves the Really Black Panthers. Again: apparently, every member's skin tone was very dark, like Martin's. They were inspired by the first *Black Panther* movie and the fact that many of the black actors in this film, including both male and female lead characters, had very dark skin. Historically and politically, they were also inspired by the Black Panther Party, established in 1966 by Huey Newton and Bobby Seale. But Martin's organization was not merely a resurrection of the old Black Panthers who told the world that "Black is beautiful." His members were the new super-black Black Panthers: ultra-ebony Americans. They went beyond the old Panthers by celebrating not just being black, but the darkest of dark skin. Their motto: "Very dark, very beautiful."

This slogan was designed to communicate the opposite of colorism. It was a way for those who experienced denigration because of their very black pigment to celebrate it—to take pride in a skin color that even some blacks looked down upon. And they very deliberately meant this celebration of super-dark flesh to be a repudiation of the white supremacist standard of beauty that had dominated the world for too long, with women of color in Africa and other parts of the world using dangerous skin bleaching chemicals to try to approximate what they had been brainwashed into thinking was the paradigm of beauty: very white skin, the whitest of white skin.

So, what were these very dark human beings doing liberating a very white guy? I have already suggested the answer. While waiting to be freed, I at first thought that the simple answer was because Martin, in sympathizing with my ordeal, had asked them to do so—and maybe also because Martin paid them handsomely to risk their lives and freedom to save a white man. But their real reason—and Martin's—was, as already indicated, that they had a special job in mind for me once I was located in another state and provided with my new identity. They helped me to radically change my appearance by providing me with an expensive toupee that looked like actual hair, not one of those cheap-looking wigs, and had me shave off my facial hair, except for my mustache. An all-points bulletin warning the public that "Aaron Levitt could be armed and dangerous" contained a photo of someone who was completely bald with a black beard. My top-of-the-line hairpiece was dirty-blond, and I was to have a matching mustache and eyebrows. They provided me with this color of hair dye—for my eyebrows and mustache—and they gave me a driver's license with a photo that looked like the new me. It belonged to Dalton Wells.

Apparently, there was a native Texan by that name, a white nationalist propagandist, a man who had vanished from public view under strange circumstances while working for the white nationalist cause in Portland, Oregon. The speculation among white nationalists was that Wells had gone into hiding because a local Antifa group had been following him, making him feel like his life was under threat. My liberators bluntly told me that members of Martin's organization—the Really Black Panthers in Portland—had executed Wells and that no one would ever discover his corpse because it had been incinerated. His ashes were put in a small biodegradable bag that was thrown into a dumpster in Portland. The RBP had evidently made other leading white nationalists disappear. I, in a Dalton Wells disguise, would be asked to help them in their mission of undermining one arm of the white nationalist movement.

Wearing that Elite Designer toupee that matched Dalton's hair, with my dyed eyebrows and mustache, I would remarkably resemble Wells. We were close to the same age, born just a few years apart. There weren't a lot of photographs of Wells floating around—so it might be difficult for those who had never met him, and had seen only photos, to notice any differences. Even those who had seen him in person might be fooled by my disguise. He had been in Portland to aggressively organize people turned off by progressive culture, working openly for months as a proud white nationalist who saw himself as a vessel of the only correct ideology. His aim was to write and publish books on white nationalism that would be widely distributed. With my new look, Martin was confident that I could now easily pass for him.

So, I would supposedly be Dalton Wells reappearing in order to continue my work in the cause of publicizing *the great replacement theory*: the idea that there was a growing threat to the white race posed by immigrants of color. Their increasing numbers were believed to contribute to white genocide. As I mentioned earlier, the core claim of those who defended this theory was that Jews were orchestrating this—that Jews were the devious agents behind pro-replacement policies and practices. All people of color in the United States, whose numbers were multiplying by the day, were seen as threats to a white future. But an increasing number of "dark aliens" from other countries, especially south of the border, were, according to these white nationalists, deliberately being brought into the country by Jews with the aim of destroying the once-dominant white culture. Dalton Wells viewed himself as a great patriot who was heroically fighting to end this Jewish project of white genocide.

But where was I, a Jew portraying Dalton Wells, supposed to reappear to begin anew my white nationalist work? I discovered that my assigned location would be one that was, fortunately, lodged in my false memory bank: Dallas. I had, in my mind, drawing from implanted memories, visited there many times while growing up in Bryan, Texas. I even remembered that, as a young man, I had relatives living in Dallas: an uncle, aunt, and cousins we frequently visited. Fictional kin—of course. And I had a bit of Texas accent. As I discovered, this was really Aaron's accent because he grew up in Houston. So, I could easily pass as a Texan. And let me repeat this: with my change in appearance, with that hairpiece and matching dyed mustache and eyebrows, I seemed to be the spitting image of Dalton Wells. Thus, I was asked to play the role of a Texas-born white nationalist ideologue who was returning from his patriotic battles in that center of progressive—anti-white—culture: Portland, Oregon.

I was to portray a Wells who had successfully recruited a significant number of bigoted Oregonians to the cause and organized acts of vandalism directed at various multicultural sites, Black Lives Matter headquarters, LGBTQIA2S+ organizations, mosques, and synagogues. That in fact is what the real Wells had effectively done, giving me in my Wells disguise bragging rights in the company of white nationalists. The Portland Really Black Panthers who assassinated Wells found a letter in his apartment that invited him to join the organization I was asked to infiltrate: the Really White Patriots. It was from the president of that organization. The RBP, whose name was created as a way of mocking the name of the RWP, knew what they were doing in exploiting Wells's reputation to achieve their subversive ends. They knew that RWP members would welcome Wells with open arms and trust him to help carry out their mission. I had, however, to do more than simply look like Dalton Wells. I had to convincingly portray him in all his bigoted brilliance. In fear and trembling, I agreed to send a response accepting the invitation to join in the work of the Really White Patriots.

So, the Really Black Panthers wanted me to be an informant in a white nationalist organization that stood for everything I despised. I was to make it my new home and serve as a spy who would communicate all of the Really White Patriots' plans to the RBP. The RWP organization was fast gaining more members and spreading hate across the nation. It was founded by a smart—maybe even brilliant—young man, now only twenty-five, Jefferson Finis Davis, who was from a small town between Dallas and Fort Worth: Granbury. He took pride in being named after the president of the Confederate States of America, a man the young Jefferson saw as a truly great patriot. Jefferson's father, Thomas Jefferson Davis, was a white supremacist who taught his son well. In high school the young Jefferson's right-wing views led him to visit a particular online white nationalist site, one more refined in its language, ideology, and strategy than those sites and groups his father favored. Jefferson would eventually oust the head of this organization that called itself the White Patriots of Texas, change its name, take over the leadership, and turn it into a national operation.

He was a budding young right-wing journalist who loved Trump but ultimately concluded that Trump didn't go far enough and was not a very wise political strategist. Jefferson thought the January 6th violent attack on the US Capitol Building was a stupid, ill-planned, and counterproductive revolt. The organization that Jefferson took over, redesigned, expanded, and developed into a national movement was smart and strategic—a very thoughtful and patient movement whose goals are revolutionary but whose means are provisionally nonviolent and well thought out. Its central head-quarters is located just outside Dallas—in an isolated rural area close to the town where Jefferson grew up. The Really White Patriots keep a low public profile in terms of hateful speech—Jefferson prohibits members from ut-tering racial slurs in public—but in secretly recorded private communica-tions with each other their racist language was very much on display. This is something I came to observe on a regular basis. In their public statements, while never using terms such as "n*****," blacks are, according to the Patri-ots, African people who simply happen to live in the United States: "African American" is for them a misnomer.

Blacks are viewed as resident aliens. People of color—not just blacks, but also people of Latino, Asian, and Middle Eastern heritage in this coun-try—pose a problem because, together, they are beginning to outnumber real Americans: white people of European stock. And Native Americans are not true Americans because they obviously lack a European heritage and are not white. Land was not stolen from them but justly conquered by those who deserved it. They see members of the LGBTQIAS2+ community as diseased human beings whose perverse ways are infecting and ruining straight white culture and corrupting children by tempting them to take up a queer life. The affirmation of queer love and trans persons is seen as part of the massive morally corrupting mission organized by progressive Jews to destroy traditional American values. Or so the literature of the RWP asserts.

White for the RWP is much more than a color. According to the Really White Patriots, even some people who look white are not *really* white: thus, their name. As the Patriots see it, although many Jews may look white, they aren't actually white because they are in fact agents of white genocide. They are a mongrel race. Jewish claims about genocide committed against Jews by the Nazis were lies told by a people who had a history of lying and deception, people who wanted to conceal their own genocidal aims. The Jews' earliest lies were about Jesus. The Patriots see their movement as a form of Christian nationalism. They quote Jesus in the eighth chapter of the Gospel of John when he is addressing "the Jews": "You belong to your father, the devil, and want to carry out your father's desires." This language, according to RWP ideology, shows that Jesus was not Jewish because in this text Jesus calls Jews descendants of Satan. So, appealing to Scripture, Patriots literally demonize Jews.

According to RWP ideology, the claim that Jesus was a Jew is simply another Jewish lie. He was a truly white man, an Aryan according to Patriot historical revisionism. And one can find in their theology a reaffirmation of the ancient charge—grounded in language found in the Gospel of Matthew, that for centuries was official Christian doctrine—that Jews are collectively responsible for the murder of Jesus. In their literature, they quote what turned out to be a very dangerous text. While standing before Pilate, who is described as washing his hands of Jesus's crucifixion, Jews, we are told in Matt 27:25, cry out, after demanding Jesus's execution, a sweeping *mea culpa*: "Let his blood be on us and on our children." This is supposedly the New Testament origin of the charge that Jews collectively, all Jews, are Christ killers, agents of deicide. This text, like the one in John, kept Christian antisemitism alive for centuries. The Patriots want to make this again normative for Christianity.

The Patriots also find in the Bible a justification for their negative view of blacks. RWP literature, appropriating a racist interpretation of Scripture used by Southern slave owners, pushes the idea that the Curse of Ham's descendants in the Bible explains why blacks are black and why they should be viewed as morally tainted. Blacks, on the RWP interpretation of Genesis, chapter 9, inherited the guilt of their ancestor Ham, and their very skin color is evidence of this. The Patriots claim that Ham performed fellatio on his father (Noah)—what Genesis literally says is that Ham uncovered his father's nakedness—thus bringing a curse on all of his descendants, made manifest by their dark pigment. Thus, the Patriots have adopted a toxic interpretation of the Ham story, making it a tale about the moral origin of black skin, a tale that provides a justification for morally denigrating all black human beings.

But the Jews are the main enemy in the eyes of the RWP because Jews are the ultimate traitors to the white race—something, to repeat, that voids the whiteness of any Jew. I, as mentioned earlier, remember myself as being pro-immigrant, a supporter of the Hebrew Immigrant Aid Society, an organization founded in the nineteenth century that not only welcomes Jewish immigrants and refugees but also people from Latin, African, and Muslim countries, people whose lives may have been, because of their political leanings, endangered in their home country. And remembering myself as a Jew who belonged to a progressive queer-welcoming synagogue, I would be viewed by members of the RWP as an agent of white genocide and a proponent of a queer culture. Since my life story was fiction, this really applied to Aaron Levitt. In fairness, I should recognize that Aaron worked for the rights of immigrants, even illegal ones, and had been LGBTQIA2S+ affirming, a strong advocate for queer rights. This was something that Aaron did that I could take pride in. I needed to remember that Aaron was more than a murderer—that he was more than his crime.

Even if I was a fictional person, I was nonetheless someone who believed in everything the RWP members hated. And I would be boldly planting myself in the midst of the RWP community to gather intelligence about their operations, communicating their plans and their targets to the RBP. If caught, my life could be endangered. They might discover who I really was. This organization has chapters in most states. RWP tentacles had even reached to Winterville. Local members of the RWP had defaced art on a wall outside of a local LGBTQIA2S+ welcoming coffee shop, ruining the art with graffiti that included the name of their organization along with white nationalist messages. They did the same to a wall of art outside the Winterville International Market operated by Somali immigrants—Muslims who had made this city their home. And a number of other sites of immigrant or queer-friendly businesses had been vandalized. The Patriots had written antisemitic graffiti and painted crosses on an exterior wall of the Winterville Reform synagogue, the one I thought I belonged to. They had also targeted a local Black Lives Matter office.

The Really White Patriots are of course part of a massive white nationalist movement that is global in reach. They are committed to the idea of "accelerationism": the belief that since Western governments are irreparably corrupt the best thing that white nationalists can do at the present time is to accelerate the demise of these regimes by sowing chaos and creating political tension. In the United States, the Patriots' interim plan is to destabilize what they see as the illegitimate US government in preparation for the long-term goal of overthrowing a multiracial, multicultural, queer-affirming, and Jewish-controlled nation state, especially when Democrats are in power. Although Republicans are preferable, most members of this party are held in disdain because they shy away from affirming white nationalist ideology.

The Patriots maintain that their white ancestors conquered America and bequeathed it to them—and no one else. Their white-centered political ideology is expressed in a manifesto that asserts "membership within the American nation is inherited through blood" (translate as "white blood"). So, "those of foreign birth" are not necessarily Americans, even if they are citizens by law. The RWP preaches that "nationhood cannot be bestowed upon those who are not of the founding European stock of our people." That's why they do not view Blacks, Latinxs, Asians, and Native Americans as "members of the Nation." And, again, those Jews who appear white are white in name only.

Their ultimate goal is to create a new country, one that will recover the vision of the founders of the American nation—men who were obviously white supremacists—and reestablish a truly white nation completely opposed to the rotting and corrupt Jewish-multicultural-multiracial-queer-loving Sodom that, in their eyes, the United States has become. Although they, for strategic reasons, avoid talking about guns or violence publicly, it is not unusual for such organizations to avoid recommending violence while spreading an ideology that may in fact encourage violence. If lone wolves are inspired by RWP ideology to violent acts against woke institutions, so much the better. That is their unpublicized secret in-house view.

Their immediate strategy is to win converts and undermine the enemy through a propaganda campaign. Leafleting cars with their fliers, covering "progressive" places with white nationalist slogans, placing antisemitic and antiqueer banners temporarily above interstate highways, and defacing art on enemy buildings are nonviolent manifestations of their immediate strategy. Members are required to physically post or distribute a certain number of fliers each month and even travel up to one hundred miles from their homes to spread their message of "taking back America." So, their main targets should by now be obvious: Jewish institutions, Muslim places of worship, LGBTQIA2S+ friendly businesses, pro-black groups such as Black Lives Matter, institutions that promote multiculturalism, and pro-immigrant organizations. The Patriots like to organize flash demonstrations across the country, and they especially enjoy targeting and disrupting Pride events.

I, a progressive Jew, was asked to hide my true identity while in the company of super-patriots who despise Jews—maybe, as already stated, Jews above all because they are viewed as the primary enemy of a patriotic white culture. I would have to pass as a racist, antisemite, and a dedicated Christian white nationalist. It helped that I didn't have what Patriots consider a stereotypically Jewish look (think of Woody Allen or Barbara Streisand), a "kike face" as some RWP members privately describe the Jewish profile. And it also helped that with my newly acquired dirty-blond hair, mustache and eyebrows I looked remarkably like a respected white nationalist whose name was familiar to many RWP members, a Texan who had made good. Still, I was feeling very nervous about doing this and wondering whether, even with my best performance, I could pull this off. Many second thoughts.

Did I really have a choice? A choice of whether or not to become a spy and spoiler? Did I feel compelled to accept the job the Really Black Panthers had assigned me? My answer is yes, but not because of coercion. Rather I felt so indebted to them that I did not hesitate to say yes—which does not mean I was unafraid of what would happen to me if the RWP discovered who I was. The truth is that I felt morally compelled to say yes. I owed RBP a lot: my life and my liberty, which I think included the freedom to turn them down. I firmly believed in their cause and felt honored that they had the confidence that I could bring off this act of deception. Of course, in short order, I would have to educate myself about the ideology of the Patriots and learn how to credibly speak their language.

My assignment reminded me of *The BlacKkKlansman,* a 2018 Spike Lee film based loosely on historical fact. I seem to have a habit of seeing my life in terms of this or that movie. (I find it surprising that NISM was able to implant so many cinematic memories: maybe these were, again, simply

Aaron's memories imported into my memory stream.) In *The BlacKkKlans-man*, an African American Colorado Springs police officer poses as a racist, as a "really white" man, in phone conversations with David Duke, the Grand Dragon of the KKK at the time (1972). He persuades Duke that he is a white supremacist who wants to join the organization. The black police officer's aim is to infiltrate the Klan to gain intelligence about their operations. Since this black policeman obviously cannot appear as himself, he recruits a white colleague in the department whose voice is similar to his to impersonate him and meet with David Duke and other Klan members, indeed to become a Klansman. The white policeman who the black officer asks to pretend to be him and infiltrate the Klan happens to be Jewish! My life was once again imitating cinematic art.

16. The Strange Case of Dr. Jekyll and Mr. Hyde

TIME PASSED AND I was beginning to adjust to my second fictional identity, Dalton Wells, to my life as an infiltrator and disruptor. Having immersed myself in this racist-antiqueer-antisemitic-islamophobic organization, I was nervously trying to play along with their bigotry, with their need to undermine all threats to what they called "a truly straight really white Christian culture." While I was facing this challenge and collecting intelligence that was used to interrupt or even prevent the Patriots' propagandistic attacks on what they considered perverse institutions, businesses, and places of worship—I began to experience deeply disturbing mental changes.

I started to have strange memories and alien emotions: subjective states I didn't recognize as my own. At first, just flashes. And then more than flashes—even if just for a minute and then they would disappear—only to reappear with a bit more force and last longer. I was having recollections that I didn't recognize as belonging to me. Scenes in Duluth. Visions of teaching in a classroom at a college there. Memories of intimate relations with a woman I didn't know. Partial memories of a different childhood. The new remembrances were not only staying longer: they were beginning to crowd out my familiar recollections, the ones I perceived as truly mine.

It became clear what was happening, and this was very scary. These metastasizing alien memories were deeply disturbing because they seemed to foreshadow my end. It was as if I had suddenly received a terminal diagnosis, with a prognosis of only a very short time to live. Yes, little by little, I was turning back into Aaron Levitt, and I wasn't able to stop this. Obviously, I couldn't go to Elizabeth Cohen and ask her to redo the procedure, to stop the reversal.

Suddenly I remembered something Elizabeth said as I walking out on her, as I was telling her I was done, refusing to undergo the reversal procedure. It was a warning that I didn't pay careful attention to at the time, something to the effect: *You will revert to Aaron Levitt, one way or the other. You don't really have a choice.* I had dismissed that as the threat she would eventually find way to require me to undergo the reversal procedure, that I would one day be legally forced, coerced, into doing this. But perhaps she was trying to tell me something else, without saying it explicitly—namely, that there was a fail-safe mechanism built into their experiment.

Maybe she was attempting to tell me that, after a certain period of time, I would automatically revert to Aaron. I had smugly condemned the stupidity of NISM researchers in assuming that their new creation would happily accommodate their request that he submit to being erased. I had not given the experimenters credit for having the foresight to anticipate my rebellion. They had, as it turns out, wisely foreseen that the subject of their experiment might refuse to undergo the reversal procedure—and they had wisely planned for this contingency. For all I knew, there was another device hidden somewhere in my body, one I was not informed about, a device that was now triggering this metamorphosis. Perhaps this device would achieve its end more slowly than a medical procedure but it would eventually achieve the same result.

Whatever the explanation, there seemed to be no way to stop this transformation back to Aaron. My heart sank and I felt sick. I had a difficult time accepting the fact that this accelerating change was happening—that I, Nathan Feldman, was daily vanishing and that my memories were increasingly being replaced by Aaron Levitt's. Evidently, his memories and personality had been lying dormant, waiting to reemerge when the time was right. I perceived Aaron Levitt as a devilish snake now shedding his temporary skin that was Nathan Feldman. Aaron Levitt was returning to life with a vengeance. What should I do? What could I do? I felt the need to take some kind of action—but, again, there seemed to be no way to stop this reversal. However, while I was still, for the most part, Nathan Feldman, I needed to act. And while I still had agency, I wanted to use it wisely.

I had dismissed Aaron as unworthy of resurrection. I had defined him in my own mind as irredeemably evil: as a very dark figure, the vicious Mr. Edward Hyde, a cruel murderer, compared to my virtuous Dr. Henry Jekyll. I had convinced myself that Aaron was a person who should never be allowed to live again. As I was feeling Aaron's growing presence—his desires, thoughts, and memories—replace mine, I was reminded of Robert Louis Stevenson's description of Jekyll's experience of involuntarily changing into Hyde—and how disturbing that was to the good doctor. How shocking to discover that what you perceived to be your dark side can reappear against your will and reassert itself permanently.

Yes, I had assumed that Aaron would remain dead and that was good riddance. I thought I had decisively prevented his resurrection and felt that was the right thing to do. After all, I, by refusing to undergo the reversal procedure, had made a choice that I believed would be equivalent to the execution of a very guilty man. I justified this by telling myself that it was an act of self-defense, and that it was also an act of justice because Aaron was a murderer the world would be better off without. Now this demonic phoenix was rising from his ashes—reappearing in opposition to what I had decided was best for everyone, namely Aaron's permanent deletion from the cosmos. I, however, still had the power to act. I could in fact once again kill this man, eliminate Aaron a second time, this time forever. Although incapable of saving myself, I possessed the power to prevent Aaron's return to life. I could do so by killing myself. An act of suicide would absolutely destroy this once-submerged evil side of me that was threatening to rise from the dead to take my place. Only my act of self-destruction could prevent the resuscitation of Aaron. That was Jekyll's solution, and I was free to do the same. Should I make my life again imitate art, imitate another fictional tale?

Surprisingly, my anger toward Aaron began to cool, and I started to think in a more balanced and less judgmental way. It occurred to me that I could practice grace, something usually attributed to Christianity but is also part of a Jewish moral worldview. Judaism emphasizes the importance of what is called in Hebrew *teshuvah*: a kind of moral rebirth that some Jewish commentators such as Maimonides describe as the process of becoming a morally different human being, a new and redeemed person. I noticed on my calendar that *Yom Kippur* was approaching: the Jewish Day of Atonement, the time when Jews try to practice *teshuvah*. *Teshuvah* literally means "return." Jews need to return to who they should be, morally speaking. Aaron could return to life if I allowed him to—and it was possible that, if I permitted him to reemerge, he might become the person he was before he committed murder, return to the kind of person he could and should be. But did Aaron really deserve to live? The Jewish view is that God graciously gifted humans with life, which none of us deserved or earned. I now had this godlike power over Aaron, the power to give him life, a life that, from the point of view of strict justice, he didn't deserve.

I was free to practice grace by providing Aaron the opportunity to live again and to atone for his grave sin: the taking of an innocent human life. I could generously give him an opportunity for redemption. Earlier I had convinced myself that justice demanded that I not restore his life, self-righteously seeing this as a way to make him pay the ultimate price for his crime. But now a more sympathetic voice within was telling me that I should pray what the Talmud tells us that God prays, something like this: *May My mercy overpower My anger, My compassion prevail over My demand for justice.* As I moved toward extinction, shouldn't I practice *imitatio dei* and be gracious rather than vindictive?

I started to ask myself who I was, as a human being who had existed for such a short time in the world, compared to Aaron, to judge Aaron: to consider myself morally superior to him, to become his judge and executioner? Perhaps I should attempt to be more charitable and let Aaron live. I found myself, while profoundly sad at my approaching end, wanting to provide Aaron with another shot at life, a new beginning, a chance to start over. Of course, without knowing it at the time, I was the one who made it possible for Aaron to now begin anew because I had fled those who wanted to revive Aaron in order to try him for murder. If I had not escaped my captors—both my captors at the jail and my captors at NISM—Aaron would be sitting in prison, probably for life. Now Aaron could have a new life where no one knew his past.

Thus, in this spirit of gracious generosity, I decided to grant Aaron life. To fully inform him about the world he would awaken to, I needed to write Aaron a letter. I didn't tell him in this letter that I had considered destroying him by killing myself. No need to share that. I found myself wanting to help him in any way I could:

Dear Aaron,

By the time you read this letter—a kind of last will and testament—I will have disappeared, as if I had never existed. I knew nothing about you when I was born on a beautiful summer morning. But you knew about me before I was created. Indeed, working with Cohen, you helped to invent me. You were coauthor with her of a fictional narrative, what I had mistakenly thought was my actual life, my actual memories. The experiment clearly gifted me with a life I would not otherwise have had. If the idea was to implant temporary false memories that felt real, then, I have to say, NISM obviously succeeded.

I wonder: Did the experimenters also build in an automatic reversal? If so, this was life-saving for you. I am writing to tell you that you now have an opportunity that was made possible by my escape. If I had not avoided undergoing the reversal procedure, you would have been restored to your true self, put on trial for murder, and now be in prison, probably serving a life-term. It was a horrible crime, but it need not define you. My hope is that you will do something truly good with your freedom. You could of course return to Winterville, courageously turn yourself in, and face the consequences of your troubling decision to take a human life. But I don't recommend that precisely because I don't think you are inherently a criminal. If I had lived long enough, I too might have, for all I know, also done something as terrible. Too many people mistakenly believe they are different, beyond this, incapable of murder. I recommend that you take advantage of this second chance and try to make a difference in this God-forsaken world. Please go out and lead a good life, a morally good life. Don't look back, look forward. I do have a challenge for you, if you are up for it, a risky one. It's a cause I've taken up. I can understand why you might not want to step in, to take my place, but I am asking you to give it serious thought, to reflect on this invitation. Some might see this as a way for you to redeem yourself. It will not be pleasant work. You have by now discovered, if you've glanced in the mirror, that you have a different look. Namely a dyed mustache and eyebrows. And, if you choose to wear it, a very authentic-looking hairpiece on the chest of drawers. You will also find a billfold on the chest containing "your" driver's license, providing you with a photo ID. Unfortunately, you have the ID of a racist who met an untimely death and whose body was made to disappear by the very radical black organization that freed me and invited me, pretending to be Dalton Wells, to spy on the white power organization that I am now asking you to consider infiltrating and disrupting . . .

In what turned out to be a very long letter, I continued to tell Aaron about my work in the Really White Patriots, providing him all the information he needed to step into the role I created. I gave him a verbal sketch of each member of this local Texas chapter of the Patriots, their backgrounds and their personality types. Who to worry about in terms of their suspicions about the man who called himself Dalton Wells. I told Aaron that, if he so chose, the Patriots' leadership would probably approve of his/Dalton's departure from the organization. But I could not rule out that this might also endanger him.

So, if he decided not to pick up where I left off, it might be prudent for him to find a way to leave town in the dark of night and carefully cover his tracks. He would need to inform the Really Black Panthers about this, so they would be aware that they have lost a key insider at the headquarters of the RWP, someone they will want to replace, if possible. I could not rule out that the RBP might also consider taking action against him. Thus, if he chose the exit option, he should try to create a new identity and leave the country, maybe move to Canada or Mexico. More than a few people might be looking for him, including Winterville detectives. After all, he had been charged with murder, and the Winterville Police Department's search for Aaron Levitt would probably go on for a long time. If he decided to stay in Dallas to take my place, I recommended that he connect with Martin Jackson and even inform him that Nathan Feldman had suddenly transitioned back to him. He need not do that but, to keep things honest, I told him that I thought he should.

A few days after I finished this letter, I started feeling increasingly confused. I was experiencing, as Nathan Feldman, profound memory loss—with a significant increase in replacement memories. This change was now accelerating. Sadly, my identity as Nathan Feldman was fading away fast. When I began telling Nathan Feldman's strange story that started on a beautiful summer morning, I observed that one's life can change in the blink of an eye. Now my eyes were blinking shut, apparently for good. I needed to lie down, to sleep . . .

17. The Spy Who Came in from the Cold

IT WAS AS IF I were waking up from a very long sleep. Or as if I had been dead and buried for a long time and was being resurrected to life from a very cold grave. What a shock to suddenly regain consciousness and find myself in a strange place, wondering how I got here. And my greatest surprise: I was not waking up in a NISM medical bed. Instead, I soon discovered that I was in a small but nice one-bedroom apartment in Dallas—in the Highland Park suburb to be exact, named for its prime perch overlooking downtown, with its hedge-lined streets and many glamorous shops. In looking around the bedroom, I found an envelope with my name on it, a very long letter inside. I carefully read the missive from my invented twin brother. After reading it, I wasn't sure what to do? He informed me that I was wanted for murder. No surprise. I felt profoundly disoriented, but also grateful that I was alive and free. The implantation experiment had worked, and so had the reversal! Nathan had refused to undergo the reversal procedure. No surprise. It was my good fortune and Nathan's bad luck that NISM's backup plan worked. The reversal had occurred without any medical intervention. But this automatic reversal had apparently taken a long time to kick in, longer than planned.

In his letter, Nathan suggested that I begin again. A new life was now possible for me. But what was I to do about the predicament Nathan left me in? It was not prison, but it was still a very unpleasant situation. Did I really want to accept Nathan's invitation to become a spy in an organization whose members hate everything I believe and value? If they discovered that I was not only a spy, but, horror of horrors, also a Jew—an angry member of the Really White Patriots might, despite the organization's provisional commitment to nonviolence, take it on himself to make me wish I'd never been born. Nathan warned me in his letter that members are vigilant in trying to catch infiltrators and that being discovered could put my life at risk. I imagined there were some Patriots who, if they discovered who I was, would want to kill me—and might very well do so.

So, given the risks, I had to ask myself: Should I continue Nathan's work? In his letter Nathan told me to whom to report: the leader I should contact in the Really White Patriots and the leader I should contact in another organization, the one I would be spying for: the Really Black Panthers. At least that organization, in naming itself, showed a sense of humor, mocking the name of the organization I would reconnoiter—assuming I accepted Nathan's invitation to continue his work. Nathan had felt a debt to the RBP because members of that organization freed him in a bold move, risking their own freedom, and maybe their lives, if there had been a shootout. Nathan felt a moral obligation to do this risky work: gathering intelligence and trying to spot any weaknesses in the RWP organization that could be exploited. Obviously, none of the members of the Really Black Panthers could pretend to be Dalton Wells. That's why they needed white allies, why they needed to recruit people like Nathan.

The aim of the RBP was, on my understanding, to disrupt the plans of the Patriots, to interfere with their sundry white nationalist projects, to make it possible for the police to catch them in the act of defacing what they considered "enemy" murals, the walls of any institution welcoming immigrants of color or affirming LGBTQIA2S+ rights, and really any place they considered alien to a genuinely America way of life. Evidently, the Patriots often do their work in the middle of the night or at times when it is unlikely anyone will catch them. Intelligence gathering would involve discovering and communicating to the RBP the Patriots' targets, with the dates and times of their planned attacks. It would involve communicating this information to branches of the RBP or their supporters in the targeted locations. I would be tasked with doing this while making sure that the Patriots could not discover the source of these leaks.

Although not a fan of the police or the FBI, the RBP often share their intelligence with both, but not necessarily. The head of the RBP wanted Nathan to know that members of his organization might, from time to time, step outside the law. They might, instead of notifying the police and FBI, take matters in their own hands and beat the hell out of Patriots they caught in the act of spreading hate. Also, they did not rule out the need to do hits on certain members of the RWP leadership and leading figures in other white nationalist or Neo-Nazi organizations. They were even thinking about taking out Jefferson Finis Davis. If I decided to take over Nathan's role, and revealed to the RBP that I was really Aaron Levitt, the RBP leadership might assume that, since I was an escaped killer, I could serve, from time to time, as one of their hitmen.

Did I really want to enter this world of risky espionage and planned assassinations? Did I actually owe Nathan this: a commitment to take up this cause, to continue his undercover work? I had given Nathan a Jewish conscience, and he evidently did not hesitate to answer the call of the Really Black Panthers. I had helped to create his value system. He was simply living out these values in a bold and courageous way. Nathan had made something of himself in his very short life. The brevity of Nathan's life reminded me of a biblical character—Abel, whose name in Hebrew is revealing: *hevel*, which means vapor. Abel disappears almost as soon as he appears in this mythical biblical story about the first murder. He has an unjustly short life, one terminated by his brother. Such was the story of Nathan's life, also cut short by his brother. Some biblical commentators believe Cain and Abel were identical twins. Nathan and I were very much like identical twins, the difference being that we occupied the same body and brain at different times. Nathan had even said this in his letter to me: that we were twin brothers.

What's the worst that could happen to me if I was caught, outed as a spy? To be honest, I doubted that someone in the RWP would actually kill me or even physically attack me. That could draw the kind of attention from the police and the FBI that would damage their long-term goals and maybe even unravel the organization. For all they knew, I could be an FBI informant. The RWP would probably simply expel me and redouble its efforts to find other infiltrators. Of course, once they outed me online as a spy and a Jew, more violent white nationalists—such as members of the virulently antisemitic American Justice Party, a friend of the Patriots—who got word about this might want to physically attack and even kill me. But who was I to condemn anyone who engaged in violence, or even committed murder? I was, after all, an escaped murderer. I had viciously taken an innocent human life. I had killed a man simply because I was a jealous lover.

A philosopher by training who taught ethics and the importance of rationality, I had committed a grossly immoral act in a fit of irrational, jealous rage. That might seem to contradict the idea that it was a calculated act, making the homicide seem more like a mindless crime of passion. In fact, I had carefully planned the killing, and my planning was fueled by anger—anger that exploded once I saw Margaret's rich, handsome lover. I had committed premeditated murder. So, I worried that if the RBP discovered this they might see me as someone capable of following orders to kill leaders in the enemy camp.

Nathan had suggested that working for the RBP could be a way to redeem my life. I had never paid for my crime—and would never have to if I remained incognito and careful. What would my life have been if a jury had convicted me of murder and sentenced me to prison? I would probably be spending the rest of my days behind bars, no good to anyone or myself. Of course, I would then be, as they say, paying my debt to society, giving justice to the victim of my crime. I could still make that choice, as Nathan also pointed out. But he had advised against it. Nathan should have been furious with me for creating his life with a plan to eventually destroy it—for joining with Elizabeth Cohen to engage in what to Nathan must have seemed like a cruel experiment, one indifferent to the feelings and fate of the creature we brought into existence. Nathan proved to be extraordinarily generous in wanting me to have a new life and a chance for redemption. I could do that if I chose to continue his work, the job of undercutting the schemes and dreams of organized bigots.

If I stepped into Nathan's shoes, would members of the Really White Patriots notice any differences in Dalton Wells's behavior and speech? Nathan had my Texas accent—which was of course supposed to be the accent of Wells. It is a very slight Southern accent, but those who know regional dialects can detect it—recognize that its origin is Texas rather than, say, Georgia. I would be impersonating a native Texan who saw himself as a truly white Patriot. I didn't really want to wear that toupee, even though it looked like real hair. I preferred having no hair. After Nathan escaped, my photo had been, from what I could discover, circulating through various media. Had I become one of America's Most Wanted? I didn't think so, but I wasn't sure.

When I left my Dallas apartment the first time, with the hairpiece in place, to explore on foot the Highland Park neighborhood where I now resided, at least temporarily, I again felt fortunate to be alive and free. Probably no one in this Dallas suburb would have recognized me even if I weren't disguised, but I couldn't take that chance. Most post offices no longer have photos of the FBI's Most Wanted. I checked the post office in my new neighborhood, and I didn't see an FBI poster. When I turned on the TV in my apartment, I didn't see my picture on the news. A Google search did not reveal any recent national or local publicity about my case. Why should people in Dallas care about a murder in a small town in Minnesota? Indeed, I wondered whether the authorities in Winterville were making much of an effort to find me. Maybe I was already a cold case.

In his letter Nathan said that if I decided not to continue his work and traveled elsewhere, I should probably stay disguised because my photo had made a *Dateline* episode a few months ago, and people were encouraged to call the police if they saw anyone who looked like the man in the photo that filled the television screen. So, it seemed that, to be safe, I would need to stay in disguise. When I googled Aaron Moshe Levitt, I did see a lot of old articles with my photo and bio—one titled "Professor of Ethics Charged with Premeditated Murder Is on the Lam."

The picture of me that was publicized nationwide—and on *Dateline*—was of someone completely bald and black-bearded. However, information about me included other identifying marks: for example, that I had scars on my left wrist, upper left arm, and my upper left thigh. The latter is hidden, but what about the long wrist scar? Was this like the mark of Cain? The *Dateline* episode had made a point of this, informing viewers that it would be another way to identify the accused who had probably changed his facial appearance. So, I needed to hide that revealing scar just as Nathan said he did by wearing an elongated red, white, and blue wristband when he wasn't wearing a long-sleeve shirt. I saw the wristband on the chest of drawers, with the initials DW + RWP. I tried it on: it completely covered the scar. I would, when wearing short-sleeve shirts, need to wear this band. And to stay in disguise, I would always need to put on the toupee. Supposedly, it was specially crafted to look like Wells's hair.

In fact, there were a number of these high-end, high-quality hairpieces in a lower chest drawer, with information about how to order others. The RBP had purchased them for Nathan. It was almost impossible to tell this was not my actual hair. And wearing a piece of such high quality was not uncomfortable. I really did look very different with dirty-blond hair and a matching mustache and eyebrows. I found the dye for my mustache and eyebrows in the second drawer of the chest, just as Nathan had stated in his letter. And, if a member of the Patriots were to discover that I wore a toupee, that would not be a reason to suspect me of being unPatriotic—only of being vain. For all they knew, Wells wore one.

What would my source of income be if I continued Nathan's work? The same as Nathan's: selling Wells's book on white nationalism. There was a 2022 work—*Taking Back America*—by Wells about the "actual" founding of the United States and how this got subverted by enemies of the white race. And he had a contract and an advance—from the same white nationalist publishing house that had issued his first book—to write a new book about the good work of the Really White Patriots. This would be another book that Wells could sell to actual and potential RWP members and of course to other white nationalists everywhere. Was I supposed to actually write a draft of this book? I didn't plan to.

Nathan was told by the RWP that one of his jobs would be to make sure copies of his 2022 book were placed on various college and high school campuses throughout the United States—by sending them to recruits at various high schools and colleges nationwide. The RWP had a long list of these recruits, with addresses. There was also an e-book that could easily be distributed. Although Nathan told me in his letter that distributing this book sickened and disturbed him, he said that he needed to do this to show that he was spreading RWP propaganda. There were many boxes of *Taking Back America* in what was now my apartment. Nathan informed me in his letter that he was trying to send out as few of these books as possible. RWP paid for the purchase of these books from Wells's publisher, with a plan to aggressively distribute many of them far and wide. RWP members nationwide were urged to buy this book for themselves and as gifts for friends—as way of financially supporting the cause, spreading the word. Nathan received a high percentage of the proceeds from the sale of *Taking Back America* and a modest salary from the RWP, more than enough to live on because the organization also paid his rent and utilities.

"Dalton Wells" was also asked to offer this book for a discount to actual and potential allies in the extreme right wing of the Republican Party, with a long list of names and addresses. Since RWP promised people on this list they would receive the book on discount, Nathan did have to send these books to alt-right Republicans once he received an order. A secretary at RWP, the only woman working for the organization, handled these orders. A large number of these books were kept in the local RWP warehouse. People who ordered *Taking Back America* were considered potential RWP members and put on a mailing list for its newsletter. There were, as it turned out, all-too-many people eager to purchase *Taking Back America*—people not only in the United States, but Canada, and actually worldwide. Nathan received significant royalties from these purchases.

The publisher had orders from all over the planet. Dalton Wells's book apparently inspired publication of *Taking Back Hungary* by Viktor Varga, a member of Fidesz, a Hungarian right-wing anti-immigrant party committed to what it calls "Christian democracy," an ideology opposed to the "unpatriotic and too tolerant" ideology of liberal democracy. The preface to that book encouraged readers to purchase a translation into Hungarian of Wells's book. Did I really want to make a living by selling books that furthered the cause of white nationalism, not only nationally but globally? Would I really have a choice about this if I decided to portray Dalton Wells? I would be engaged in the paradoxical task of spreading white nationalist ideology while also seeking to undercut the tactics and thwart the plans of the RWP.

Stepping into Nathan's place, I would, by selling a book I detested, be able to make enough to pay for necessities and even have money left over for some luxuries. Nathan, in the guise of Wells, had informed the white nationalist publisher that he had moved to Dallas and provided his new address. An advance—a check for $20,000—for a book on the RWP had been sent from the publisher to Nathan. It was now in my possession. That would be a problem because I had no plan to write the projected book. I would have to stall, or send the check back. The wealthy ultra-right-wing publisher of *Taking Back America*—who was urging "Dalton Wells" to complete the second book—was more interested in spreading the word than making a profit for his publishing house. In a generous arrangement, Dalton/Nathan was getting 60 percent of the profits from his first book. The RWP were getting 30 percent. Again: that would of course be Dalton Wells's only book since I had no intention of ghost writing the second.

Taking Back America explained the "true" story of the founding of the country—how it was not stolen from Indigenous people but belonged by right to white conquerors from Europe. So, it mirrored the RWP's ideology. Again, although Nathan found pushing this book nauseating, this was part of the act that made him credible to the group. He was, after all, making a living by promoting Christian white nationalism. Although I did not need to indiscriminately send out these books as suggested by the RWP, I would need to make sure white nationalists or their sympathizers who ordered these books got their copies. Most were ordered from the publisher, not from me or RWP. This white nationalist propaganda work was a necessary evil, a skillful way for Nathan to convince those around him that he was one of them. So, I would have to continue this as my way of making a living and making myself credible. But not only would I have to do this filthy work for the RWP with a smile, I might also have to, in fulfilling obligations to the

RBP, suspend my view that all human life should be respected by taking the life of this or that white nationalist.

Of course, I had already, in murdering Samuel Shaw, contradicted my ethical view about the value of the life of every person. At least the Patriots did not have a policy of promoting violence, and would probably never ask me to commit murder. Indeed, members were not even allowed to own guns. And no one could become a member of the RWP who had a criminal record. I did not yet have such a record because I was never convicted of murder. I would now be Dalton Wells, not Aaron Levitt. And as long as I could successfully play the role of Dalton Wells, I would not run the risk of ever being caught and convicted of murder. I did not, however, want to play the role of Dalton Wells indefinitely.

Despite its official avoidance of anything suggesting violence, the fact is that the RWP organization has a military aura about it. When in public for a protest or a flash demonstration, members wear a uniform: a tan hat, a white face covering—and a red, white, and blue jacket with RWP patches over a white shirt. Also, khakis and military-style boots. Nathan had one of these uniforms hanging in his closet. I also saw a pair of RWP boots, with the initials of the organization on them. The military theme was obvious when they secretly conducted simulated hand-to-hand combat training, performed on gated private property at their rural training facilities throughout the country. They also practice battle formation drills, wielding shields adorned with their logo: a Christian cross with an R on its left arm, a W on the right arm, and a P at the foot of the cross—with this logo superimposed on the red stripes of an image of the American flag of first thirteen colonies. As one of their few full-time propagandists and ideologues, Dalton Wells was exempt from having to participate in this military training. But they wanted Dalton to have a uniform just in case revolution came in his lifetime. Maybe they thought he didn't require military training. The real Dalton Wells was known to be a crack sharpshooter, having received military training in the Army.

RWP would-be combatants constantly train secretly so they will be ready when the revolution comes. Members of RWP who train at different concealed private places throughout the country are given instructions in the use of a variety of weapons, weapons that they are not allowed to take with them, to own. When the revolution comes, the organization has a supplier who will provide them with rapid-fire weapons, grenade launchers, and armed drones. One of my duties as a spy would be to secretly video these military-style practices and send the videos to the RBP. The Patriots' ultimate aim is, when the time is right, to achieve victory by revolutionary violence—to eventually overthrown what they perceive to be an illegitimate government and replace it with a new order that will "reclaim America": reestablish American society as it was originally intended to be. The Patriots are very smart in their patience and call for a multigenerational process. This is Jefferson Finis Davis's wise strategy. The RWP is prepared to wait for the right time to light the torch of revolution. The failure of the Trump-sanctioned January 6th insurrection showed Davis the danger and idiocy of premature action. RWP's interim task is to recruit true patriots, to significantly increase RWP membership, and to aggressively distribute propaganda describing their values and their vision for the restoration of America.

My RBP task was, working with other infiltrators, to subvert the long-term strategy of the RWP by undercutting and disrupting their day-to-day tactics. I would apparently be only one of number of underminers in their ranks spying on different chapters throughout the country. After thinking about it carefully, I, because of my strong opposition to the mission of RWP, became fully committed to the mission of the Really Black Panthers. I of course remained very anxious about what I was doing and wondering if I could really pull this off. My training, after all, was as an academic, a teacher of philosophy and a scholar, with no preparation to be an agent of espionage. I was used to living in safety and not taking risks. If I was found out, I could be a target of RWP's wrath. Even if they did not kill me, they could make my life miserable. In truth, I found this a frightening mission. I wasn't sure I possessed Nathan's courage.

If the RWP discovered my true identity and did a quick google search, they would discover that I was charged with murder. They would also find out that I was a member of the enemy camp—and, worst of all, a Jew. But they would not discover, unless I revealed it, that I worked for RBP. Most important for them, they would have in their possession a man with a price on his head. They could then simply hold me and report to the Winterville Police Department that they had apprehended Aaron Levitt, the accused murderer of Samuel Shaw. And identifying me as a member of a white nationalist organization would not help my reputation or my legal case. And, to protect the RBP, I could not tell anyone I was a spy. Some might suspect that I was not only a murderer but also a self-hating Jew who worked for an antisemitic cause, a supreme form of betrayal of the Jewish people. People might speculate that I had disowned my Jewishness—and what could be a better way to do that than becoming a Christian white nationalist. The RWP would then, after shaming me, receive the $30,000 reward the Shaw family had promised anyone with information that led to my arrest. The Patriots would then enrich themselves at my expense. And I would have to go through a murder trial with my conviction almost a certainty. My shame would be increased if people believed that I was not only a murderer but a Jew who denied his heritage, who had in fact promoted antisemitism.

18. Dirty Hands

I DECIDED TO INFORM Martin Jackson about my reemergence—which would be for him the surprising and disturbing announcement of Nathan's death. I communicated with him on the same secure RBP email account and laptop that Nathan used. Messages sent or received disappear within minutes after they are sent or received: they cannot ever be retrieved. I could have called him on a special RBP cell phone on which unretrievable texts also disappear shortly after they are sent or received. I chose emailing Martin instead of calling him because I wanted to give Martin time to adjust to this shocking information—time to absorb and process what would be for Martin very bad, very sad news. This would give him breathing space to think about how he should respond to me. I imagined Martin feeling not only great sadness, but also great anger: anger that I was alive and Nathan was not. This automatic reversion was not something he could have anticipated.

I had of course known from the beginning that if everything went according to plan the reversion was inevitable—that in the event that Nathan refused to undergo the reversal procedure, the transformation back to me would, after a certain period of time, automatically occur. I told Martin in my email that this had been built into what NISM secretly called "the Nathan Feldman Project." Otherwise, I informed Martin, I would never have consented to be an experimental subject. Nathan, in his long letter, had told me about Martin's role in preventing the reversal procedure, in saving his life by liberating him from his captors—how the van taking him to NISM was intercepted by Martin's comrades.

Martin of course had believed that by freeing Nathan and helping him create a new identity he would be preventing a reversal from ever occurring. I'm sure he assumed, as did Nathan, that a reversal would require a medical procedure. I also knew that Martin would, in my case, understand the term *reversal* the way that word is sometimes defined: a change for the worst. From Nathan's letter, it was clear that he and Martin had become good friends—indeed very close, caring deeply about each other. I was acutely aware that telling Martin about the reversal would be equivalent to informing him about the death of someone he came to love.

After I informed him of Nathan's passing, Martin, in his email response, demanded that we meet. I suspected that Martin would not only be mourning the death of Nathan but also wondering if I was up to the task of continuing Nathan's work. Or, given the risks, whether I was willing to do so—although I told him in the email that I planned to carry on with Nathan's espionage activity. Thus, I needed to reassure him in person that I was not only truly on board but that I was up to the challenge. I knew that if I refused to step into Nathan's place Martin could try to coerce me, indeed blackmail me, into doing so. He could threaten to out me to the Winterville Police Department. I could then of course out Martin as the man behind Aaron's/Nathan's escape. But we didn't need to enter this tit-for-tat war because I was more than willing, in the role of spy, to join in the fight against the Really White Patriots. Indeed, I informed Martin that, in my Dalton Wells disguise, I had already attended a number of RWP meetings.

Still Martin wanted to meet me. He emailed the date he was to arrive in Dallas. The two of us would have to be extraordinarily careful. We agreed to meet at the Carlyle Hotel in downtown Dallas, a five-star establishment a few blocks from the Arts District. He had reserved a suite for three nights because he knew that we would probably need to continue our discussion over several days. There was a lot we had to cover, including plans for the future, but I felt one reason he wanted to spend time with me in face-to-face conversations was to take my full measure, discern my level of commitment, and see if I was as savvy as Nathan.

I did not say this to Martin, but the truth was that I had the same skills and abilities as Nathan because we possessed the same brain—even if our memories and personalities were different. We had the same level of intelligence. I created Nathan in my image, but with different memories and different character traits. So, yes there were differences: Nathan was his own person, a distinctive individual. But, in terms of my capacity to take over for Nathan, there should be no problem. In fact, as already indicated, I might have, in my darkest hour, demonstrated a capacity that Nathan probably lacked: the willingness to take a human life. I had, before I ever committed murder, actually seen this potential in me at an early age, although, until that tragic night, had never acted on it. I had recognized in myself a Cain dimension—a tendency to feel flashes of rage that inclined me to want to destroy those who angered me, a recurrent murderous disposition that I had kept in check until that night.

This part of me that had, over the years, wanted to assert itself when certain people did or said things that I thought were outrageous, terribly wrong, or simply disrespectful of me. Seething on the inside—wanting to destroy those who triggered my rage—I had been able to put a lid on it and, unlike the mythical Cain character, not even show this on my face. Most important, I had somehow been able to keep what was going on inside of me from manifesting itself in the form of a deed. But my potential for violent behavior finally became actualized when I discovered that the woman who I thought loved only me really favored another man. I suddenly became Cain. In that famous mythical biblical story, Cain was furious because God had favored his brother Abel's offering over his own. In an act of jealous rage, Cain murdered his brother whom he thought had been unfairly favored. The Hebrew literally says that, before the murder, Cain became "very hot and his face fell," language that refers to a feeling of hostility within him that was boiling over, something that was clearly manifested in his demeanor, in his face.

Because I could recall from my own past many times when I had experienced flashes of rage that could have turned violent—I well understood the emotions this biblical character was described as experiencing: jealousy, fury, and a strong desire to destroy the source of these feelings. But this famous biblical tale was also a story about a human capacity to rule over even our most violent emotions. This view of the possibility of self-control is found in God's instruction to Cain—whose anger toward God would have actually made more sense—to monitor and control his urge to commit murder. In Genesis, God is quoted as saying to Cain: "Sin is crouching at the door, but you can master it."

The claim is that Cain could have resisted his murderous urge, that he was free to act otherwise—for example, to be his brother's keeper rather than his brother's killer. This is a bold claim about the reality of human freedom in the face of powerful emotions. Even at the moment he was feeling "very hot," Cain could still have chosen not to act on his violent urges. But Cain elected not to heed this warning and let his fury get the best of him. Refusing to be Abel's keeper, he became instead his brother's executioner.

That night in Samuel Shaw's home, I was clearly not my brother's keeper when I too let rage get the best of me. Like Cain I was feeling jealous fury because, in my case, a woman had preferred Samuel Shaw's offering over mine, had favored him over me. Looking back, I believe that I did make a choice: the choice to act on my feelings of hatred and jealousy. As a Sartrean, I believe in radical freedom and reject the idea that emotions are causal forces over which we have no control. Still, for those of us who experience a rage so powerful that we also feel impelled to act on it—self-control, although not impossible, can be very difficult.

Knowing this about myself, I wanted, working with Elizabeth Cohen, to shape Nathan in such a way that he would not resemble this part of me. I informed her about my history of feelings of murderous rage while denying that I ever acted on these emotions. Using recent medical advances that had been made in brain research, neurosurgeons were able to correct an imbalance between my weak prefrontal cortical control and the excessive bottom-up signals of negative affect (known as reactive aggression) in my limbic region, including my amygdala. In sum, they eliminated my tendency to experience potentially violent anger. This was for me a special benefit of Elizabeth's grand experiment. Unlike the implantation of temporary false memories, that change in my brain was permanent. It brought an end to my recurring murderous inclinations that finally broke free in my furious homicidal attack on Samuel Shaw.

Although I have come to think this was a mistake, I didn't tell Martin that my tendency to feel violent rage, the result of an imbalance in my brain, had been corrected—that I now in fact had a strong inhibition to violent reactions and lacked any disposition to violence. As mentioned already, I assumed that the RBP, knowing that I took a life, might wish, on some occasions, to access my capacity to kill. I thought that Martin would see this as an asset, and, wanting to win him over, I did not disabuse him of this mistaken belief: that I was killer material. I was praying that the RBP would never call upon me to kill. Again, although it was foolish and would come back to bite me, I wanted Martin to think I still had a dark side. Nathan, in his long letter to me, said he had originally viewed me as his Edward Hyde personality, but that he had changed his mind about that.

I was in fact, before the experiment, a Jekyll and Hyde personality. I had let Hyde murder Samuel Shaw. But Hyde had now been medically excised. So, Nathan was in a sense right when he concluded I was not really a Hyde personality. Advanced neurosurgery had permanently changed this region of my brain. Martin Jackson no doubt believed that Aaron Levitt, given his history, was capable of murder and, indeed, Martin, unfortunately for me, would not forget this. Let me repeat: not wanting to weaken the case for my usefulness, I didn't inform Jackson that I was not the same person as the Aaron Levitt who committed murder.

Also, in his letter to me, Nathan had informed me how Martin, like us, was a bourgeois socialist who had expensive tastes, even owning and racing sports cars. How he had been denied tenure by colleagues who were probably jealous of his academic and financial success in publishing radical sociology textbooks that were much in demand. How he was not only a progressive Jew, but also the person who created the radical ultra-black group that I would be working for, an organization that never ruled out operating outside the law, and even arranged for especially dangerous racists to be eliminated from the world. That's why I feared that the RBP might want to use me for lethal purposes. They apparently had never asked Nathan to undertake such work, but I knew they would see me as a different kettle of fish.

After Martin informed me that he was traveling from Winterville to meet with me, I informed the local members of this chapter of the RWP that I was going to take off a few days to be with relatives who would be flying into Dallas and that, since I did not have the room to host them in my small apartment in Highland Park, I planned to enjoy their company in a downtown Dallas hotel, reserving rooms for all of us for a three-day period, suggesting that we had a lot of catching up to do because we had not been together in a while. I said that we planned to enjoy the good food at many fancy restaurants in downtown Dallas—and that we would be attending a Dallas Mavericks game. That's what I told my new bigoted buddies. I didn't tell them the name of the hotel, and I wasn't asked to do so. I thought that members of this local RWP chapter trusted me, trusted Dalton Wells. With one exception, that conviction was correct.

When I arrived at the Carlyle late in the morning, I asked the clerk if I could check in early. It was a bit after eleven. She happily accommodated me. The two-bedroom suite—including also a kitchen and living room— Martin had reserved was, fortunately, open for immediate occupation. I took an elevator to the suite, on the fifth floor. Martin was to arrive sometime after two. I was hungry—so I quickly tossed my clothes bag on a chair in the living room and went to the lobby to look for a place to eat. I was told that the hotel restaurant, the Carlyle Cask Bar and Kitchen, had great food. It was a place that served many dishes with a Southern flair: comfort food, including fried green tomatoes. But the diverse menu also included Japanese entrées such as Wagyu strip steak. The waitress informed me that Wagyu was a Japanese word which translates as "cow or cattle" and "when the meat is cooked to perfection, it was one of the most coveted steaks in the world." I already knew about this special beef but let the waitress give her obviously well-rehearsed Wagyu testimonial. Even Arby's was pushing this remarkable meat in a TV sandwich ad. Wagyu beef was prepared at the Carlyle grill in a way that gave it an extraordinary juicy and sweet flavor. This was made possible by using marbled cuts from the short loin. These boneless cuts become very tender when cooked in their own fat in a cast iron pan for only a few minutes until medium rare. I ordered this special beef—six thinly sliced pieces—along with a generous serving of perfectly steamed olive-oiled asparagus—not too limp or too stiff—and a small loaf of the restaurant's specially baked Jewish rye bread, seasoned with whole caraway fruits and glazed with egg wash. The only thing Jewish on the menu.

Although I thought that a vegan diet was the most ethical and healthy way to eat—kosher rules made no sense to me, except for the requirement to make the death of kosher animals as painless as possible—I sometimes in my eating practices ignored ethics, just as I occasionally ignored my awareness that beef is a less-than-healthy food. And I had also developed, in my early twenties, a love of whiskey, which I had a long history of drinking daily in moderation. The Carlyle bar, I was delighted to discover, had 200 whiskey options, even having a whiskey-themed décor. It also offered an extensive craft beer and wine menu. But I chose to treat myself to the Glenmorangie Signet, considered the best whiskey in the world because of, among other ingredients, its use of high-roasted chocolate malt barley. I felt fortunate to be conscious again, alive to enjoy these special pleasures I had indulged in so often in my once privileged life.

I discovered that Martin shared my love for fine, even expensive, food and drink, having a palate similar to that of Nathan. Nathan simply inherited the taste preferences that are found in my cerebral cortex, specifically the gustatory organization of my insula. That meant that Martin and I would at least share that in common. Thus, Martin would find that my tastes in food and drink were the same as Nathan's—and that I, like the two of them, was a political radical with a disposition to epicurean indulgences. Our motto could have been "Eat well, drink up, and be a good socialist."

That was, after all, the legacy of Friedrich Engels, who once boasted to Karl Marx's daughter, Laura, that on his seventieth birthday he, along with a few good socialist friends, consumed sixteen bottles of champagne and dozens of oysters. There is no reason why one cannot enjoy the finer things of life while fighting for an egalitarian society. We epicurean democratic socialists envision a just world where all people can enjoy gustatory delights. In the meantime, we see no point in denying these pleasures to ourselves. Socialists need not be ascetics.

After lunch, feeling a bit sleepy and also somewhat anxious about meeting Martin, I went to the suite to get some rest—and to practice, while lying down, breath meditation, something that usually relaxed me. The whiskey I consumed at lunch eventually calmed my nerves, enabling me to fall asleep. I had of course chosen the smaller of the two bedrooms, the one with the queen bed. At around 2:45 that afternoon I heard a knock on the door that woke me. It was Martin. What immediately struck me was how dark his skin was, something that gave real meaning to the name of the organization he created.

Martin and I would have to confine ourselves to this suite when engaged in conversation. We could not be seen talking together in public, outside this private space. On the chance that one of the Really White Patriots might see me in the hotel, I could not be seen with a black man. So, our meetings always had to be behind closed doors. That meant that when eating together we would have to order room service. When eating at the hotel restaurant, we needed to sit at separate tables. And if eating outside the hotel, we needed to go our separate ways. I discovered that Martin was a master chef who for one evening meal ordered the ingredients needed to prepare for us an Italian dinner—creamy tomato basil chicken and orzo— that turned out to be very tasty.

On that first afternoon, we sat together for a long conversation in the spacious living room of our suite. Martin was cool toward me and still probably skeptical about the degree of my commitment to the cause. Although I of course looked exactly like Nathan, he knew that, no matter how much I had shaped Nathan to be like me, Nathan and I were clearly different human beings. From his perspective, I was different from Nathan for at least two very dark reasons: I had brutally murdered an innocent human being and I was responsible for the reversion of Nathan to me, resulting in the death of Nathan. Two acts of homicide. But he needed my services and so would have to swallow his dislike for me. I saw my challenge as convincing him of my dedication to the RBP mission and my competence to carry on Nathan's work. I think I succeeded in both—but that didn't mean he ceased feeling less than warm toward me. Understandable. The important thing was that I seemed to convince Martin that he could count on me—that I could and would deliver.

But, while Martin and I were building trust, there was apparently at least one member of the Really White Patriots who did not fully trust me, who had his suspicions. He was a Patriot who I thought had my number, although he never expressed this distrust to me—and, fortunately, there was no evidence he shared his suspicions with anyone in the organization. It was something about the way he looked at me, something skeptical in his stare. Nathan, in his description of members of the RWP, said that I should be wary of this man: James Robinson. What I had working for me was what Nathan had described as Robinson's cautiousness: he knew things could blow up in his face and destroy the morale of the organization if he falsely accused a fellow member.

I think his super-suspicious nature made him suspicious of everyone and even of his own suspicions. Robinson knew he needed to tread softly. He clearly would not charge a fellow RWP member with being a traitor without solid evidence. From what Nathan told me in his letter, Robinson would never ever, in the absence of proof, casually share with any fellow Patriot his doubts about the man who said he was Dalton Wells. That view of him would be confirmed later, after I returned from my hotel conference with Martin, at a Really White Patriots meeting where Robinson was missing. Although everyone was concerned about what happened to him, there weren't any members who reported that Robinson had told them that he had questioned my *bona fides*.

The attention now was on Robinson because of his absence: he had never missed a meeting. Members were puzzling over why he had suddenly become incommunicado. Perhaps he been taken somewhere against his will; maybe he was being questioned by the FBI or other authorities. Had Antifa kidnapped him? Or had he left under his own power for some unknown reason? His sudden failure to communicate was worrisome to Patriots, including Jefferson Davis. Thus, far from there being any evidence that Robinson had planted in any member's mind questions about me, RWP members were, if anything, wondering about Robinson, about his inexplicable disappearance and failure to respond to emails, calls, and texts—perhaps even harboring suspicions about him.

Robinson was hardly a candidate for betrayal. He was a talented white nationalist propagandist whose target demographic was young people, from high school to university populations, especially those tilting right who were looking for a cause that offered the excitement of actually doing something illegal without taking great risks. Dalton Wells and James Robinson were probably competing to see who could enlist the greatest number of recruits from the same demographic. Robinson, like the real Wells, knew that there were many young white men who were feeling angry and confused, needing an enemy to blame for everything bad happening to them—and who could be convinced to take action against their true enemy. What enemy? Why not blacks? Why not all people of color? Why not queers? Why not Muslims? And, above all, why not Jews, because of course Jews were behind everything that was wrong with this country—and the world?

Robinson regularly did a podcast where he eloquently made his case about the rising threat to white culture. Instead of books, he had created slick, attractive brochures about the work of the Patriots that were printed by the thousands. He sent these to members in RWP chapters throughout the country, asking people to put them on cars in college parking lots and on cars at high school campuses. His brochures were competing with Dalton Wells's book for white nationalist attention. So, perhaps what I saw as suspicion was really jealousy, jealousy because of my/Dalton's book that was selling so well. Robinson, very competitive, was all over social media with his message of why the Really White Patriots were the new right wave of a promising very white future—a vision of a purified America.

His brochures included photos of Patriots in uniform, sending the message that those disenchanted with the powers that be can become part of an organization whose members, when in action, dress smartly—and organize flash demonstrations against unpatriotic places and events: against any manifestation of anti-white culture. These brochures invite true patriots to join a community of like-minded white men who are doing work that could not be more important: reclaiming America. Robinson was a master at reeling in both disoriented, vulnerable young white men desperately looking for a cause and super-confident young "really white" guys who were disillusioned with the Republican Party, even at its most Trumpist.

Thus, the Really White Patriots appealed to young white men looking for a truly bold and smart right-wing organization—young men who were frustrated with the impotence of electoral politics, young men willing to live outside the law but not in a way that might bring prison time. But, even if interested in joining the cause, those seeking to become members of the RWP would have to go through a rigorous vetting process that weeded out not only undesirables (the mentally ill, criminals, addicts, those with low IQs, etc.) but also sober, mentally healthy, and intelligent individuals who might be WINOs: white in name only.

This was a measure of Jefferson Davis's thoroughness and savvy. There were background checks, long interviews, and even IQ tests. Superficial whiteness—a white pigment—was not enough. Individuals needed to be what the name of the organization signals: truly white patriots. They needed to be white at the very core of their being. They also needed to be well-educated and fully informed about and convinced by RWP's white nationalist ideology. Wells's book was required reading, with a quiz at the end, requiring a score of at least 90 percent! And people like Robinson stayed acutely alert to the possibility of false friends: those who, under the cover of white skin, and mouthing the right words, wanted to join the RWP in order to undermine the organization's mission, to betray the cause. The "Benedict Arnolds" of the White Race. People like me.

Robinson took pride in his ability to detect and expose phonies and spies, to get the goods on them. He had done so in the recent past to great acclaim. That was what he was up to when he arrived at the Carlyle. He probably wanted to confirm for himself that I was actually vacationing and socializing with relatives. In truth, I would wager that Robinson's actual aim was to confirm his worst—and of course insightful—suspicions about me. Clearly, his instincts were good; he had perceived something questionable about me that others had missed. Robinson was obviously at the Carlyle to play his role as catcher of spies. I discovered his presence by accident. As luck would have it, while looking down from an upper level, the mezzanine, I saw him talking to a hotel clerk, no doubt pretending to be my friend or a relative, asking about the Wells party.

Seeing him rattled me. I tried to calm myself and to figure out how to handle this. Maybe there would be no problem. I thought at first that per- haps this was just one of the many downtown hotels he was checking out and would leave as soon as he couldn't find evidence that I was registered at the Carlyle. Since there was no room under my name, I at first told myself that he would strike out. Nothing to worry about. He would then scout other downtown hotels. Would he really investigate every downtown inn? Then it suddenly occurred to me that it was probably not happenstance that he was visiting this particular hotel. I began to suspect that he knew with certainty that I was staying at the Carlyle, maybe under a false name. My best guess was that, at one of our RWP meetings, perhaps just before my trip to downtown Dallas—which I of course had described as a vacation— he had stealthily placed a GPS tracking device under my car and, using that, had located my vehicle in the Carlyle underground parking garage. I later confirmed this when I looked under my car. It was a lucky break that I saw him first, giving me time to work with Martin to prepare a plan for our escape or a way to neutralize Robinson. It also taught me the lesson of daily checking under my car, even under the hood.

If Robinson discovered that Martin and I were in the same suite, the game would be over. I would be finished and the work Nathan had started would have to be aborted. It would be a significant intelligence loss since my location, this Dallas RWP chapter, was the headquarters of the organization, the place of command and control where Jefferson Davis's orders were sent to members in other chapters throughout the country. We had a decision to make: whether to quit and quickly leave town if Robinson discovered I was meeting with Martin—again, just my association with an ebony human being was enough to blow my cover—or find a way to prevent him from delivering a message about my betrayal.

I knew that once Robinson discovered that my car was in Carlyle hotel parking he would not leave until he found me. What would have made him deeply suspicious was that, although my car was there, I had not registered for a room in my name and there was no Wells party. That would have convinced him I was hiding something. Robinson no doubt had a photo of me he could show around. I'm sure that he was determined to track me down in order to demand that I explain myself. Or, if he saw me with Martin, he might immediately notify those in leadership. I could of course try to come up with a story to explain everything that looked suspicious, but I doubted that I could be convincing.

Martin and I decided on an extreme solution to our problem. I knew that I could make myself bait to lure Robinson to our suite. I would walk around the hotel lobby, making myself visible, have coffee in the restaurant, and then return to the room, presumably with Robinson on my trail, on my tail. It was a large enough place for Robinson to easily conceal himself while watching and following me. He could place himself in the mezzanine overlooking the lobby, to watch for me, the place where I had first spotted him. While walking around the lobby I made a point of not looking mindful, of not being aware of my surroundings, doing what so many do: focusing entirely on my cellphone screen, barely looking forward—and not looking to the right or to the left, not to mention behind me. I wanted to appear oblivious to everything around me.

I assumed that Robinson would see the floor number I had punched on an elevator in the lobby area and then make his way up, carefully shadowing me to find out which room I entered. Since there was a large lounge area on the fifth floor, with vending machines filled with a variety of treats and drinks, my plan was to linger there, to give Robinson the time he needed to ride the elevator to our floor. Again, he would see that I was totally focused on my phone screen as I was getting something from a vending machine, and then he would watch me slowly make my way to the suite. I sensed but did not know for sure that Robinson was following me.

Assuming that he was watching me from afar, after walking slowly down the hall, I then unlocked the door and entered the suite. Now that he knew my exact location, what would Robinson do? He could of course return to the lobby and try to find out who was in Suite 506, but he might just knock on our door. We were prepared if he did the latter. Indeed, that was crucial to our plan. But what if Robinson decided to go to the lobby to discover the name of the person who reserved Suite 506. If he did that, it could be the end of everything. Googling "Martin Jackson," Robinson would find more than enough to confirm his suspicions about me.

Although many Martin Jacksons would come up on Google, he would see at the top of the page, just under a Wikipedia description of a British drummer with that name, a Martin L. Jackson. Robinson would notice that this Jackson also had a Wikipedia page—with a photo, a picture that would be enough to tell Robinson he was on the right track—providing information about Martin's publications and radical activist history. Martin L. Jackson would be described as an archenemy of white nationalism and author of many leftist textbooks. Robinson would see that this Jackson was a champion of critical race theory. There was even a reference to the Really Black Panthers and how the name was invented as a way of mocking the name the Really White Patriots. My spy mission would be finished.

We had wagered that, instead of returning to the lobby to try to find out who was in Suite 506, Robinson would simply knock on the door he saw me enter. Fortunately for us but not for Robinson, he chose to do that. I let him in. Once he entered, we proceeded according to plan. Martin was a fifth-degree black belt who knew how to incapacitate a person in a flash, to render his opponent unconscious or, if necessary, lifeless. Our aim was the latter. When he knocked, I opened the door which Martin was behind, greeting Robinson with a smile. Why did I smile? Martin then quickly shut the door and, before Robinson could scream, performed what in martial arts is called a rear naked choke, cutting off the flow of blood to Robinson's brain by putting pressure on the arteries in his neck. In a matter of minutes Robinson lost consciousness, and Martin kept this choke hold for five minutes. Martin then let the body collapse to the floor. To confirm that he was dead, Martin checked Robinson's pulse while he lay motionless on the floor—and then Martin looked up at me, indicating with his head that the deed was done.

I was thankful that I wasn't asked to kill Robinson, but I was now of course a party to yet another homicide. I tried to convince myself that if murder means deliberately taking an innocent human life, this was not murder. James Robinson's life was a guilty one because he was an agent of hateful propaganda. Ironically, so was I! From the perspective of criminal law, we committed murder. Martin's act satisfied the conditions of *actus reus* and *mens rea*. It was clearly a voluntary act of premeditated murder, and I had assisted in this homicide. I was thus equally guilty. Martin and I had coldly calculated that the continuation of my role as spy was more important than this man's life. My medically altered amygdala didn't prevent me from participating in another murder. I felt no rage toward Robinson. Indeed, I had inappropriately smiled. I had, with Martin, dispassionately decided that Robinson needed to die.

I continued to find ways, in my own mind, to justify the murder of Robinson. I thought: if someone could have killed Joseph Goebbels, Hitler's supreme propagandist of racism and antisemitism, would that have been wrong? Although that too, legally speaking, would also have been murder, wouldn't it have been justified? I think many would say yes. This is how I privately reasoned, how I continued to rationalize killing another human being. Martin and I didn't have lot of time to deliberate before we decided what to do about Robinson, but we had both agreed on this homicidal course of action.

Getting rid of the body was our next task. We had to make a corpse disappear, fast. This was a skill that the Really Black Panthers already possessed. I was told that they had mastered this morbid art. Each chapter was provided with a manual about how to carefully remove all traces of a body. After all, I was playing my role as infiltrator only because members of the

RBP in Portland had made Dalton Wells vanish. Martin had RBP comrades in the Dallas area, a group he had arranged to meet with on this visit. He was in fact planning to make Dallas the new headquarters of the RBP, to be closer to the headquarters of the RWP. His plan was to move to Dallas in the near future. A transplanted Texan, Martin had grown up in San Antonio and then, after flunking out of the University of Houston College of Medicine, moved to Austin to work toward a PhD in sociology at UT. Upon completion of his doctorate, he found, in a tight academic job market, a tenure-track position at Winterville State University. He never adjusted to the frigid weather. So, he was more than ready to return to the relatively warm winters of his home state, even to Dallas with its occasional ice storms and snow—and its now ultra-hot summers due to climate change. He wanted to flee the brutal Winterville winters that seemed never to end.

Two Dallas Panthers were prepared to take on the task of making Robinson's corpse disappear. Their day jobs: morticians. They concealed and brought in tools for dismembering the body so that it could fit into two large suitcases with rollers. They then moved the sundered body—upper torso in one luggage bag and lower torso in the other—to their hearse in underground hotel parking. These Panthers did the same thing with Robinson's remains as the Panthers in Portland did with Wells's corpse: cremated the sundered body, placed the ashes in a small biodegradable bag, and threw this into a dumpster in the back of their mortuary. Panthers in different states ran funeral parlors with onsite cremation services. The hearse transported Wells's body parts to a funeral home in a predominantly black Dallas suburb. Many Panthers were trained morticians. Usually located in African American neighborhoods, the main clientele of these Panther funeral homes were people in the black community. The funeral business is lucrative and stable because one never runs out of customers. A significant percentage of the profits from these RBP-run mortuaries go into RBP coffers. The Panthers also try, while making a profit, to keep the costs of funerals as low as possible for their black customers. But, increasingly, a side practice of these businesses was cremating the bodies of murdered white nationalists whose disappearance the RBP wanted to remain a mystery. When members disappear without a trace from a community of white nationalists, it can spook members of this community and give them second thoughts about what they are doing.

Such are the more macabre aspects of this work. Life and death decisions sometimes had to made to keep things running smoothly. I was not proud of what we did to James Robinson, but I had carefully thought through our options—as did Martin—and we agreed that this was necessary. As Jews, we both believed in the value of human life, even the lives of racists. But as Jews, we were not pacifists. We believed that if Jews in Germany in larger numbers had, early on, worked against the Nazis, had joined with resistance fighters, had participated in efforts to assassinate Hitler and key leaders in the SS—and to disrupt the Nazi propaganda machine before it could reach greater numbers of potential converts—things might have been different. Maybe. Maybe not. Even the great Lutheran theologian Dietrich Bonhoeffer, once a committed pacifist, had finally concluded that it was morally necessary to try to kill Hitler—that if there was any chance of success, it was worth the risk of being executed as well as the moral costs. Of course, Bonhoeffer paid with his life. The point is that it is sometimes impossible in the real world, when you are fighting evil, to avoid what Sartre called—in a play wrote he wrote with this name—"dirty hands," by which he meant bloody hands: hands that, *in extremis*, are used to kill dangerous political opponents.

19. East of Eden

I DIDN'T KNOW HOW long I could get away with doing this constructively subversive work, but I thought, to honor the memory of Nathan, who I now considered my beloved dead brother, Abel to my Cain, I needed to give it my best shot, to continue this as long as I could handle the stress and believed I was doing real damage to the RWP project. Was it a way to redeem a life that resembled that of Cain in more ways than one? Clearly now living very much to the east of Eden, I had three deaths on my conscience. I had cruelly murdered Samuel Shaw and had a scar on my left wrist to remind me of this—and to repeat something already said, a kind of mark of Cain. I had also participated in an experiment that created and then destroyed Nathan Feldman's innocent life. And I had assisted in the murder of James Robinson. Whatever terrible things he said or wrote, Robinson was still a human being. Was I, now thrice guilty of murder, actually morally worse than Cain?

If I was Cain, I was nonetheless now doing something positive with my life. Even Cain does not disappear from the biblical narrative after he commits what is, according to biblical myth, the first murder. Although God disowns Cain, God does not kill him. Indeed, Cain goes on to found the first city, very far from Eden, to make a new life for himself, a life where God was completely absent. I had felt the absence of God in my life long before I took three human lives. Would the presence of the Jewish God in my life have made me less likely to commit murder? Jews often, out of reverence, substitute the word Adonai or LORD because they don't know how to pronounce the Hebrew personal name of God: YHVH. A blasphemous question: Is this reverence morally justifiable? Is the felt absence of Adonai in the lives of many Jews really a great moral loss, a loss that makes them more prone disrespect life? I think not. After all, the great unpronounce-able One of the Tanakh, the Jewish Bible, commands the mass murder of

Canaanites, including children and infants. Let us pray that biblical geno-cides are as mythical as the story of the ten plagues and the parted sea. The God of some Jewish Scriptures, whether a fictional character or a reality, has dirty hands. Maybe it would be better to have no Creator at all than a God guilty of so much bloodshed.

This is the God Leonard Cohen boldly and defiantly complained to in one of the most Jewish songs he ever wrote, mentioned earlier. In what could be described as a boldly defiant prayer, in words addressed to the God of the Tanakh, Cohen sings accusatory words in the title song of his last album: "You want it darker." Here Cohen is clearly playing the role of Jacob/Israel: he shows himself to be a courageous God wrestler. One of the great contributions of Judaism to monotheism—that Christianity and Islam did not pick up on—is the Jewish practice of God-wrestling, even God-bashing, in the name of justice. In fairness to Jewish Scripture, I am well aware of another, very different, image of God in the Tanakh, the God I can believe in on the rare occasions when I can believe, namely a God who commands love of the stranger and protection of the most vulnerable. A good God of life, justice, kindness, and compassion. Our Scripture seems to have conflicting theologies, different images of YHVH. The second image of God is worth morally imitating while the first image breeds murder and genocide.

God or no God, wanting to be redeem myself, I was trying, in my own very limited way, to make up for the lives I had taken, to show that my life was now, morally speaking, *relatively* good. I convinced myself that, even if this risky undercover job did not fully redeem me, there was still a lot to be said for my decision to stay and work for the Really Black Panthers, to help thwart the plans of the Really White Patriots. It was the praxis of impure justice. It was work that was morally ambiguous and two-faced. I had to present before the RWP the confident face of a strong proponent of white nationalism and even appear to enthusiastically push a bigoted ideology that pleased them—and I had, before the RBP, to present the face of a gutsy enemy of the RWP, an infiltrator who was even willing to kill in the cause of the RBP. Although only one was my true face—even though my heart was with the RBP mission and that alone—doing their bidding meant that my hands would never be entirely clean. The James Robinsons of this world might, from time to time, need to be murdered. I told myself I was working for a truly just cause, even if the means employed were not always just. Of course, as I kept reminding myself, one has to be careful not to get carried away when fighting evil. Nietzsche had warned: "He who fights with monsters should look to it that he himself does not become a monster." That's advice worth keeping in mind, although not always possible to follow. We should not forget that the book in which we find these words is titled *Beyond Good and Evil*.

I am now dwelling in a world that is totally alien to my former life as an academic where I safely wrote articles and books that called for a socialist revolution. I played the role of radical professor, but to be honest, I, instead of engaging in radical action, often withdrew to the cocoon of my cozy booklined philosophy office. It was the comfortable life of a professor of philosophy who urged students to adopt a defiant attitude toward an unjust society, to work for radical social change—while I, for the most part, sat on the sidelines. I took pride in refusing to be the politically neutral teacher that many outside the university say academia should make normative. But I was never the kind of social radical who took to the streets or risked being arrested. I had loved teaching philosophy in a politically radical but comfortable and safe way. The Catholic university I worked at was surprisingly progressive and never discouraged me from making social justice central to my teaching. I would probably still be doing this for a living—teaching social revolution while not taking great risks—if I had not been let go by the financially struggling University of St. Mary. If they had kept me on, I would not have moved to Winterville. Eventually tiring of a commuter love relationship, I would, have, if had retained my teaching job in Duluth, probably found a woman to love who lived in that port city bordering Lake Superior. In that case, I might not have irrationally tried to save a failed relationship by killing Samuel Shaw. I was clearly not Margaret Newman's one true love.

I have come to conclude that my now risky and morally impure life as a spy and spoiler is a far better way than academia to pursue my Jewish-Buddhist-Marxist commitment to social justice. There is a lot to be said in support of spending one's days and nights in the praxis of fucking with and fucking up the projects, plans, and dreams of Christian white nationalists. It gives me great pleasure to now be one of those progressive activists despised by the radical right, working in the midst of and against those who see themselves as the only truly enlightened patriots. It is my small, messy contribution to what Jews call *tikkun olam*: repairing a damaged world.

My life as a mole—tasked with frustrating the goals of the RWP—has helped me sleep better at night, even as I sadly remember that I helped to create a new human being while knowing that he would be erased once neuroscience was done with him. I recognize that Nathan's life, no matter how brief or how fictional, did count as a valuable human life—as much as that of Samuel Shaw and, in my opinion, more than that of James Robinson. Despite his implanted memories and his fictional character, Nathan Feldman was a real person who deserved to live as much as Aaron Levitt. It comforts me that I can continue what Nathan started, as a way of paying tribute to what he accomplished in his all-too-short time on earth.

www.ingramcontent.com/pod-product-compliance
Lightning Source LLC
Chambersburg PA
CBHW051139020726
47501CB00005B/1591